THE FRANKLIN LIBRARY
OF MYSTERY MASTERPIECES

GHOSTLY TALES

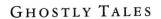

"To be half so terrible as a good murder story," Henry James once noted, "a good ghost story . . . must be connected at a hundred points with the common objects of life." This quote best illustrates James's approach to the art of mystery fiction. He strove to recreate reality, but with a twist—to show a "normal" situation gone wrong. The four short stories included in this volume present this technique at its finest.

In "The Turn of the Screw," James's best-known tale (and one of the most famous short stories in the English language), a naive young woman journeys to Bly Manor, in the English countryside, to serve as governess to two young children. The lovely gothic mansion, the beautiful and angelic children, and the kindly old housekeeper all are common enough— until two recalcitrant ghosts begin paying violent visits to the governess and her young charges.

This technique of shattering a calm reality with the supernatural is used to equal effect in the other stories included in this Franklin Mystery edition of *Ghostly Tales*. In "Owen Wingrave," a young man who defies his family is haunted by the portrait of an ancestor; in "Sir Dominick Ferrand," a writer buys a used desk only to discover a mysterious cache of letters hidden within it; and in "The Last of the Valerii," an ancient Roman statue drives a newlywed Count to madness.

James incorporated into each of his stories the technique that his brother, the philosopher William James, was the first to call "stream of consciousness." This approach was especially effective in his ghostly tales, in which we view eerie happenings through the eyes of a protagonist who is too addled by the mysterious events to report them objectively. Reality and perception become so closely entwined that the reader is soon as confused as the narrator, adding even more mystery and tension to the tale.

Born in New York City in 1843, James was a child of privilege. His father, the son of one of America's first millionaires, was a respected philosopher and theologian. The family traveled extensively in Europe during Henry's childhood, exposing the young boy to the culture and history of the Western world. After briefly studying law at Harvard, James decided to devote himself entirely to the life of letters. In 1876 he moved to London, where he joined the British literati. His neighbor for a time was the poet Robert Browning, who complained that James spent so much time socializing that he could not possibly be serious about writing.

The transatlantic nature of James's career is best exemplified by his commitment to the war effort in World War I. By 1916, James had become a naturalized British subject, due, in part, to his devotion to England. He housed Belgian refugees, visited hospitals, and helped found the American ambulance service (despite his own failing health). James, who had contracted pneumonia, received England's prestigious Order of Merit, awarded to him on his deathbed. He died February 28, 1916; the epitaph on his gravestone in Cambridge, Massachusetts, reads, "Novelist and interpreter of his generation on both sides of the sea."

Lionized in life, Henry James has become even more respected in the decades since his death. T. S. Eliot, another author claimed by both America and England, once observed that "James did not provide us with 'ideas,' but with another world of thought and feeling." Although he never married or produced any children, the James line lives on in the many novels and stories he created during his half-century career as one of the greatest writers in the English language.

The Editors

HENRY JAMES

GHOSTLY
TALES

ILLUSTRATED BY SCOTT REYNOLDS

THE FRANKLIN LIBRARY
FRANKLIN CENTER, PENNSYLVANIA

CONTENTS

GHOSTLY TALES

THE TURN OF
THE SCREW

The story had held us, round the fire, sufficiently breath-less, but except the obvious remark that it was grue-some, as, on Christmas Eve in an old house, a strange tale should essentially be, I remember no comment uttered till somebody happened to say that it was the only case he had met in which such a visitation had fallen on a child. The case, I may mention, was that of an apparition in just such an old house as had gathered us for the occasion—an ap-pearance, of a dreadful kind, to a little boy sleeping in the room with his mother and waking her up in the terror of it; waking her not to dissipate his dread and soothe him to sleep again, but to encounter also, herself, before she had suc-ceeded in doing so, the same sight that had shaken him. It was this observation that drew from Douglas—not immedi-ately, but later in the evening—a reply that had the inter-esting consequence to which I call attention. Someone else told a story not particularly effective, which I saw he was not following. This I took for a sign that he had himself something to produce and that we should only have to wait. We waited in fact till two nights later; but that same evening, before we scattered, he brought out his mind.

"I quite agree—in regard to Griffin's ghost, or whatever it was—that its appearing first to the little boy, at so tender an age, adds a particular touch. But it's not the first occurrence of its charming kind that I know to have involved a child. If the child gives the effect another turn of the screw, what do you say to *two* children—?"

"We say, of course," somebody exclaimed, "that they give two turns! Also that we want to hear about them."

I can see Douglas there before the fire, to which he had got up to present his back, looking down at his interlocutor with his hands in his pockets. "Nobody but me, till now, has ever heard. It's quite too horrible." This, naturally, was declared by several voices to give the thing the utmost price, and our friend, with quiet art, prepared his triumph by turning his eyes over the rest of us and going on: "It's beyond everything. Nothing at all that I know touches it."

"For sheer terror?" I remember asking.

He seemed to say it was not so simple as that; to be really at a loss how to qualify it. He passed his hand over his eyes, made a little wincing grimace. "For dreadful—dreadfulness!"

"Oh, how delicious!" cried one of the women.

He took no notice of her; he looked at me, but as if, instead of me, he saw what he spoke of. "For general uncanny ugliness and horror and pain."

"Well then," I said, "just sit right down and begin."

He turned round to the fire, gave a kick to a log, watched it an instant. Then as he faced us again: "I can't begin. I shall have to send to town." There was a unanimous groan at this, and much reproach; after which, in his preoccupied way, he explained. "The story's written. It's in a locked drawer—it has not been out for years. I could write to my man and enclose the key; he could send down the packet as he finds it." It was to me in particular that he appeared to propound this—appeared almost to appeal for aid not to hesitate. He had broken a thickness of ice, the formation of many a writer; had had his reasons for a long silence. The others resented postponement, but it was just his scruples that charmed me. I adjured him to write by the first post and to agree with us for an early hearing; then I asked him if the experience in question had been his own. To this his answer was prompt. "Oh, thank God, no!"

"And is the record yours? You took the thing down?"

"Nothing but the impression. I took that *here*"—he tapped his heart. "I've never lost it."

"Then your manuscript—?"

"Is in old, faded ink, and in the most beautiful hand." He hung fire again. "A woman's. She has been dead these twenty years. She sent me the pages in question before she died." They were all listening now, and of course there was somebody to be arch, or at any rate to draw the inference. But if he put the inference by without a smile it was also without irritation. "She was a most charming person, but she was ten years older than I. She was my sister's governess," he quietly said. "She was the most agreeable woman I've ever known in her position; she would have been worthy of any whatever. It was long ago, and this episode was long before. I was at Trinity, and I found her at home on my coming down the second summer. I was much there that year—it was a beautiful one; and we had, in her off-hours, some strolls and talks in the garden—talks in which she struck me as awfully clever and nice. Oh yes; don't grin: I liked her extremely and am glad to this day to think she liked me too. If she hadn't she wouldn't have told me. She had never told anyone. It wasn't

7

simply that she said so, but that I knew she hadn't. I was sure; I could see. You'll easily judge why when you hear."

"Because the thing had been such a scare?"

He continued to fix me. "You'll easily judge," he repeated: "*you* will."

I fixed him too. "I see. She was in love."

He laughed for the first time. "You *are* acute. Yes, she was in love. That is, she had been. That came out—she couldn't tell her story without its coming out. I saw it, and she saw I saw it; but neither of us spoke of it. I remember the time and the place—the corner of the lawn, the shade of the great beeches and the long, hot summer afternoon. It wasn't a scene for a shudder; but oh—!" He quitted the fire and dropped back into his chair.

"You'll receive the packet Thursday morning?" I inquired.

"Probably not till the second post."

"Well then; after dinner—"

"You'll all meet me here?" He looked us round again. "Isn't anybody going?" It was almost the tone of hope.

"Everybody will stay!"

"*I* will—and *I* will!" cried the ladies whose departure had been fixed. Mrs. Griffin, however, expressed the need for a little more light. "Who was it she was in love with?"

"The story will tell," I took upon myself to reply.

"Oh, I can't wait for the story!"

"The story *won't* tell," said Douglas; "not in any literal, vulgar way."

"More's the pity, then. That's the only way I ever understand."

"Won't *you* tell, Douglas?" somebody else inquired.

He sprang to his feet again. "Yes—tomorrow. Now I must go to bed. Good-night." And quickly catching up a

candlestick, he left us slightly bewildered. From our end of
the great brown hall we heard his step on the stair; whereupon
Mrs. Griffin spoke. "Well, if I don't know who she was in
love with, I know who *he* was."

"She was ten years older," said her husband.

"*Raison de plus*—at that age! But it's rather nice, his long
reticence."

"Forty years!" Griffin put in.

"With this outbreak at last."

"The outbreak," I returned, "will make a tremendous
occasion of Thursday night"; and everyone so agreed with
me that, in the light of it, we lost all attention for everything
else. The last story, however incomplete and like the mere
opening of a serial, had been told; we handshook and "can-
dlestuck," as somebody said, and went to bed.

I knew the next day that a letter containing the key had,
by the first post, gone off to his London apartments; but in
spite of—or perhaps just on account of—the eventual dif-
fusion of this knowledge we quite let him alone till after
dinner, till such an hour of the evening, in fact, as might best
accord with the kind of emotion in which our hopes were
fixed. Then he became as communicative as we could desire
and indeed gave us his best reason for being so. We had it
from him again before the fire in the hall, as we had had our
mild wonders of the previous night. It appeared that the
narrative he had promised to read us really required for a
proper intelligence a few words of prologue. Let me say here
distinctly, to have done with it, that this narrative, from an
exact transcript of my own made much later, is what I shall
presently give. Poor Douglas, before his death—when it was
in sight—committed to me the manuscript that reached him
on the third of these days and that, on the same spot, with
immense effect, he began to read to our hushed little circle

on the night of the fourth. The departing ladies who had said they would stay didn't, of course, thank heaven, stay: they departed, in consequence of arrangements made, in a rage of curiosity, as they professed, produced by the touches with which he had already worked us up. But that only made his little final auditory more compact and select, kept it, round the hearth, subject to a common thrill.

The first of these touches conveyed that the written statement took up the tale at a point after it had, in a manner, begun. The fact to be in possession of was therefore that his old friend, the youngest of several daughters of a poor country parson, had, at the age of twenty, on taking service for the first time in the schoolroom, come up to London, in trepidation, to answer in person an advertisement that had already placed her in brief correspondence with the advertiser. This person proved, on her presenting herself, for judgment, at a house in Harley Street, that impressed her as vast and imposing—this prospective patron proved a gentleman, a bachelor in the prime of life, such a figure as had never risen, save in a dream or an old novel, before a fluttered, anxious girl out of a Hampshire vicarage. One could easily fix his type; it never, happily, dies out. He was handsome and bold and pleasant, off-hand and gay and kind. He struck her, inevitably, as gallant and splendid, but what took her most of all and gave her the courage she afterwards showed was that he put the whole thing to her as a kind of favour, an obligation he should gratefully incur. She conceived him as rich, but as fearfully extravagant—saw him all in a glow of high fashion, of good looks, of expensive habits, of charming ways with women. He had for his own town residence a big house filled with the spoils of travel and the trophies of the chase; but it was to his country home, an old family place in Essex, that he wished her immediately to proceed.

He had been left, by the death of their parents in India, guardian to a small nephew and a small niece, children of a younger, a military brother, whom he had lost two years before. These children were, by the strangest of chances for a man in his position—a lone man without the right sort of experience or a grain of patience—very heavily on his hands. It had all been a great worry and, on his own part doubtless, a series of blunders, but he immensely pitied the poor chicks and had done all he could; had in particular sent them down to his other house, the proper place for them being of course the country, and kept them there, from the first, with the best people he could find to look after them, parting even with his own servants to wait on them and going down himself, whenever he might, to see how they were doing. The awkward thing was that they had practically no other relations and that his own affairs took up all his time. He had put them in possession of Bly, which was healthy and secure, and had placed at the head of their little establishment—but below stairs only—an excellent woman, Mrs. Grose, whom he was sure his visitor would like and who had formerly been maid to his mother. She was now housekeeper and was also acting for the time as superintendent to the little girl, of whom, without children of her own, she was, by good luck, extremely fond. There were plenty of people to help, but of course the young lady who should go down as governess would be in supreme authority. She would also have, in holidays, to look after the small boy, who had been for a term at school—young as he was to be sent, but what else could be done?—and who, as the holidays were about to begin, would be back from one day to the other. There had been for the two children at first a young lady whom they had had the misfortune to lose. She had done for them quite beautifully—she was a most respectable person—till her death, the great awkwardness of which had, precisely, left no alternative but the school for little Miles. Mrs. Grose, since then, in the way of manners and things, had done as she could for Flora; and there were, further, a cook, a housemaid, a dairywoman, an old pony, an old groom, and an old gardner, all likewise thoroughly respectable.

So far had Douglas presented his picture when someone put a question. "And what did the former governess die of?— of so much respectability?"

Our friend's answer was prompt. "That will come out. I don't anticipate."

"Excuse me—I thought that was just what you *are* doing."

"In her successor's place," I suggested, "I should have wished to learn if the office brought with it—"

"Necessary danger to life?" Douglas completed my thought. "She did wish to learn, and she did learn. You shall hear tomorrow what she learnt. Meanwhile, of course, the prospect struck her as lightly grim. She was young, untried, nervous: it was a vision of serious duties and little company, of really great loneliness. She hesitated—took a couple of days to consult and consider. But the salary offered much exceeded her modest measure, and on a second interview she faced the music, she engaged." And Douglas, with this, made a pause that, for the benefit of the company, moved me to throw in—

"The moral of which was of course the seduction exercised by the splendid young man. She succumbed to it."

He got up and, as he had done the night before, went to the fire, gave a stir to a log with his foot, then stood a moment with his back to us. "She saw him only twice."

"Yes, but that's just the beauty of her passion."

A little to my surprise, on this, Douglas turned round to me. "It *was* the beauty of it. There were others," he went

on, "who hadn't succumbed. He told her frankly all his difficulty—that for several applicants the conditions had been
prohibitive. They were, somehow, simply afraid. It sounded
dull—it sounded strange; and all the more so because of his
main condition."

"Which was—?"

"That she should never trouble him—but never, never:
neither appeal nor complain nor write about anything; only
meet all questions herself, receive all moneys from his so-
licitor, take the whole thing over and let him alone. She
promised to do this, and she mentioned to me that when,
for a moment, disburdened, delighted, he held her hand,
thanking her for the sacrifice, she already felt rewarded."

"But was that all her reward?" one of the ladies asked.

"She never saw him again."

"Oh!" said the lady; which, as our friend immediately left
us again, was the only other word of importance contributed
to the subject till, the next night, by the corner of the hearth,
in the best chair, he opened the faded red cover of a thin
old-fashioned gilt-edged album. The whole thing took indeed
more nights than one, but on the first occasion the same lady
put another question. "What is your title?"

"I haven't one."

"Oh, *I* have!" I said. But Douglas, without heeding me,
had begun to read with a fine clearness that was like a ren-
dering to the ear of the beauty of his author's hand.

I

I remember the whole beginning as a succession of flights
and drops, a little see-saw of the right throbs and the wrong.
After rising, in town, to meet his appeal, I had at all events

a couple of very bad days—found myself doubtful again, felt indeed sure I had made a mistake. In this state of mind I spent the long hours of bumping, swinging coach that carried me to the stopping-place at which I was to be met by a vehicle from the house. This convenience, I was told, had been ordered, and I found, toward the close of the June afternoon, a commodious fly in waiting for me. Driving at that hour, on a lovely day, through a country to which the summer sweetness seemed to offer me a friendly welcome, my fortitude mounted afresh and, as we turned into the avenue, encountered a reprieve that was probably but a proof of the point to which it had sunk. I suppose I had expected, or had dreaded, something so melancholy that what greeted me was a good surprise. I remember as a most pleasant impression the broad, clear front, its open windows and fresh curtains and the pair of maids looking out; I remember the lawn and the bright flowers and the crunch of my wheels on the gravel and the clustered tree-tops over which the rooks circled and cawed in the golden sky. The scene had a greatness that made it a different affair from my own scant home, and there immediately appeared at the door, with a little girl in her hand, a civil person who dropped me as decent a curtsey as if I had been the mistress or a distinguished visitor. I had received in Harley Street a narrower notion of the place, and that, as I recalled it, made me think the proprietor still more of a gentleman suggested that what I was to enjoy might be something beyond his promise.

I had no drop again till the next day, for I was carried triumphantly through the following hours by my introduction to the younger of my pupils. The little girl who accompanied Mrs. Grose appeared to me on the spot a creature so charming as to make it a great fortune to have to do with her. She was the most beautiful child I had ever seen, and I afterwards wondered that my employer had not told me more of her. I slept little that night—I was too much excited; and this astonished me too, I recollect, remained with me, adding to my sense of the liberality with which I was treated. The large, impressive room, one of the best in the house, the great state bed, as I almost felt it, the full, figured draperies, the long glasses in which, for the first time, I could see myself from head to foot, all struck me—like the extraordinary charm of my small charge—as so many things thrown in. It was thrown in as well, from the first moment, that I should get on with Mrs. Grose in a relation over which, on my way, in the coach, I fear I had rather brooded. The only thing indeed that in this early outlook might have made me shrink again was the clear circumstance of her being so glad to see me. I perceived within half an hour that she was so glad—stout, simple, plain, clean, wholesome woman—as to be positively on her guard against showing it too much. I wondered even then a little why she should wish not to show it, and that, with reflection, with suspicion, might of course have made me uneasy.

But it was a comfort that there could be no uneasiness in a connection with anything so beatific as the radiant image of my little girl, the vision of whose angelic beauty had probably more than anything else to do with the restlessness that, before morning, made me several times rise and wander about my room to take in the whole picture and prospect; to watch, from my open window, the faint summer dawn, to look at such portions of the rest of the house as I could catch, and to listen, while, in the fading dusk, the first birds began to twitter, for the possible recurrence of a sound or two, less natural and not without, but within, that I had fancied I heard. There had been a moment when I believed I recognized, faint and far, the cry of a child; there had been another when I found myself just consciously starting as at the passage, before my door, of a light footstep. But these fancies were not marked enough not to be thrown off, and it is only in the light, or the gloom, I should rather say, of other and subsequent matters that they now come back to me. To watch, teach, "form" little Flora would too evidently be the making of a happy and useful life. It had been agreed between us downstairs that after this first occasion I should have her as a matter of course at night, her small white bed being already arranged, to that end, in my room. What I had undertaken was the whole care of her, and she had remained, just this last time, with Mrs. Grose only as an effect of our consideration for my inevitable strangeness and her natural timidity. In spite of this timidity—which the child herself, in the oddest way in the world, had been perfectly frank and brave about, allowing it, without a sign of uncomfortable consciousness, with the deep, sweet serenity indeed of one of Raphael's holy infants, to be discussed, to be imputed to her and to determine us—I felt quite sure she would presently like me. It was part of what I already liked Mrs. Grose herself for, the pleasure I could see her feel in my admiration and wonder as I sat at supper with four tall candles and with my pupil, in a high chair and a bib, brightly facing me, between them, over bread and milk. There were naturally things that in Flora's presence could pass between us only as prodigious and gratified looks, obscure and roundabout allusions.

"And the little boy—does he look like her? Is he too so very remarkable?"

One wouldn't flatter a child. "Oh, miss, *most* remarkable. If you think well of this one!"—and she stood there with a plate in her hand, beaming at our companion, who looked from one of us to the other with placid heavenly eyes that contained nothing to check us.

"Yes; if I do—?"

"You *will* be carried away by the little gentleman!"

"Well, that, I think, is what I came for—to be carried away. I'm afraid, however," I remember feeling the impulse to add, "I'm rather easily carried away. I was carried away in London!"

I can still see Mrs. Grose's broad face as she took this in. "In Harley Street?"

"In Harley Street."

"Well, miss, you're not the first—and you won't be the last."

"Oh, I've no pretension," I could laugh, "to being the only one. My other pupil, at any rate, as I understand, comes back tomorrow?"

"Not tomorrow—Friday, miss. He arrives, as you did, by the coach, under care of the guard, and is to be met by the same carriage."

I forthwith expressed that the proper as well as the pleasant and friendly thing would be therefore that on the arrival of the public conveyance I should be in waiting for him with his little sister; an idea in which Mrs. Grose concurred so heartily that I somehow took her manner as a kind of comforting pledge—never falsified, thank heaven!—that we should on every question be quite at one. Oh, she was glad I was there!

What I felt the next day was, I suppose, nothing that could be fairly called a reaction from the cheer of my arrival; it was probably at the most only a slight oppression produced by a fuller measure of the scale, as I walked round them, gazed up at them, took them in, of my new circumstances. They had, as it were, an extent and mass for which I had not been prepared and in the presence of which I found myself, freshly, a little scared as well as a little proud. Lessons, in this agitation, certainly suffered some delay; I reflected that my first duty was, by the gentlest arts I could contrive, to win the child into the sense of knowing me. I spent the day with her out-of-doors; I arranged with her, to her great satisfaction, that it should be she, she only, who might show me the place. She showed it step by step and room by room and secret by secret, with droll, delightful, childish talk about it and with the result, in half an hour, of our becoming immense friends. Young as she was, I was struck, throughout our little tour, with her confidence and courage with the way, in empty chambers and dull corridors, on crooked staircases that made me pause and even on the summit of an old machicolated square tower that made me dizzy, her morning music, her disposition to tell me so many more things than she asked, rang out and led me on. I have not seen Bly since the day I left it, and I dare say that to my older and more informed eyes it would now appear sufficiently contracted. But as my little conductress, with her hair of gold and her frock of blue, danced before me round corners and pattered down passages, I had the view of a castle of romance inhabited by a rosy sprite, such a place as would somehow, for diversion of the young idea, take all colour out of storybooks and fairy-tales. Wasn't it just a storybook over which I had fallen a-doze and a-dream? No; it was a big, ugly, antique, but convenient house, embodying a few features of a building still older, half replaced and half utilized, in which I had the fancy of our being almost as lost as a handful of passengers in a great drifting ship. Well, I was, strangely, at the helm!

II

This came home to me when, two days later, I drove over with Flora to meet, as Mrs. Grose said, the little gentleman;

and all the more for an incident that, presenting itself the second evening, had deeply disconcerted me. The first day had been, on the whole, as I have expressed, reassuring; but I was to see it wind up in keen apprehension. The postbag, that evening—it came late—contained a letter for me, which, however, in the hand of my employer, I found to be composed but of a few words enclosing another, addressed to himself, with a seal still unbroken. "This, I recognize, is from the head-master, and the head-master's an awful bore. Read him, please; deal with him; but mind you don't report. Not a word. I'm off!" I broke the seal with a great effort—so great a one that I was a long time coming to it; took the unopened missive at last up to my room and only attacked it just before going to bed. I had better have let it wait till morning, for it gave me a second sleepless night. With no counsel to take, the next day, I was full of distress; and it finally got so the better of me that I determined to open myself at least to Mrs. Grose.

"What does it mean? The child's dismissed his school."

She gave me a look that I remarked at the moment; then, visibly, with a quick blankness, seemed to try to take it back. "But aren't they all—?"

"Sent home—yes. But only for the holidays. Miles may never go back at all."

Consciously, under my attention, she reddened. "They won't take him?"

"They absolutely decline."

At this she raised her eyes, which she had turned from me; I saw them fill with good tears. "What has he done?"

I hesitated; then I judged best simply to hand her my letter—which, however, had the effect of making her, without taking it, simply put her hands behind her. She shook her head sadly. "Such things are not for me, miss."

My counsellor couldn't read! I winced at my mistake, which I attenuated as I could, and opened my letter again to repeat it to her; then, faltering in the act and folding it up once more, I put it back in my pocket. "Is he really *bad?*"

The tears were still in her eyes. "Do the gentlemen say so?"

"They go into no particulars. They simply express their regret that it should be impossible to keep him. That can have only one meaning." Mrs. Grose listened with dumb emotion; she forbore to ask me what this meaning might be; so that, presently, to put the thing with some coherence and with the mere aid of her presence to my own mind, I went on: "That he's an injury to the others."

At this, with one of the quick turns of simple folk, she suddenly flamed up. "Master Miles!—*him* an injury?"

There was such a flood of good faith in it that, though I had not yet seen the child, my very fears made me jump to the absurdity of the idea. I found myself, to meet my friend the better, offering it, on the spot, sarcastically. "To his poor little innocent mates!"

"It's too dreadful," cried Mrs. Grose, "to say such cruel things! Why, he's scarce ten years old."

"Yes, yes; it would be incredible."

She was evidently grateful for such a profession. "See him, miss, first. *Then* believe it!" I felt forthwith a new impatience to see him; it was the beginning of a curiosity that, for all the next hours, was to deepen almost to pain. Mrs. Grose was aware, I could judge, of what she had produced in me, and she followed it up with assurance. "You might as well believe it of the little lady. Bless her," she added the next moment—"*look* at her!"

I turned and saw that Flora, whom, ten minutes before, I had established in the schoolroom with a sheet of white paper, a pencil, and a copy of nice "round O's," now presented herself to view at the open door. She expressed in her little way an extraordinary detachment from disagreeable duties, looking to me, however, with a great childish light that seemed to offer it as a mere result of the affection she had conceived for my person, which had rendered necessary that she should follow me. I needed nothing more than this to feel the full force of Mrs. Grose's comparison, and, catching my pupil in my arms, covered her with kisses in which there was a sob of atonement.

None the less, the rest of the day, I watched for further occasion to approach my colleague, especially as, toward evening, I began to fancy she rather sought to avoid me. I overtook her, I remember, on the staircase; we went down together, and at the bottom I detained her, holding her there with a hand on her arm. "I take what you said to me at noon as a declaration that *you've* never known him to be bad."

She threw back her head; she had clearly, by this time, and very honestly, adopted an attitude. "Oh, never known him—I don't pretend *that!*"

I was upset again. "Then you *have* known him—?"

"Yes indeed, miss, thank God!"

On reflection I accepted this. "You mean that a boy who never is—?"

"Is no boy for *me!*"

I held her tighter. "You like them with the spirit to be naughty?" Then, keeping pace with her answer, "So do I!" I eagerly brought out. "But not to the degree to contaminate—"

"To contaminate?"—my big word left her at a loss. I explained it. "To corrupt."

She stared, taking my meaning in; but it produced in her an odd laugh. "Are you afraid he'll corrupt *you?*" She put the question with such a fine bold humour that, with a laugh, a little silly doubtless, to match her own, I gave way for the time to the apprehension of ridicule.

But the next day, as the hour for my drive approached, I cropped up in another place. "What was the lady who was here before?"

"The last governess? She was also young and pretty—almost as young and almost as pretty, miss, even as you."

"Ah, then, I hope her youth and her beauty helped her!" I recollect throwing off. "He seems to like us young and pretty!"

"Oh, he *did*," Mrs. Grose assented: "it was the way he liked everyone!" She had no sooner spoken indeed than she caught herself up. "I mean that's *his* way—the master's."

I was struck. "But of whom did you speak first?"

She looked blank, but she coloured. "Why, of *him*."

"Of the master?"

"Of who else?"

There was so obviously no one else that the next moment I had lost my impression of her having accidentally said more than she meant; and I merely asked what I wanted to know. "Did *she* see anything in the boy—?"

"That wasn't right? She never told me."

I had a scruple, but I overcame it. "Was she careful—particular?"

Mrs. Grose appeared to try to be conscientious. "About some things—yes."

"But not about all?"

Again she considered. "Well, miss—she's gone. I won't tell tales."

"I quite understand your feeling," I hastened to reply; but I thought it, after an instant, not opposed to this concession to pursue: "Did she die here?"

"No—she went off."

I don't know what there was in this brevity of Mrs. Grose's that struck me as ambiguous. "Went off to die?" Mrs. Grose looked straight out of the window, but I felt that, hypothetically, I had a right to know what young persons engaged for Bly were expected to do. "She was taken ill, you mean, and went home?"

"She was not taken ill, so far as appeared, in this house. She left it, at the end of the year, to go home, as she said, for a short holiday, to which the time she had put in had certainly given her a right. We had then a young woman—a nursemaid who had stayed on and who was a good girl and clever; and *she* took the children altogether for the interval. But our young lady never came back, and at the very moment I was expecting her I heard from the master that she was dead."

I turned this over. "But of what?"

"He never told me! But please, miss," said Mrs. Grose, "I must get to my work."

III

Her thus turning her back on me was fortunately not, for my just preoccupations, a snub that could check the growth of our mutual esteem. We met, after I had brought home little Miles, more intimately than ever on the ground of my stupefaction, my general emotion: so monstrous was I then ready to pronounce it that such a child as had now been revealed to me should be under an interdict. I was a little late on the scene, and I felt, as he stood wistfully looking out for me before the door of the inn at which the coach had put him down, that I had seen him, on the instant, without and within, in the great glow of freshness, the same positive fragrance of purity, in which I had, from the first moment, seen his little sister. He was incredibly beautiful, and Mrs. Grose had put her finger on it: everything but a sort of passion of tenderness for him was swept away by his presence. What I then and there took him to my heart for was something divine that I have never found to the same degree in any child—his indescribable little air of knowing nothing in the world but love. It would have been impossible to carry a bad name with a greater sweetness of innocence, and by the time I had got back to Bly with him I remained merely bewildered—so far, that is, as I was not outraged—by the sense of the horrible letter locked up in my room, in a drawer. As soon as I could compass a private word with Mrs. Grose I declared to her that it was grotesque.

She promptly understood me. "You mean the cruel charge—?"

"It doesn't live an instant. My dear woman, *look* at him!"

She smiled at my pretension to have discovered his charm. "I assure you, miss, I do nothing else! What will you say, then?" she immediately added.

"In answer to the letter?" I had made up my mind. "Nothing."

"And to his uncle?"

I was incisive. "Nothing."

"And to the boy himself?"

I was wonderful. "Nothing."

She gave with her apron a great wipe to her mouth. "Then I'll stand by you. We'll see it out."

"We'll see it out!" I ardently echoed, giving her my hand to make it a vow.

She held me there a moment, then whisked up her apron again with her detached hand. "Would you mind, miss, if I used the freedom—"

"To kiss me? No!" I took the good creature in my arms and, after we had embraced like sisters, felt still more fortified and indignant.

This, at all events, was for the time: a time so full that, as I recall the way it went, it reminds me of all the art I now need to make it a little distinct. What I look back at with amazement is the situation I accepted. I had undertaken, with my companion, to see it out, and I was under a charm, apparently, that could smooth away the extent and the far and difficult connections of such an effort. I was lifted aloft on a great wave of infatuation and pity. I found it simple, in my ignorance, my confusion, and perhaps my conceit, to assume that I could deal with a boy whose education for the world was all on the point of beginning. I am unable even to remember at this day what proposal I framed for the end of his holidays and the resumption of his studies. Lessons with me, indeed, that charming summer, we all had a theory that he was to have; but I now feel that, for weeks, the lessons must have been rather my own. I learnt something—at first certainly—that had not been one of the teachings of my small, smothered life; learnt to be amused, and even amusing, and not to think for the morrow. It was the first time, in a manner, that I had known space and air and freedom, all the music of summer and all the mystery of nature. And then there was consideration—and consideration was sweet. Oh, it was a trap—not designed, but deep—to my imagination, to my delicacy, perhaps to my vanity; to whatever, in me, was most excitable. The best way to picture it all is to say that I was off my guard. They gave me so little trouble—they were of a gentleness so extraordinary. I used to speculate—but even this with a dim disconnectedness—as to how the rough future (for all futures are rough!) would handle them and might bruise them. They had the bloom of health and happiness; and yet, as if I had been in charge of a pair of little grandees, of princes of the blood, for whom everything, to be right, would have to be enclosed and protected, the only form that, in my fancy, the after-years could take for them was that of a romantic, a really royal extension of the garden and the park. It may be, of course, above all, that what suddenly broke into this gives the previous time a charm of stillness—that hush in which something gathers or crouches. The change was actually like the spring of a beast.

In the first weeks the days were long; they often, at their finest, gave me what I used to call my own hour, the hour when, for my pupils, tea-time and bed-time having come and gone, I had, before my final retirement, a small interval alone. Much as I liked my companions, this hour was the thing in the day I liked most; and I liked it best of all when, as the light faded—or rather, I should say, the day lingered and the last calls of the last birds sounded, in a flushed sky, from the old trees—I could take a turn into the grounds and enjoy, almost with a sense of property that amused and flattered me, the beauty and dignity of the place. It was a pleasure at these moments to feel myself tranquil and justified; doubtless, perhaps, also to reflect that by my discretion, my quiet good sense and general high propriety, I was giving pleasure—if he ever thought of it!—to the person to whose pressure I had responded. What I was doing was what he had earnestly hoped and directly asked of me, and that I *could*, after all, do it proved even a greater joy than I had expected. I dare say I fancied myself, in short, a remarkable young woman and took comfort in the faith that this would more publicly appear. Well, I needed to be remarkable to offer a front to the remarkable things that presently gave their first sign.

It was plump, one afternoon, in the middle of my very hour: the children were tucked away and I had come out for my stroll. One of the thoughts that, as I don't in the least shrink now from noting, used to be with me in these wanderings was that it would be as charming as a charming story suddenly to meet someone. Someone would appear there at the turn of a path and would stand before me and smile and approve. I didn't ask more than that—I only asked that he should *know;* and the only way to be sure he knew would be to see it, and the kind light of it, in his handsome face. That was exactly present to me—by which I mean the face was—when, on the first of these occasions, at the end of a long June day, I stopped short on emerging from one of the plantations and coming into view of the house. What arrested me on the spot—and with a shock much greater than any vision had allowed for—was the sense that my imagination had, in a flash, turned real. He did stand there!—but high up, beyond the lawn and at the very top of the tower to which, on that first morning, little Flora had conducted me. This tower was one of a pair—square, incongruous, crenelated structures— that were distinguished, for some reason, though I could see little difference, as the new and the old. They flanked opposite ends of the house and were probably architectural absurdities, redeemed in a measure indeed by not being wholly disengaged nor of a height too pretentious, dating, in their gingerbread antiquity, from a romantic revival that was already a respectable past. I admired them, had fancies about them, for we could all profit in a degree, especially when they loomed through the dusk, by the grandeur of their actual battlements; yet it was not at such an elevation that the figure I had so often invoked seemed most in place.

It produced in me, this figure, in the clear twilight, I remember, two distinct gasps of emotion, which were, sharply, the shock of my first and that of my second surprise. My second was a violent perception of the mistake of my

first: the man who met my eyes was not the person I had
precipitately supposed. There came to me thus a bewilderment of vision of which, after these years, there is no living
view that I can hope to give. An unknown man in a lonely
place is a permitted object of fear to a young woman privately
bred; and the figure that faced me was—a few more seconds
assured me—as little any one else I knew as it was the image
that had been in my mind. I had not seen it in Harley Street—
I had not seen it anywhere. The place, moreover, in the
strangest way in the world, had, on the instant, and by the
very fact of its appearance, become a solitude. To me at least,
making my statement here with a deliberation with which I
have never made it, the whole feeling of the moment returns.
It was as if, while I took in—what I did take in—all the rest
of the scene had been stricken with death. I can hear again,
as I write, the intense hush in which the sounds of evening
dropped. The rooks stopped cawing in the golden sky and
the friendly hour lost, for the minute, all its voice. But there
was no other change in nature, unless indeed it were a change
that I saw with a stranger sharpness. The gold was still in the
sky, the clearness in the air, and the man who looked at me
over the battlements was as definite as a picture in a frame.
That's how I thought, with extraordinary quickness, of each
person that he might have been and that he was not. We
were confronted across our distance quite long enough for
me to ask myself with intensity who then he was and to feel,
as an effect of my inability to say, a wonder that in a few
instants more became intense.

The great question, or one of these, is, afterwards, I know,
with regard to certain matters, the question of how long they
have lasted. Well, this matter of mine, think what you will
of it, lasted while I caught at a dozen possibilities, none of
which made a difference for the better, that I could see, in

there having been in the house—and for how long, above all?—a person of whom I was in ignorance. It lasted while I just bridled a little with the sense that my office demanded that there should be no such ignorance and no such person. It lasted while this visitant, at all events—and there was a touch of the strange freedom, as I remember, in the sign of familiarity of his wearing no hat—seemed to fix me, from his position, with just the question, just the scrutiny through the fading light, that his own presence provoked. We were too far apart to call to each other, but there was a moment at which, at shorter range, some challenge between us, breaking the hush, would have been the right result of our straight mutual stare. He was in one of the angles, the one away from the house, very erect, as it struck me, and with both hands on the ledge. So I saw him as I see the letters I form on this page; then, exactly, after a minute, as if to add to the spectacle, he slowly changed his place—passed, looking at me hard all the while, to the opposite corner of the platform. Yes, I had the sharpest sense that during this transit he never took his eyes from me, and I can see at this moment the way his hand, as he went, passed from one of the crenelations to the next. He stopped at the other corner, but less long, and even as he turned away still markedly fixed me. He turned away; that was all I knew.

IV

It was not that I didn't wait, on this occasion, for more, for I was rooted as deeply as I was shaken. Was there a "secret" at Bly—a mystery of Udolpho or an insane, an unmentionable relative kept in unsuspected confinement? I can't say how long I turned it over, or how long, in a confusion of curiosity and dread, I remained where I had had my collision; I only recall that when I re-entered the house darkness had quite closed in. Agitation, in the interval, certainly had held me and driven me, for I must, in circling about the place, have walked three miles; but I was to be, later on, so much more overwhelmed that this mere dawn of alarm was a comparatively human chill. The most singular part of it in fact— singular as the rest had been—was the part I became, in the hall, aware of in meeting Mrs. Grose. This picture comes back to me in the general train—the impression, as I received it on my return, of the wide white panelled space, bright in the lamplight and with its portraits and red carpet, and of the good surprised look of my friend, which immediately told me she had missed me. It came to me straightway, under her contact, that, with plain heartiness, mere relieved anxiety at my appearance, she knew nothing whatever that could bear upon the incident I had there ready for her. I had not suspected in advance that her comfortable face would pull me up, and I somehow measured the importance of what I had seen by my thus finding myself hesitate to mention it. Scarce anything in the whole history seems to me so odd as this fact that my real beginning of fear was one, as I may say, with the instinct of sparing my companion. On the spot, accordingly, in the pleasant hall and with her eyes on me, I, for a reason that I couldn't then have phrased, achieved an inward revolution—offered a vague pretext for my lateness and, with the plea of the beauty of the night and of the heavy dew and wet feet, went as soon as possible to my room.

Here it was another affair; here, for many days after, it was a queer affair enough. There were hours, from day to day—or at least there were moments, snatched even from clear duties—when I had to shut myself up to think. It was not so much yet that I was more nervous than I could bear to be as that I was remarkably afraid of becoming so; for the truth I had now to turn over was, simply and clearly, the truth that I could arrive at no account whatever of the visitor with whom I had been so inexplicably and yet, as it seemed to me, so intimately concerned. It took little time to see that I could sound without forms of inquiry and without exciting remark any domestic complication. The shock I had suffered must have sharpened all my senses; I felt sure, at the end of three days and as the result of mere closer attention, that I had not been practised upon by the servants nor made the object of any "game." Of whatever it was that I knew nothing was known around me. There was but one sane inference: someone had taken a liberty rather gross. That was what, repeatedly, I dipped into my room and locked the door to say to myself. We had been, collectively, subject to an intrusion; some unscrupulous traveller, curious in old houses, had made his way in unobserved, enjoyed the prospect from the best point of view, and then stolen out as he came. If he had given me such a bold hard stare, that was but a part of his indiscretion. The good thing, after all, was that we should surely see no more of him.

This was not so good a thing, I admit, as not to leave me to judge that what, essentially, made nothing else much signify was simply my charming work. My charming work was just my life with Miles and Flora, and through nothing could I so like it as through feeling that I could throw myself into it in trouble. The attraction of my small charges was a constant joy, leading me to wonder afresh at the vanity of my original fears, the distaste I had begun by entertaining for the probable grey prose of my office. There was to be no grey prose, it appeared, and no long grind; so how could work not be charming that presented itself as daily beauty? It was all the romance of the nursery and the poetry of the schoolroom. I don't mean by this, of course, that we studied only fiction and verse; I mean I can express no otherwise the sort of interest my companions inspired. How can I describe that except by saying that instead of growing used to them—and it's a marvel for a governess: I call the sisterhood to witness!— I made constant fresh discoveries. There was one direction, assuredly, in which these discoveries stopped: deep obscurity continued to cover the region of the boy's conduct at school. It had been promptly given me, I have noted, to face that mystery without a pang. Perhaps even it would be nearer the truth to say that—without a word—he himself had cleared it up. He had made the whole charge absurd. My conclusion bloomed there with the real rose-flush of his innocence: he was only too fine and fair for the little horrid, unclean school-world, and he had paid a price for it. I reflected acutely that the sense of such differences, such superiorities of quality, always, on the part of the majority—which could include even stupid, sordid head-masters—turns infallibly to the vindictive.

Both the children had a gentleness (it was their only fault, and it never made Miles a muff) that kept them—how shall I express it?—almost impersonal and certainly quite unpunishable. They were like the cherubs of the anecdote, who had—morally, at any rate—nothing to whack! I remember feeling with Miles in especial as if he had had, as it were, no history. We expect of a small child a scant one, but there was in this beautiful little boy something extraordinarily sensitive, yet extraordinarily happy, that, more than in any creature of his age I have seen, struck me as beginning anew each day. He had never for a second suffered. I took this as a direct disproof of his having really been chastised. If he had been wicked he would have "caught" it, and I should have caught it by the rebound—I should have found the trace. I found nothing at all, and he was therefore an angel. He never spoke of his school, never mentioned a comrade or a master; and I, for my part, was quite too much disgusted to allude to them. Of course I was under the spell, and the wonderful part is that, even at the time, I perfectly knew I was. But I gave myself up to it; it was an antidote to any pain, and I had more pains than one. I was in receipt in these days of disturbing letters from home, where things were not going well. But with my children, what things in the world mattered? That was the question I used to put to my scrappy retirements. I was dazzled by their loveliness.

There was a Sunday—to get on—when it rained with such force and for so many hours that there could be no procession to church; in consequence of which, as the day declined, I had arranged with Mrs. Grose that, should the evening show improvement, we would attend together the late service. The rain happily stopped, and I prepared for our walk, which, through the park and by the good road to the village, would be a matter of twenty minutes. Coming downstairs to meet my colleague in the hall, I remembered a pair of gloves that had required three stitches and that had received them—with a publicity perhaps not edifying—while I sat with the children at their tea, served on Sundays, by exception, in that cold, clean temple of mahogany and brass, the "grown-up" dining-room. The gloves had been dropped there, and I turned in to recover them. The day was grey enough, but the afternoon light still lingered, and it enabled me, on crossing the threshold, not only to recognize, on a chair near the wide window, then closed, the articles I wanted, but to become aware of a person on the other side of the window and looking straight in. One step into the room had sufficed; my vision was instantaneous; it was all there. The person looking straight in was the person who had already appeared to me. He appeared thus again with I won't say greater distinctness, for that was impossible, but with a nearness that represented a forward stride in our intercourse and made me, as I met him, catch my breath and turn cold. He was the same—he was the same, and seen, this time, as he had been seen before, from the waist up, the window, though the dining-room was on the ground-floor, not going down to the terrace on which he stood. His face was close to the glass, yet the effect of this better view was, strangely, only to show me how intense the former had been. He remained but a few seconds—long enough to convince me he also saw and recognized; but it was as if I had been looking at him for years and had known him always. Something, however, happened this time that had not happened before; his stare into my face, through the glass and across the room, was as deep and hard as then, but it quitted me for a moment during which I could still watch it, see it fix successively several other things. On the spot there came to me the added shock of a certitude that it was not for me he had come there. He had come for someone else.

The flash of this knowledge—for it was knowledge in the midst of dread—produced in me the most extraordinary effect, started, as I stood there, a sudden vibration of duty and courage. I say courage because I was beyond all doubt already far gone. I bounded straight out of the door again, reached that of the house, got, in an instant, upon the drive, and, passing along the terrace as fast as I could rush, turned a corner and came full in sight. But it was in sight of nothing now—my visitor had vanished. I stopped, I almost dropped, with the real relief of this; but I took in the whole scene— I gave him time to reappear. I call it time, but how long was it? I can't speak to the purpose today of the duration of these things. That kind of measure must have left me: they couldn't have lasted as they actually appeared to me to last. The terrace and the whole place, the lawn and the garden beyond it, all I could see of the park, were empty with a great emptiness. There were shrubberies and big trees, but I remember the clear assurance I felt that none of them concealed him. He was there or was not there: not there if I didn't see him. I got hold of this; then, instinctively, instead of returning as I had come, went to the window. It was confusedly present to me that I ought to place myself where he had stood. I did so; I applied my face to the pane and looked, as he had looked, into the room. As if, at this moment, to show me exactly what his range had been, Mrs. Grose, as I had done for himself just before, came in from the hall. With this I had the full image of a repetition of what had already occurred. She saw me as I had seen my own visitant; she pulled up short as I had done; I gave her something of the shock that I had received. She turned white, and this made me ask myself if I had blanched as much. She stared, in short, and retreated on just *my* lines, and I knew she had then passed out and come round to me and that I should presently meet her. I remained where I was, and while I waited I thought of more things than one. But there's only one I take space to mention. I wondered why *she* should be scared.

V

Oh, she let me know as soon as, round the corner of the house, she loomed again into view. "What in the name of goodness is the matter—?" She was now flushed and out of breath.

I said nothing till she came quite near. "With me?" I must have made a wonderful face. "Do I show it?"

"You're as white as a sheet. You look awful."

I considered; I could meet on this, without scruple, any innocence. My need to respect the bloom of Mrs. Grose's had dropped, without a rustle, from my shoulders, and if I wavered for the instant it was not with what I kept back. I put out my hand to her and she took it; I held her hard a little, liking to feel her close to me. There was a kind of support in the shy heave of her surprise. "You came for me for church, of course, but I can't go."

"Has anything happened?"

"Yes. You must know now. Did I look very queer?"

"Through this window? Dreadful!"

"Well," I said, "I've been frightened." Mrs. Grose's eyes expressed plainly that *she* had no wish to be, yet also that she knew too well her place not to be ready to share with me any marked inconvenience. Oh, it was quite settled that she *must* share! "Just what you saw from the dining-room a minute ago was the effect of that. What *I* saw—just before—was much worse."

Her hand tightened. "What was it?"

"An extraordinary man. Looking in."

"What extraordinary man?"

"I haven't the least idea."

Mrs. Grose gazed round us in vain. "Then where is he gone?"

"I know still less."

"Have you seen him before?"

"Yes—once. On the old tower."

She could only look at me harder. "Do you mean he's a stranger?"

"Oh, very much!"

"Yet you didn't tell me?"

"No—for reasons. But now that you've guessed—"

Mrs. Grose's round eyes encountered this charge. "Ah, I haven't guessed!" she said very simply. "How can I if *you* don't imagine?"

"I don't in the very least."

"You've seen him nowhere but on the tower?"

"And on this spot just now."

Mrs. Grose looked round again. "What was he doing on the tower?"

"Only standing there and looking down at me."

She thought a minute. "Was he a gentleman?"

I found I had no need to think. "No." She gazed in deeper wonder. "No."

"Then nobody about the place? Nobody from the village?"

"Nobody—nobody. I didn't tell you, but I made sure."

She breathed a vague relief: this was, oddly, so much to the good. It only went indeed a little way. "But if he isn't a gentleman—"

"What *is* he? He's a horror."

"A horror?"

"He's—God help me if I know *what* he is!"

Mrs. Grose looked round once more; she fixed her eyes on the duskier distance, then, pulling herself together, turned to me, with abrupt inconsequence. "It's time we should be at church."

"Oh, I'm not fit for church!"

"Won't it do you good?"

"It won't do *them*—!" I nodded at the house.

"The children?"

"I can't leave them now."

"You're afraid—?"

I spoke boldly. "I'm afraid of *him*."

Mrs. Grose's large face showed me, at this, for the first

time, the far-away faint glimmer of a consciousness more acute: I somehow made out in it the delayed dawn of an idea I myself had not given her and that was as yet quite obscure to me. It comes back to me that I thought instantly of this as something I could get from her; and I felt it to be connected with the desire she presently showed to know more. "When was it—on the tower?"

"About the middle of the month. At this same hour."

"Almost at dark," said Mrs. Grose.

"Oh no, not nearly. I saw him as I see you."

"Then how did he get in?"

"And how did he get out?" I laughed. "I had no opportunity to ask him! This evening, you see," I pursued, "he has not been able to get in."

"He only peeps?"

"I hope it will be confined to that!" She had now let go my hand; she turned away a little. I waited an instant; then I brought out: "Go to church. Good-bye. I must watch."

Slowly she faced me again. "Do you fear for them?"

We met in another long look. "Don't *you?*" Instead of answering she came nearer to the window and, for a minute, applied her face to the glass. "You see how he could see," I meanwhile went on.

She didn't move. "How long was he here?"

"Till I came out. I came to meet him."

Mrs. Grose at last turned round, and there was still more in her face. "*I* couldn't have come out."

"Neither could I!" I laughed again. "But I did come. I have my duty."

"So have I mine," she replied; after which she added: "What is he like?"

"I've been dying to tell you. But he's like nobody."

"Nobody?" she echoed.

"He has no hat." Then seeing in her face that she already, in this, with a deeper dismay, found a touch of picture, I quickly added stroke to stroke. "He has red hair, very red, close-curling, and a pale face, long in shape, with straight, good features and little, rather queer whiskers that are as red as his hair. His eyebrows are, somehow, darker; they look particularly arched and as if they might move a good deal. His eyes are sharp, strange—awfully; but I only know clearly that they're rather small and very fixed. His mouth's wide, and his lips are thin, and except for his little whiskers he's quite clean-shaven. He gives me a sort of sense of looking like an actor."

"An actor!" It was impossible to resemble one less, at least, than Mrs. Grose at that moment.

"I've never seen one, but so I suppose them. He's tall, active, erect," I continued, "but never—no, never!—a gentleman."

My companion's face had blanched as I went on; her round eyes started and her mild mouth gaped. "A gentleman?" she gasped, confounded, stupefied: "a gentleman *he?*"

"You know him then?"

She visibly tried to hold herself. "But he *is* handsome?"

I saw the way to help her. "Remarkably!"

"And dressed—?"

"In somebody's clothes. They're smart, but they're not his own."

She broke into a breathless affirmative groan. "They're the master's!"

I caught it up. "You *do* know him?"

She faltered but a second. "Quint!" she cried.

"Quint?"

"Peter Quint—his own man, his valet, when he was here!"

"When the master was?"

39

Gaping still, but meeting me, she pieced it all together. "He never wore his hat, but he did wear—well, there were waistcoasts missed! They were both here—last year. Then the master went, and Quint was alone."

I followed, but halting a little. "Alone?"

"Alone with *us*." Then, as from a deeper depth, "In charge," she added.

"And what became of him?"

She hung fire so long that I was still more mystified. "He went too," she brought out at last.

"Went where?"

Her expression, at this, became extraordinary. "God knows where! He died."

"Died?" I almost shrieked.

She seemed fairly to square herself, plant herself more firmly to utter the wonder of it. "Yes. Mr. Quint is dead."

VI

It took of course more than that particular passage to place us together in presence of what we had now to live with as we could—my dreadful liability to impressions of the order so vividly exemplified, and my companion's knowledge, henceforth—a knowledge half consternation and half compassion—of that liability. There had been, this evening, after the revelation that left me, for an hour, so prostrate—there had been, for either of us, no attendance on any service but a little service of tears and vows, of prayers and promises, a climax to the series of mutual challenges and pledges that had straightway ensued on our retreating together to the schoolroom and shutting ourselves up there to have everything out. The result of our having everything out was simply to reduce our situation to the last rigour of its elements. She herself had seen nothing, not the shadow of a shadow, and nobody in the house but the governess was in the governess's plight; yet she accepted without directly impugning my sanity the truth as I gave it to her, and ended by showing me, on this ground, an awe-stricken tenderness, an expression of the sense of my more than questionable privilege, of which the very breath has remained with me as that of the sweetest of human charities.

What was settled between us, accordingly, that night, was that we thought we might bear things together; and I was not even sure that, in spite of her exemption, it was she who had the best of the burden. I knew at this hour, I think, as well as I knew later what I was capable of meeting to shelter my pupils; but it took me some time to be wholly sure of what my honest ally was prepared for to keep terms with so compromising a contract. I was queer company enough—quite as queer as the company I received; but as I trace over what we went through I see how much common ground we must have found in the one idea that, by good fortune, *could* steady us. It was the idea, the second movement, that led me straight out, as I may say, of the inner chamber of my dread. I could take the air in the court, at least, and there Mrs. Grose could join me. Perfectly can I recall now the particular way strength came to me before we separated for the night. We had gone over and over every feature of what I had seen.

"He was looking for someone else, you say—someone who was not you?"

"He was looking for little Miles." A portentous clearness now possessed me. "*That's* whom he was looking for."

"But how do you know?"

"I know, I know, I know!" My exaltation grew. "And *you* know, my dear!"

She didn't deny this, but I required, I felt, not even so much telling as that. She resumed in a moment, not at any rate: "What if *he* should see him?"

"Little Miles? That's what he wants!"

She looked immensely scared again. "The child?"

"Heaven forbid! The man. He wants to appear to *them*." That he might was an awful conception, and yet, somehow, I could keep it at bay; which, moreover, as we lingered there, was what I succeeded in practically proving. I had an absolute certainty that I should see again what I had already seen, but something within me said that by offering myself bravely as the sole subject of such experience, by accepting, by inviting, by surmounting it all, I should serve as an expiatory victim and guard the tranquillity of my companions. The children, in especial, I should thus fence about and absolutely save. I recall one of the last things I said that night to Mrs. Grose.

"It does strike me that my pupils have never mentioned—"

She looked at me hard as I musingly pulled up. "His having been here and the time they were with him?"

"The time they were with him, and his name, his presence, his history, in any way."

"Oh, the little lady doesn't remember. She never heard or knew."

"The circumstances of his death?" I thought with some intensity. "Perhaps not. But Miles would remember—Miles would know."

"Ah, don't try him!" broke from Mrs. Grose.

I returned her the look she had given me. "Don't be afraid." I continued to think. "It *is* rather odd."

"That he has never spoken of him?"

"Never by the least allusion. And you tell me they were 'great friends'?"

"Oh, it wasn't *him!*" Mrs. Grose with emphasis declared. "It was Quint's own fancy. To play with him, I mean—to spoil him." She paused a moment; then she added: "Quint was much too free."

This gave me, straight from my vision of his face—*such a face!*—a sudden sickness of disgust. "Too free with *my* boy?"

"Too free with everyone!"

I forebore, for the moment, to analyze this description further than by the reflection that a part of it applied to several of the members of the household, of the half-dozen maids and men who were still of our small colony. But there was everything, for our apprehension, in the lucky fact that no discomfortable legend, no perturbation of scullions, had ever, within anyone's memory, attached to the kind old place. It had neither bad name nor ill fame, and Mrs. Grose, most apparently, only desired to cling to me and to quake in silence. I even put her, the very last thing of all, to the test. It was when, at midnight, she had her hand on the schoolroom door to take leave. "I have it from you then—for it's of great importance—that he was definitely and admittedly bad?"

"Oh, not admittedly. *I* knew it—but the master didn't."

"And you never told him?"

"Well, he didn't like tale-bearing—he hated complaints. He was terribly short with anything of the kind, and if people were all right to *him*—"

"He wouldn't be bothered with more?" This squared well enough with my impression of him: he was not a trouble-loving gentleman, nor so very particular perhaps about some of the company *he* kept. All the same, I pressed my interlocutress. "I promise you *I* would have told!"

She felt my discrimination. "I dare say I was wrong. But, really, I was afraid."

"Afraid of what?"

"Of things that man could do. Quint was so clever—he was so deep."

I took this in still more than, probably, I showed. "You weren't afraid of anything else? Not of his effect—!"

"His effect?" she repeated with a face of anguish and waiting while I faltered.

"On innocent little precious lives. They were in your charge."

"No, they were not in mine!" she roundly and distressfully returned. "The master believed in him and placed him here because he was supposed not to be well and the country air so good for him. So he had everything to say. Yes"—she let me have it—"even about *them*."

"Them—that creature?" I had to smother a kind of howl. "And you could bear it!"

"No. I couldn't—and I can't now!" And the poor woman burst into tears.

A rigid control, from the next day, was, as I have said, to follow them; yet how often and how passionately, for a week, we came back together to the subject! Must as we had discussed it that Sunday night, I was, in the immediate later hours in especial—for it may be imagined whether I slept—still haunted with the shadow of something she had not told me. I myself had kept back nothing, but there was a word Mrs. Grose had kept back. I was sure, moreover, by morning, that this was not from a failure of frankness, but because on every side there were fears. It seems to me indeed, in retrospect, that by the time the morrow's sun was high I had restlessly read into the facts before us almost all the meaning they were to receive from subsequent and more cruel occurrences. What they gave me above all was just the sinister figure of the living man—the dead one would keep awhile!—

and of the months he had continuously passed at Bly, which, added up, made a formidable stretch. The limit of this evil time had arrived only when, on the dawn of a winter's morning, Peter Quint was found, by a labourer going to early work, stone dead on the road from the village: a catastrophe explained—superficially at least—by a visible wound to his head; such a wound as might have been produced—and as, on the final evidence, *had* been—by a fatal slip, in the dark and after leaving the public house, on the steepish icy slope, a wrong path altogether, at the bottom of which he lay. The icy slope, the turn mistaken at night and in liquor, accounted for much—practically, in the end and after the inquest and boundless chatter, for everything; but there had been matters in his life—strange passages and perils, secret disorders, vices more than suspected—that would have accounted for a good deal more.

I scarce know how to put my story into words that shall be a credible picture of my state of mind; but I was in these days literally able to find a joy in the extraordinary flight of heroism the occasion demanded of me. I now saw that I had been asked for a service admirable and difficult; and there would be a greatness in letting it be seen—oh, in the right quarter!—that I could succeed where many another girl might have failed. It was an immense help to me—I confess I rather applaud myself as I look back!—that I saw my service so strongly and so simply. I was there to protect and defend the little creatures in the world the most bereaved and the most loveable, the appeal of whose helplessness had suddenly become only too explicit, a deep, constant ache of one's own committed heart. We were cut off, really, together; we were united in our danger. They had nothing but me, and I—well, I had *them*. It was in short a magnificent chance. This chance presented itself to me in an image richly material. I was a screen—I was to stand before them. The more I saw, the less they would. I began to watch them in a stifled suspense, a disguised excitement that might well, had it continued too long, have turned to something like madness. What saved me, as I now see, was that it turned to something else altogether. It didn't last as suspense—it was superseded by horrible proofs. Proofs, I say, yes—from the moment I really took hold.

This moment dated from an afternoon hour that I happened to spend in the grounds with the younger of my pupils alone. We had left Miles indoors, on the red cushion of a deep window-seat; he had wished to finish a book, and I had been glad to encourage a purpose so laudable in a young man whose only defect was an occasional excess of the restless. His sister, on the contrary, had been alert to come out, and I strolled with her half an hour, seeking the shade, for the sun was still high and the day exceptionally warm. I was aware afresh, with her, as we went, of how, like her brother, she contrived—it was the charming thing in both children—to let me alone without appearing to drop me and to accompany me without appearing to surround. They were never importunate and yet never listless. My attention to them all really went to seeing them amuse themselves immensely without me: this was a spectacle they seemed actively to prepare and that engaged me as an active admirer. I walked in a world of their invention—they had no occasion whatever to draw upon mine; so that my time was taken only with being, for them, some remarkable person or thing that the game of the moment required and that was merely, thanks to my superior, my exalted stamp, a happy and highly distinguished sinecure. I forget what I was on the present occasion; I only remember that I was something very important and very quiet and that Flora was playing very hard. We were on the edge of the lake, and, as we had lately begun geography, the lake was the Sea of Azof.

Suddenly, in these circumstances, I became aware that, on the other side of the Sea of Azof, we had an interested spectator. The way this knowledge gathered in me was the strangest thing in the world—the strangest, that is, except the very much stranger in which it quickly merged itself. I had sat down with a piece of work—for I was something or other that could sit—on the old stone bench which overlooked the pond; and in this position I began to take in with certitude, and yet without direct vision, the presence, at a distance, of a third person. The old trees, the thick shrubbery, made a great and pleasant shade, but it was all suffused with the brightness of the hot, still hour. There was no ambiguity in anything; none whatever, at least, in the conviction I from one moment to another found myself forming as to what I should see straight before me and across the lake as a consequence of raising my eyes. They were attached at this juncture to the stitching in which I was engaged, and I can feel once more the spasm of my effort not to move them till I should so have steadied myself as to be able to make up my mind what to do. There was an alien object in view—a figure whose right of presence I instantly, passionately questioned. I recollect counting over perfectly the possibilities, reminding myself that nothing was more natural, for instance, than the appearance of one of the men about the place, or even of a messenger, a postman or a tradesman's boy, from the village. That reminder had as little effect on my practical certitude as I was conscious—still even without looking—of its having upon the character and attitude of our visitor. Nothing was more natural than that these things should be the other things that they absolutely were not.

Of the positive identity of the apparition I would assure

myself as soon as the small clock of my courage should have ticked out the right second; meanwhile, with an effort that was already sharp enough, I transferred my eyes straight to little Flora, who, at the moment, was about ten yards away. My heart had stood still for an instant with the wonder and terror of the question whether she too would see; and I held my breath while I waited for what a cry from her, what some sudden innocent sign either of interest or of alarm, would tell me. I waited, but nothing came; then, in the first place— and there is something more dire in this, I feel, than in anything I have to relate—I was determined by a sense that, within a minute, all sounds from her had previously dropped; and, in the second, by the circumstance that, also within the minute, she had, in her play, turned her back to the water. This was her attitude when I at last looked at her—looked with the confirmed conviction that we were still, together, under direct personal notice. She had picked up a small flat piece of wood, which happened to have in it a little hole that had evidently suggested to her the idea of sticking in another fragment that might figure as a mast and make the thing a boat. This second morsel, as I watched her, she was very markedly and intently attempting to tighten in its place. My apprehension of what she was doing sustained me so that after some seconds I felt I was ready for more. Then I again shifted my eyes—I faced what I had to face.

VII

I got hold of Mrs. Grose as soon after this as I could; and I can give no intelligible account of how I fought out the interval. Yet I still hear myself cry as I fairly threw myself into her arms: "They *know*—it's too monstrous: they know, they know!"

"And what on earth—?" I felt her incredulity as she held me.

"Why, all that *we* know—and heaven knows what else besides!" Then, as she released me, I made it out to her, made it out perhaps only now with full coherency even to myself. "Two hours ago, in the garden"—I could scarce articulate—"Flora *saw!*"

Mrs. Grose took it as she might have taken a blow in the stomach. "She has told you?" she panted.

"Not a word—that's the horror. She kept it to herself! The child of eight, *that* child!" Unutterable still, for me, was the stupefaction of it.

Mrs. Grose, of course, could only gape the wider. "Then how do you know?"

"I was there—I saw with my eyes: saw that she was perfectly aware."

"Do you mean aware of *him?*"

"No—of *her*." I was conscious as I spoke that I looked prodigious things, for I got the slow reflection of them in my companion's face. "Another person—this time; but a figure of quite as unmistakable horror and evil: a woman in black, pale and dreadful!—with such an air also, and such a face!—on the other side of the lake. I was there with the child—quiet for the hour; and in the midst of it she came."

"Came how—from where?"

"From where they come from! She just appeared and stood there—but not so near."

"And without coming nearer?"

"Oh, for the effect and the feeling, she might have been as close as you!"

My friend, with an odd impulse, fell back a step. "Was she someone you've never seen?"

"Yes. But someone the child has. Someone *you* have." Then, to show how I had thought it all out: "My predecessor—the one who died."

"Miss Jessel?"

"Miss Jessel. You don't believe me?" I pressed.

She turned right and left in her distress. "How can you be sure?"

This drew from me, in the state of my nerves, a flash of impatience. "Then ask Flora—*she's* sure!" But I had no sooner spoken than I caught myself up. "No, for God's sake, *don't!* She'll say she isn't—she'll lie!"

Mrs. Grose was not too bewildered instinctively to protest. "Ah, how *can* you?"

"Because I'm clear. Flora doesn't want me to know."

"It's only then to spare you."

"No, no—there are depths, depths! The more I go over it, the more I see in it, and the more I see in it the more I fear. I don't know what I *don't* see—what I *don't* fear!"

Mrs. Grose tried to keep up with me. "You mean you're afraid of seeing her again!"

"Oh, no; that's nothing—now!" Then I explained. "It's of *not* seeing her."

But my companion only looked wan. "I don't understand you."

"Why, it's that the child may keep it up—and that the child assuredly *will*—without my knowing it."

At the image of this possibility Mrs. Grose for a moment collapsed, yet presently to pull herself together again, as if from the positive force of the sense of what, should we yield an inch, there would really be to give way to. "Dear, dear—

we must keep our heads! And after all, if she doesn't mind it—!" She even tried a grim joke. "Perhaps she likes it!"

"Likes *such* things—a scrap of an infant!"

"Isn't it just a proof of her blessed innocence?" my friend bravely inquired.

She brought me, for the instant, almost round. "Oh, we must clutch at *that*—we must cling to it! If it isn't a proof of what you say, it's a proof of—God knows what! For the woman's a horror of horrors."

Mrs. Grose, at this, fixed her eyes a minute on the ground; then at last raising them, "Tell me how you know," she said.

"Then you admit it's what she was?" I cried.

"Tell me how you know," my friend simply repeated.

"Know? By seeing her! By the way she looked."

"At you, do you mean—so wickedly?"

"Dear me, no—I could have borne that. She gave me never a glance. She only fixed the child."

Mrs. Grose tried to see it. "Fixed her?"

"Ah, with such awful eyes!"

She stared at mine as if they might really have resembled them. "Do you mean of dislike?"

"God help us, no. Of something much worse."

"Worse than dislike?"—this left her indeed at a loss.

"With a determination—indescribable. With a kind of fury of intention."

I made her turn pale. "Intention?"

"To get hold of her." Mrs. Grose—her eyes just lingering on mine—gave a shudder and walked to the window; and while she stood there looking out I completed my statement. "*That's* what Flora knows."

After a little she turned round. "The person was in black, you say?"

"In mourning—rather poor, almost shabby. But—yes—

with extraordinary beauty." I now recognized to what I had at last, stroke by stroke, brought the victim of my confidence, for she quite visibly weighed this. "Oh, handsome—very, very," I insisted; "wonderfully handsome. But infamous."

She slowly came back to me. "Miss Jessel—*was* infamous." She once more took my hand in both her own, holding it as tight as if to fortify me against the increase of alarm I might draw from this disclosure. "They were both infamous," she finally said.

So, for a little, we faced it once more together; and I found absolutely a degree of help in seeing it now so straight. "I appreciate," I said, "the great decency of your not having hitherto spoken; but the time has certainly come to give me the whole thing." She appeared to assent to this, but still only in silence; seeing which I went on: "I must have it now. Of what did she die? Come, there was something between them."

"There was everything."

"In spite of the difference—?"

"Oh, of their rank, their condition"—she brought it woefully out. "*She* was a lady."

I turned it over; I again saw. "Yes—she was a lady."

"And he so dreadfully below," said Mrs. Grose.

I felt that I doubtless needn't press too hard, in such company, on the place of a servant in the scale; but there was nothing to prevent an acceptance of my companion's own measure of my predecessor's abasement. There was a way to deal with that, and I dealt; the more readily for my full vision—on the evidence—of our employer's late clever, good-looking "own" man; impudent, assured, spoiled, depraved. "The fellow was a hound."

Mrs. Grose considered as if it were perhaps a little a case for a sense of shades. "I've never seen one like him. He did what he wished."

"With *her?*"

"With them all."

It was as if now in my friend's own eyes Miss Jessel had again appeared. I seemed at any rate, for an instant, to see their evocation of her as distinctly as I had seen her by the pond; and I brought out with decision: "It must have been also what *she* wished!"

Mrs. Grose's face signified that it had been indeed, but she said at the same time: "Poor woman—she paid for it!"

"Then you do know what she died of?" I asked.

"No—I know nothing. I wanted not to know; I was glad enough I didn't; and I thanked heaven she was well out of this!"

"Yet you had, then, your idea—"

"Of her real reason for leaving? Oh, yes—as to that. She couldn't have stayed. Fancy it here—for a governess! And afterwards I imagined—and I still imagine. And what I imagine is dreadful."

"Not so dreadful as what *I* do," I replied; on which I must have shown her—as I was indeed but too conscious—a front of miserable defeat. It brought out again all her compassion for me, and at the renewed touch of her kindness my power to resist broke down. I burst, as I had, the other time, made her burst, into tears; she took me to her motherly breast, and my lamentation overflowed. "I don't do it!" I sobbed in despair; "I don't save or shield them! It's far worse than I dreamed—they're lost!"

VIII

What I had said to Mrs. Grose was true enough: there were in the matter I had put before her depths and possibilities that I lacked resolution to sound; so that when we met once more in the wonder of it we were of a common mind about the duty of resistance to extravagant fancies. We were to keep our heads if we should keep nothing else—difficult indeed as that might be in the face of what, in our prodigious experience, was least to be questioned. Late that night, while the house slept, we had another talk in my room, when she went all the way with me as to its being beyond doubt that I had seen exactly what I had seen. To hold her perfectly in the pinch of that, I found I had only to ask her how, if I had "made it up," I came to be able to give, of each of the persons appearing to me, a picture disclosing, to the last detail, their special marks—a portrait on the exhibition of which she had instantly recognized and named them. She wished, of course—small blame to her!—to sink the whole subject; and I was quick to assure her that my own interest in it had now violently taken the form of a search for the way to escape from it. I encountered her on the ground of a probability that with recurrence—for recurrence we took for granted— I should get used to my danger, distinctly professing that my personal exposure had suddenly become the least of my discomforts. It was my new suspicion that was intolerable; and yet even to this complication the later hours of the day had brought a little ease.

On leaving her, after my first outbreak, I had of course returned to my pupils, associating the right remedy for my dismay with that sense of their charm which I had already found to be a thing I could positively cultivate and which had never failed me yet. I had simply, in other words, plunged afresh into Flora's special society and there become aware— it was almost a luxury!—that she could put her little conscious hand straight upon the spot that ached. She had looked at me in sweet speculation and then had accused me to my face

of having "cried." I had supposed I had brushed away the
ugly signs: but I could literally—for the time, at all events—
rejoice, under this fathomless charity, that they had not entirely disappeared. To gaze into the depths of blue of the
child's eyes and pronounce their loveliness a trick of pre-
mature cunning was to be guilty of a cynicism in preference
to which I naturally preferred to abjure my judgment and,
so far as might be, my agitation. I couldn't abjure for merely
wanting to, but I could repeat to Mrs. Grose—as I did there,
over and over, in the small hours—that with their voices in
the air, their pressure on one's heart and their fragrant faces
against one's cheek, everything fell to the ground but their
incapacity and their beauty. It was a pity that, somehow, to
settle this once for all, I had equally to re-enumerate the signs
of subtlety that, in the afternoon, by the lake, had made a
miracle of my show of self-possession. It was a pity to be
obliged to re-investigate the certitude of the moment itself
and repeat how it had come to me as a revelation that the
inconceivable communion I then surprised was a matter, for
either party, of habit. It was a pity that I should have had to
quaver out again the reasons for my not having, in my delusion, so much as questioned that the little girl saw our
visitant even as I actually saw Mrs. Grose herself, and that
she wanted, by just so much as she did thus see, to make me
suppose she didn't, and at the same time, without showing
anything, arrive at a guess as to whether I myself did! It was
a pity that I needed once more to describe the portentous
little activity by which she sought to divert my attention—
the perceptible increase of movement, the greater intensity
of play, the singing, the gabbling of nonsense, and the invitation to romp.

Yet if I had not indulged, to prove there was nothing in
it, in this review, I should have missed the two or three dim

elements of comfort that still remained to me. I should not for instance have been able to asseverate to my friend that I was certain—which was so much to the good—that *I* at least had not betrayed myself. I should not have been prompted, by stress of need, by desperation of mind,—I scarce know what to call it,—to invoke such further aid to intelligence as might spring from pushing my colleague fairly to the wall. She had told me, bit by bit, under pressure, a great deal; but a small shifty spot on the wrong side of it all still sometimes brushed my brow like the wing of a bat; and I remember how on this occasion—for the sleeping house and the concentration alike of our danger and our watch seemed to help—I felt the importance of giving the last jerk to the curtain. "I don't believe anything so horrible," I recollect saying; "no, let us put it definitely, my dear, that I don't. But if I did, you know, there's a thing I should require now, just without sparing you the least bit more—oh, not a scrap, come!—to get out of you. What was it you had in mind when, in our distress, before Miles came back, over the letter from his school, you said, under my insistence, that you didn't pretend for him that he had not literally *ever* been 'bad'? He has *not* literally 'ever,' in these weeks that I myself have lived with him and so closely watched him; he has been an imperturbable little prodigy of delightful, loveable goodness. Therefore you might perfectly have made the claim for him if you had not, as it happened, seen an exception to take. What was your exception, and to what passage in your personal observation of him did you refer?"

It was a dreadfully austere inquiry, but levity was not our note, and, at any rate, before the grey dawn admonished us to separate I had got my answer. What my friend had had in mind proved to be immensely to the purpose. It was neither more nor less than the circumstance that for a period of

several months Quint and the boy had been perpetually together. It was in fact the very appropriate truth that she had
ventured to criticize the propriety, to hint at the incongruity,
of so close an alliance, and even to go so far on the subject
as a frank overture to Miss Jessel. Miss Jessel had, with a
most strange manner, requested her to mind her business,
and the good woman had, on this, directly approached little
Miles. What she had said to him, since I pressed, was that
she liked to see young gentlemen not forget their station.

I pressed again, of course, at this. "You reminded him
that Quint was only a base menial?"

"As you might say! And it was his answer, for one thing,
that was bad."

"And for another thing?" I waited. "He repeated your
words to Quint?"

"No, not that. It's just that he *wouldn't!*" she could still
impress upon me. "I was sure, at any rate," she added, "that
he didn't. But he denied certain occasions."

"What occasions?"

"When they had been about together quite as if Quint
were his tutor—and a very grand one—and Miss Jessel only
for the little lady. When he had gone off with the fellow, I
mean, and spent hours with him."

"He then prevaricated about it—he said he hadn't?" Her
assent was clear enough to cause me to add in a moment: "I
see. He lied."

"Oh!" Mrs. Grose mumbled. This was a suggestion that
it didn't matter; which indeed she backed up by a further
remark. "You see, after all, Miss Jessel didn't mind. She didn't
forbid him."

I considered. "Did he put that to you as a justification?"

At this she dropped again. "No, he never spoke of it."

"Never mentioned her in connection with Quint?"

She saw, visibly flushing, where I was coming out. "Well, he didn't show anything. He denied," she repeated; "he denied."

Lord, how I pressed her now! "So that you could see he knew what was between the two wretches?"

"I don't know—I don't know!" the poor woman groaned.

"You do know, you dear thing," I replied; "only you haven't my dreadful boldness of mind, and you keep back, out of timidity and modesty and delicacy, even the impression that, in the past, when you had, without my aid, to flounder about in silence, most of all made you miserable. But I shall get it out of you yet! There was something in the boy that suggested to you," I continued, "that he covered and concealed their relationship."

"Oh, he couldn't prevent—"

"Your learning the truth? I dare say! But, heavens," I fell, with vehemence, a-thinking, "what it shows that they must, to that extent, have succeeded in making of him!"

"Ah, nothing that's not nice *now!*" Mrs. Grose lugubriously pleaded.

"I don't wonder you looked queer," I persisted, "when I mentioned to you the letter from his school!"

"I doubt if I looked as queer as you!" she retorted with homely force. "And if he was so bad then as that comes to, how is he such an angel now?"

"Yes, indeed—and if he was a fiend at school! How, how, how? Well," I said in my torment, "you must put it to me again, but I shall not be able to tell you for some days. Only, put it to me again!" I cried in a way that made my friend stare. "There are directions in which I must not for the present let myself go." Meanwhile I returned to her first example—the one to which she had just previously referred—of the boy's happy capacity for an occasional slip. "If Quint—on your remonstrance at the time you speak of—was a base menial, one of the things Miles said to you, I find myself guessing, was that you were another." Again her admission was so adequate that I continued: "And you forgave him that?"

"Wouldn't *you?*"

"Oh, yes!" And we exchanged there, in the stillness, a sound of the oddest amusement. Then I went on: "At all events, while he was with the man—"

"Miss Flora was with the woman. It suited them all!"

It suited me too, I felt, only too well; by which I mean that it suited exactly the particularly deadly view I was in the very act of forbidding myself to entertain. But I so far succeeded in checking the expression of this view that I will throw, just here, no further light on it than may be offered by the mention of my final observation to Mrs. Grose. "His having lied and been impudent are, I confess, less engaging specimens that I had hoped to have from you of the outbreak in him of the little natural man. Still," I mused, "they must do, for they make me feel more than ever that I must watch."

It made me blush, the next minute, to see in my friend's face how much more unreservedly she had forgiven him than her anecdote struck me as presenting to my own tenderness an occasion for doing. This came out when, at the schoolroom door, she quitted me. "Surely you don't accuse *him*—"

"Of carrying on an intercourse that he conceals from me? Ah, remember that, until further evidence, I now accuse nobody." Then, before shutting her out to go, by another passage, to her own place, "I must just wait," I wound up.

I X

I waited and waited, and the days, as they elapsed, took something from my consternation. A very few of them, in fact, passing, in constant sight of my pupils, without a fresh incident, sufficed to give to grievous fancies and even to odious memories a kind of brush of the sponge. I have spoken of the surrender to their extraordinary childish grace as a thing I could actively cultivate, and it may be imagined if I neglected now to address myself to this source for whatever it would yield. Stranger than I can express, certainly, was the effort to struggle against my new lights; it would doubtless have been, however, a greater tension still had it not been so frequently successful. I used to wonder how my little charges could help guessing that I thought strange things about them; and the circumstance that these things only made them more interesting was not by itself a direct aid to keeping them in the dark. I trembled lest they should see that they *were* so immensely more interesting. Putting things at the worst, at all events, as in meditation I so often did, any clouding of their innocence could only be—blameless and fore-doomed as they were—a reason the more for taking risks. There were moments when, by an irresistible impulse, I found myself catching them up and pressing them to my heart. As soon as I had done so I used to say to myself: "What will they think of that? Doesn't it betray too much?" It would have been easy to get into a sad, wild tangle about how much I might betray; but the real account, I feel, of the hours of peace that I could still enjoy was that the immediate charm of my companions was a beguilement still effective even under the shadow of the possibility that it was studied. For if it occurred to me that I might occasionally excite suspicion by the little outbreaks of my sharper passion for them, so too I remember wondering if I mightn't see a queerness in the traceable increase of their own demonstrations.

They were at this period extravagantly and preternaturally fond of me; which, after all, I could reflect, was no more than

a graceful response in children perpetually bowed over and
hugged. The homage of which they were so lavish succeeded,
in truth, for my nerves, quite as well as if I never appeared
to myself, as I may say, literally to catch them at a purpose
in it. They had never, I think, wanted to do so many things
for their poor protectress; I mean—though they got their
lessons better and better, which was naturally what would
please her most—in the way of diverting, entertaining, sur-
prising her; reading her passages, telling her stories, acting
her charades, pouncing out at her, in disguises, as animals
and historical characters, and above all astonishing her by the
"pieces" they had secretly got by heart and could interminably
recite. I should never get to the bottom—were I to let myself
go even now—of the prodigious private commentary, all
under still more private correction, with which, in these days,
I overscored their full hours. They had shown me from the
first a facility for everything, a general faculty which, taking
a fresh start, achieved remarkable flights. They got their little
tasks as if they loved them, and indulged, from the mere
exuberance of the gift, in the most unimposed little miracles
of memory. They not only popped out at me as tigers and
as Romans, but as Shakespeareans, astronomers, and navi-
gators. This was so singularly the case that it had presumably
much to do with the fact as to which, at the present day, I
am at a loss for a different explanation: I allude to my unnatural composure on the subject of another school for Miles.
What I remember is that I was content not, for the time, to
open the question, and that contentment must have sprung
from the sense of his perpetually striking show of cleverness.
He was too clever for a bad governess, for a parson's daughter, to spoil; and the strangest if not the brightest thread in
the pensive embroidery I just spoke of was the impression
I might have got, if I had dared to work it out, that he was

under some influence operating in his small intellectual life as a tremendous incitement.

If it was easy to reflect, however, that such a boy could postpone school, it was at least as marked that for such a boy to have been "kicked out" by a school-master was a mystification without end. Let me add that in their company now—and I was careful almost never to be out of it—I could follow no scent very far. We lived in a cloud of music and love and success and private theatricals. The musical sense in each of the children was of the quickest, but the elder in especial had a marvellous knack of catching and repeating. The school-room piano broke into all gruesome fancies; and when that failed there were confabulations in corners, with a sequel of one of them going out in the highest spirits in order to "come in" as something new. I had had brothers myself, and it was no revelation to me that little girls could be slavish idolaters of little boys. What surpassed everything was that there was a little boy in the world who could have for the inferior age, sex, and intelligence so fine a consideration. They were extraordinarily at one, and to say that they never either quarrelled or complained is to make the note of praise coarse for their quality of sweetness. Sometimes, indeed, when I dropped into coarseness, I perhaps came across traces of little understandings between them by which one of them should keep me occupied while the other slipped away. There is a *naïf* side, I suppose, in all diplomacy; but if my pupils practised upon me, it was surely with the minimum of grossness. It was all in the other quarter that, after a lull, the grossness broke out.

I find that I really hang back; but I must take my plunge. In going on with the record of what was hideous at Bly, I not only challenge the most liberal faith—for which I little care; but—and this is another matter—I renew what I myself suffered, I again push my way through it to the end. There came suddenly an hour after which, as I look back, the affair seems to me to have been all pure suffering; but I have at least reached the heart of it, and the straightest road out is doubtless to advance. One evening—with nothing to lead up or to prepare it—I felt the cold touch of the impression that had breathed on me the night of my arrival and which, much lighter then, as I have mentioned, I should probably have made little of in memory had my subsequent sojourn been less agitated. I had not gone to bed; I sat reading by a couple of candles. There was a roomful of old books at Bly—last-century fiction, some of it, which, to the extent of a distinctly deprecated renown, but never to so much as that of a stray specimen, had reached the sequestered home and appealed to the unavowed curiosity of my youth. I remember that the book I had in my hand was Fielding's *Amelia;* also that I was wholly awake. I recall further both a general conviction that it was horribly late and a particular objection to looking at my watch. I figure, finally, that the white curtain draping, in the fashion of those days, the head of Flora's little bed, shrouded, as I had assured myself long before, the perfection of childish rest. I recollect in short that, though I was deeply interested in my author, I found myself, at the turn of a page and with his spell all scattered, looking straight up from him and hard at the door of my room. There was a moment during which I listened, reminded of the faint sense I had had, the first night, of there being something undefineably astir in the house, and noted the soft breath of the open casement just move the half-drawn blind. Then, with all the marks of a deliberation that must have seemed magnificent had there been anyone to admire it, I laid down my book, rose to my feet, and, taking a candle, went straight out of the room and, from the passage, on which my light made little impression, noiselessly closed and locked the door.

I can say now neither what determined nor what guided

me, but I went straight along the lobby, holding my candle high, till I came within sight of the tall window that presided over the great turn of the staircase. At this point I precipitately found myself aware of three things. They were practically simultaneous, yet they had flashes of succession. My candle, under a bold flourish, went out, and I perceived, by the uncovered window, that the yielding dusk of earliest morning rendered it unnecessary. Without it, the next instant, I saw that there was someone on the stair. I speak of sequences, but I required no lapse of seconds to stiffen myself for a third encounter with Quint. The apparition had reached the landing half-way up and was therefore on the spot nearest the window, where at sight of me, it stopped short and fixed me exactly as it had fixed me from the tower and from the garden. He knew me as well as I knew him; and so, in the cold, faint twilight, with a glimmer in the high glass and another on the polish of the oak stair below, we faced each other in our common intensity. He was absolutely, on this occasion, a living, detestable, dangerous presence. But that was not the wonder of wonders; I reserve this distinction for quite another circumstance: the circumstance that dread had unmistakably quitted me and that there was nothing in me there that didn't meet and measure him.

I had plenty of anguish after that extraordinary moment, but I had, thank God, no terror. And he knew I had not— I found myself at the end of an instant magnificently aware of this. I felt, in a fierce rigour of confidence, that if I stood my ground a minute I should cease—for the time, at least— to have him to reckon with; and during the minute, accordingly, the thing was as human and hideous as a real interview: hideous just because it *was* human, as human as to have met alone, in the small hours, in a sleeping house, some enemy, some adventurer, some criminal. It was the dead silence of our long gaze at such close quarters that gave the whole horror, huge as it was, its only note of the unnatural. If I had met a murderer in such a place and at such an hour, we still at least would have spoken. Something would have passed, in life, between us; if nothing had passed one of us would have moved. The moment was so prolonged that it would have taken but little more to make me doubt if even *I* were in life. I can't express what followed it save by saying that the silence itself—which was indeed in a manner an attestation of my strength—became the element into which I saw the figure disappear; in which I definitely saw it turn as I might have seen the low wretch to which it had once belonged turn on receipt of an order, and pass, with my eyes on the villainous back that no hunch could have more disfigured, straight down the staircase and into the darkness in which the next bend was lost.

X

I remained awhile at the top of the stair, but with the effect presently of understanding that when my visitor had gone, he had gone: then I returned to my room. The foremost thing I saw there by the light of the candle I had left burning was that Flora's little bed was empty; and on this I caught my breath with all the terror that, five minutes before, I had been able to resist. I dashed at the place in which I had left her lying and over which (for the small silk counterpane and the sheets were disarranged) the white curtains had been deceivingly pulled forward; then my step, to my unutterable relief, produced an answering sound: I perceived an agitation of the window-blind, and the child, ducking down, emerged rosily from the other side of it. She stood there in so much of her candour and so little of her nightgown, with her pink bare feet and the golden glow of her curls. She looked intensely grave, and I had never had such a sense of losing an advantage acquired (the thrill of which had just been so prodigious) as on my consciousness that she addressed me with a reproach. "You naughty: where *have* you been?"—instead of challenging her own irregularity I found myself arraigned and explaining. She herself explained, for that matter, with the loveliest, eagerest simplicity. She had known suddenly, as she lay there, that I was out of the room, and had jumped up to see what had become of me. I had dropped, with the joy of her reappearance, back into my chair—feeling then, and then only, a little faint; and she had pattered straight over to me, thrown herself upon my knee, given herself to be held with the flame of the candle full in the wonderful little face that was still flushed with sleep. I remember closing my eyes an instant, yieldingly, consciously, as before the excess of something beautiful that shone out of the blue of her own. "You were looking for me out of the window?" I said. "You thought I might be walking in the grounds?"

"Well, you know, I thought someone was"—she never blanched as she smiled out that at me.

Oh, how I looked at her now! "And did you see anyone?"

"Ah, *no!*" she returned, almost with the full privilege of childish inconsequence, resentfully, though with a long sweetness in her little drawl of the negative.

At that moment, in the state of my nerves, I absolutely believed she lied; and if I once more closed my eyes it was before the dazzle of the three or four possible ways in which I might take this up. One of these, for a moment, tempted me with such singular intensity that, to withstand it, I must have gripped my little girl with a spasm that, wonderfully, she submitted to without a cry or a sign of fright. Why not break out at her on the spot and have it all over?—give it to her straight in her lovely little lighted face? "You see, you see, you *know* that you do and that you already quite suspect I believe it; therefore why not frankly confess it to me, so that we may at least live with it together and learn perhaps, in the strangeness of our fate, where we are and what it means?" This solicitation dropped, alas, as it came: if I could immediately have succumbed to it I might have spared my-self—well you'll see what. Instead of succumbing I sprang again to my feet, looked at her bed, and took a helpless middle way. "Why did you pull the curtain over the place to make me think you were still there?"

Flora luminously considered; after which, with her little divine smile: "Because I don't like to frighten you!"

"But if I had, by your idea, gone out—?"

She absolutely declined to be puzzled; she turned her eyes to the flame of the candle as if the question were as irrelevant, or at any rate as impersonal, as Mrs. Marcet or nine-times-nine. "Oh, but you know," she quite adequately answered, "that you might come back, you dear, and that you *have!*" And after a little, when she had got into bed, I had, for a long time, by almost sitting on her to hold her hand, to prove that I recognized the pertinence of my return.

You may imagine the general complexion, from that mo-ment, of my nights. I repeatedly sat up till I didn't know when; I selected moments when my room-mate unmistakably slept, and, stealing out, took noiseless turns in the passage and even pushed as far as to where I had last met Quint. But I never met him there again; and I may as well say at once that I on no other occasion saw him in the house. I just missed, on the staircase, on the other hand, a different ad-venture. Looking down it from the top I once recognized the presence of a woman seated on one of the lower steps with her back presented to me, her body half bowed and her head, in an attitude of woe, in her hands. I had been there but an instant, however, when she vanished without looking round at me. I knew, none the less, exactly what dreadful face she had to show; and I wondered whether, if instead of being above I had been below, I should have had, for going up, the same nerve I had lately shown Quint. Well, there continued to be plenty of chance for nerve. On the eleventh night after my latest encounter with that gentleman—they were all numbered now—I had an alarm that perilously skirted it and that indeed, from the particular quality of its unexpectedness, proved quite my sharpest shock. It was precisely the first night during this series that, weary with watching, I had felt that I might again without laxity lay myself down at my old hour. I slept immediately and, as I afterwards knew, till about one o'clock; but when I woke it was to sit straight up, as completely roused as if a hand had shook me. I had left a light burning, but it was now out, and I felt an instant certainty that Flora had extinguished it. This brought me to my feet and straight, in the darkness, to her bed, which I found she had left. A glance at the window enlightened me further, and the striking of a match completed the picture.

The child had again got up—this time blowing out the taper, and had again, for some purpose of observation or response, squeezed in behind the blind and was peering out into the night. That she now saw—as she had not, I had satisfied myself, the previous time—was proved to me by the fact that she was disturbed neither by my reillumination nor by the haste I made to get into slippers and into a wrap. Hidden, protected, absorbed, she evidently rested on the sill—the casement opened forward—and gave herself up. There was a great still moon to help her, and this fact had counted in my quick decision. She was face to face with the

apparition we had met at the lake, and could now communicate with it as she had not then been able to do. What I,
on my side, had to care for was, without disturbing her, to
reach, from the corridor, some other window in the same
quarter. I got to the door without her hearing me; I got out
of it, closed it and listened, from the other side, for some
sound from her. While I stood in the passage I had my eyes
on her brother's door, which was but ten steps off and which,
indescribably, produced in me a renewal of the strange impulse that I lately spoke of as my temptation. What if I should
go straight in and march to *his* window?—what if, by risking
to his boyish bewilderment a revelation of my motive, I
should throw across the rest of the mystery the long halter
of my boldness?

This thought held me sufficiently to make me cross to
his threshold and pause again. I preternaturally listened; I
figured to myself what might portentously be; I wondered if
his bed were also empty and he too were secretly at watch.
It was a deep, soundless minute, at the end of which my
impulse failed. He was quiet; he might be innocent; the risk
was hideous; I turned away. There was a figure in the
grounds—a figure prowling for a sight, the visitor with whom
Flora was engaged; but it was not the visitor most concerned
with my boy. I hesitated afresh, but on other grounds and
only a few seconds; then I had made my choice. There were
empty rooms at Bly, and it was only a question of choosing
the right one. The right one suddenly presented itself to me
as the lower one—though high above the gardens—in the
solid corner of the house that I have spoken of as the old
tower. This was a large, square chamber, arranged with some
state as a bedroom, the extravagant size of which made it
so inconvenient that it had not for years, though kept
by Mrs. Grose in exemplary order, been occupied. I had often

admired it and I knew my way about in it; I had only, after just faltering at the first chill of gloom of its disuse, to pass across it and unbolt as quietly as I could one of the shutters. Achieving this transit, I uncovered the glass without a sound and, applying my face to the pane, was able, the darkness without being much less than within, to see that I commanded the right direction. Then I saw something more. The moon made the night extraordinarily penetrable and showed me on the lawn a person, diminished by distance, who stood there motionless and as if fascinated, looking up to where I had appeared—looking, that is, not so much straight at me as at something that was apparently above me. There was clearly another person above me—there was a person on the tower; but the presence on the lawn was not in the least what I had conceived and had confidently hurried to meet. The presence on the lawn—I felt sick as I made it out—was poor little Miles himself.

XI

It was not till late next day that I spoke to Mrs. Grose; the rigour with which I kept my pupils in sight making it often difficult to meet her privately, and the more as we each felt the importance of not provoking—on the part of the servants quite as much as on that of the children—any suspicion of a secret flurry or of a discussion of mysteries. I drew a great security in this particular from her mere smooth aspect. There was nothing in her fresh face to pass on to others my horrible confidences. She believed me, I was sure, absolutely: if she hadn't I don't know what would have become of me, for I couldn't have borne the business alone. But she was a magnificent monument to the blessing of a want of imagination, and if she could see in our little charges nothing but their beauty and amiability, their happiness and cleverness, she had no direct communication with the sources of my trouble. If they had been at all visibly blighted or battered, she would doubtless have grown, on tracing it back, haggard enough to match them; as matters stood, however, I could feel her, when she surveyed them, with her large white arms folded and the habit of serenity in all her look, thank the Lord's mercy that if they were ruined the pieces would still serve. Flights of fancy gave place, in her mind, to a steady fireside glow, and I had already begun to perceive how, with the development of conviction that—as time went on without a public accident—our young things could, after all, look out for themselves, she addressed her greatest solicitude to the sad case presented by their instructress. That, for myself, was a sound simplification: I could engage that, to the world, my face should tell no tales, but it would have been, in the conditions, an immense added strain to find myself anxious about hers.

At the hour I now speak of she had joined me, under pressure, on the terrace, where, with the lapse of the season, the afternoon sun was now agreeable; and we sat there together while, before us, at a distance, but within call if we wished, the children strolled to and fro in one of their most manageable moods. They moved slowly, in unison, below us, over the lawn, the boy, as they went, reading aloud from a story-book and passing his arm round his sister to keep her quite in touch. Mrs. Grose watched them with positive placidity; then I caught the suppressed intellectual creak with which she conscientiously turned to take from me a view of the back of the tapestry. I had made her a receptacle of lurid things, but there was an odd recognition of my superiority— my accomplishments and my function—in her patience under my pain. She offered her mind to my disclosures as, had I wished to mix a witch's broth and proposed it with assurance, she would have held out a large clean saucepan. This had become thoroughly her attitude by the time that, in my recital of the events of the night, I reached the point of what Miles had said to me when, after seeing him, at such a monstrous hour, almost on the very spot where he happened now to be, I had gone down to bring him in; choosing then, at the window, with a concentrated need of not alarming the house, rather that method than a signal more resonant. I had left her meanwhile in little doubt of my small hope of representing with success even to her actual sympathy my sense of the real splendour of the little inspiration with which, after I had got him into the house, the boy met my final articulate challenge. As soon as I appeared in the moonlight on the terrace, he had come to me as straight as possible; on which I had taken his hand without a word and led him, through the dark spaces, up the staircase where Quint had so hungrily hovered for him, along the lobby where I had listened and trembled, and so to his forsaken room.

Not a sound, on the way, had passed between us, and I had wondered—oh, *how* I had wondered!—if he were groping about in his little mind for something plausible and not too grotesque. It would tax his invention, certainly, and I felt, this time, over his real embarrassment, a curious thrill of triumph. It was a sharp trap for the inscrutable! He couldn't play any longer at innocence; so how the deuce would he get out of it? There beat in me indeed, with the passionate throb of this question, an equal dumb appeal as to how the deuce *I* should. I was confronted at last, as never yet, with all the risk attached even now to sounding my own horrid note. I remember in fact that as we pushed into his little chamber, where the bed had not been slept in at all and the window, uncovered to the moonlight, made the place so clear that there was no need of striking a match—I remember how I suddenly dropped, sank upon the edge of the bed from the force of the idea that he must know how he really, as they say, "had" me. He could do what he liked, with all his cleverness to help him, so long as I should continue to defer to the old tradition of the criminality of those caretakers of the young who minister to superstitions and fears. He "had" me indeed, and in a cleft stick; for who would ever absolve me, who would consent that I should go unhung, if, by the faintest tremor of an overture, I were the first to introduce into our perfect intercourse an element so dire? No, no: it was useless to attempt to convey to Mrs. Grose, just as it is scarcely less so to attempt to suggest here, how, in our short, stiff brush in the dark, he fairly shook me with admiration. I was of course thoroughly kind and merciful; never, never yet had I placed on his little shoulders hands of such tenderness as those with which, while I rested against the bed, I held him there well under fire. I had no alternative but, in form at least, to put it to him.

"You must tell me now—and all the truth. What did you go out for? What were you doing there?"

I can still see his wonderful smile, the whites of his beautiful eyes, and the uncovering of his little teeth shine to me in the dusk. "If I tell you why, will you understand?" My heart, at this, leaped into my mouth. *Would* he tell me why? I found no sound on my lips to press it, and I was aware of replying only with a vague, repeated, grimacing nod. He was gentleness itself, and while I wagged my head at him he stood there more than ever a little fairy prince. It was his brightness indeed that gave me a respite. Would it be so great if he were really going to tell me? "Well," he said at last, "just exactly in order that you should do this."

"Do what?"

"Think me—for a change—*bad!*" I shall never forget the sweetness and gaiety with which he brought out the word, nor how, on top of it, he bent forward and kissed me. It was practically the end of everything. I met his kiss and I had to make, while I folded him for a minute in my arms, the most stupendous effort not to cry. He had given exactly the account of himself that permitted least of my going behind it, and it was only with the effect of confirming my acceptance of it that, as I presently glanced about the room, I could say—

"Then you didn't undress at all?"

He fairly glittered in the gloom. "Not at all. I sat up and read."

"And when did you go down?"

"At midnight. When I'm bad I *am* bad!"

"I see, I see—it's charming. But how could you be sure I would know it?"

"Oh, I arranged that with Flora." His answers rang out with a readiness! "She was to get up and look out."

"Which is what she did do." It was I who fell into the trap!

"So she disturbed you, and, to see what she was looking at, you also looked—you saw."

"While you," I concurred, "caught your death in the night air!"

He literally bloomed so from this exploit that he could afford radiantly to assent. "How otherwise should I have been bad enough?" he asked. Then, after another embrace, the incident and our interview closed on my recognition of all the reserves of goodness that, for his joke, he had been able to draw upon.

XII

The particular impression I had received proved in the morning light, I repeat, not quite successfully presentable to Mrs. Grose, though I reinforced it with the mention of still another remark that he had made before we separated. "It all lies in a half-a-dozen words," I said to her, "words that really settle the matter. 'Think, you know, what I *might* do!' He threw that off to show me how good he is. He knows down to the ground what he 'might' do. That's what he gave them a taste of at school."

"Lord, you do change!" cried my friend.

"I don't change—I simply make it out. The four, depend upon it, perpetually meet. If on either of these last nights you had been with either child, you would clearly have understood. The more I've watched and waited the more I've felt that if there were nothing else to make it sure it would be made so by the systematic silence of each. *Never,* by a slip of the tongue, have they so much as alluded to either of their old friends, any more than Miles has alluded to his expulsion. Oh yes, we may sit here and look at them, and they may show off to us there to their fill; but even while they pretend to be lost in their fairy-tale they're steeped in their vision of the dead restored. He's not reading to her," I declared; "they're talking of *them*—they're talking horrors! I go on, I know, as if I were crazy; and it's a wonder I'm not. What I've seen would have made *you* so; but it has only made me more lucid, made me get hold of still other things."

My lucidity must have seemed awful, but the charming creatures who were victims of it, passing and repassing in their interlocked sweetness, gave my colleague something to hold on by; and I felt how tight she held as, without stirring in the breath of my passion, she covered them still with her eyes. "Of what other things have you got hold?"

"Why, of the very things that have delighted, fascinated, and yet, at bottom, as I now so strangely see, mystified and troubled me. Their more than earthly beauty, their absolutely unnatural goodness. It's a game," I went on; "it's a policy and a fraud!"

"On the part of little darlings—?"

"As yet mere lovely babies? Yes, mad as that seems!" The very act of bringing it out really helped me to trace it—follow it all up and piece it all together. "They haven't been good—they've only been absent. It has been easy to live with them, because they're simply leading a life of their own. They're not mine—they're not ours. They're his and they're hers!"

"Quint's and that woman's?"

"Quint's and that woman's. They want to get to them."

Oh, how, at this, poor Mrs. Grose appeared to study them! "But for what?"

"For the love of all the evil that, in those dreadful days, the pair put into them. And to ply them with that evil still, to keep up the work of demons, is what brings the others back."

"Laws!" said my friend under her breath. The exclamation was homely, but it revealed a real acceptance of my further proof of what, in the bad time—for there had been a worse even than this!—must have occurred. There could have been no such justification for me as the plain assent of her experience to whatever depth of depravity I found credible in our brace of scoundrels. It was in obvious submission of memory that she brought out after a moment: "They *were* rascals! But what can they now do?" she pursued.

"Do?" I echoed so loud that Miles and Flora, as they

passed at their distance, paused an instant in their walk and looked at us. "Don't they do enough?" I demanded in a lower tone, while the children, having smiled and nodded and kissed hands to us, resumed their exhibition. We were held by it a minute; then I answered: "They can destroy them!" At this my companion did turn, but the inquiry she launched was a silent one, the effect of which was to make me more explicit. "They don't know, as yet, quite how—but they're trying hard. They're seen only across, as it were, and beyond—in strange places and on high places, the top of towers, the roof of houses, the outside of windows, the further edge of pools; but there's a deep design, on either side, to shorten the distance and overcome the obstacle; and the success of the tempters is only a question of time. They've only to keep to their suggestions of danger."

"For the children to come?"

"And perish in the attempt!" Mrs. Grose slowly got up, and I scrupulously added: "Unless, of course, we can prevent!"

Standing there before me while I kept my seat, she visibly turned things over. "Their uncle must do the preventing. He must take them away."

"And who's to make him?"

She had been scanning the distance, but she now dropped on me a foolish face. "You, miss."

"By writing to him that his house is poisoned and his little nephew and niece mad?"

"But if they *are,* miss?"

"And if I am myself, you mean? That's charming news to be sent him by a governess whose prime undertaking was to give him no worry."

Mrs. Grose considered, following the children again. "Yes, he do hate worry. That was the great reason—"

"Why those fiends took him in so long? No doubt, though

his indifference must have been awful. As I'm not a fiend, at any rate, I shouldn't take him in."

My companion, after an instant and for all answer, sat down again and grasped my arm. "Make him at any rate come to you."

I stared. "To *me*?" I had a sudden fear of what she might do. " 'Him'?"

"He ought to *be* here—he ought to help."

I quickly rose, and I think I must have shown her a queerer face than ever yet. "You see me asking him for a visit?" No, with her eyes on my face she evidently couldn't. Instead of it even—as a woman reads another—she could see what I myself saw: his derision, his amusement, his contempt for the break-down of my resignation at being left alone and for the fine machinery I had set in motion to attract his attention to my slighted charms. She didn't know—no one knew—how proud I had been to serve him and to stick to our terms; yet she none the less took the measure, I think, of the warning I now gave her. "If you should so lose your head as to appeal to him for me—"

She was really frightened. "Yes, miss?"

"I would leave, on the spot, both him and you."

XIII

It was all very well to join them, but speaking to them proved quite as much as ever an effort beyond my strength—offered, in close quarters, difficulties as insurmountable as before. This situation continued a month, and with new aggravations and particular notes, the note above all, sharper and sharper, of the small ironic consciousness on the part of my pupils. It was not, I am as sure today as I was sure then, my mere

infernal imagination: it was absolutely traceable that they
were aware of my predicament and that this strange relation
made, in a manner, for a long time, the air in which we moved.
I don't mean that they had their tongues in their cheeks or
did anything vulgar, for that was not one of their dangers: I
do mean, on the other hand, that the element of the unnamed
and untouched became, between us, greater than any other,
and that so much avoidance could not have been so successfully effected without a great deal of tacit arrangement. It
was as if, at moments, we were perpetually coming into sight
of subjects before which we must stop short, turning suddenly
out of alleys that we perceived to be blind, closing with a
little bang that made us look at each other—for, like all bangs,
it was something louder than we had intended—the doors
we had indiscreetly opened. All roads lead to Rome, and
there were times when it might have struck us that almost
every branch of study or subject of conversation skirted forbidden ground. Forbidden ground was the question of the
return of the dead in general and of whatever, in especial,
might survive, in memory, of the friends little children had
lost. There were days when I could have sworn that one of
them had, with a small invisible nudge, said to the other: "She
thinks she'll do it this time—but she *won't!*" To "do it" would
have been to indulge for instance—and for once in a way—
in some direct reference to the lady who had prepared them
for my discipline. They had a delightful endless appetite for
passages in my own history, to which I had again and again
treated them; they were in possession of everything that had
ever happened to me, had had, with every circumstance the
story of my smallest adventures and of those of my brothers
and sisters and of the cat and the dog at home, as well
as many particulars of the eccentric nature of my father, of
the furniture and arrangement of our house, and of the

conversation of the old women of our village. There were things enough, taking one with another, to chatter about, if one went very fast and knew by instinct when to go round. They pulled with an art of their own the strings of my invention and my memory; and nothing else perhaps, when I thought of such occasions afterwards, gave me so the suspicion of being watched from under cover. It was in any case over *my* life, *my* past, and *my* friends alone that we could take anything like our ease—a state of affairs that led them sometimes without the least pertinence to break out into sociable reminders. I was invited—with no visible connection—to repeat afresh Goody Gosling's celebrated *mot* or to confirm the details already supplied as to the cleverness of the vicarage pony.

It was partly at such junctures as these and partly at quite different ones that, with the turn my matters had now taken, my predicament, as I have called it, grew most sensible. The fact that the days passed for me without another encounter ought, it would have appeared, to have done something toward soothing my nerves. Since the light brush, that second night on the upper landing, of the presence of a woman at the foot of the stair, I had seen nothing, whether in or out of the house, that one had better not have seen. There was many a corner round which I expected to come upon Quint, and many a situation that, in a merely sinister way, would have favoured the appearance of Miss Jessel. The summer had turned, the summer had gone; the autumn had dropped upon Bly and had blown out half our lights. The place, with its grey sky and withered garlands, its bared spaces and scattered dead leaves, was like a theatre after the performance—all strewn with crumpled playbills. There were exactly states of the air, conditions of sound and of stillness, unspeakable impressions of the *kind* of ministering moment, that brought back to me, long enough to catch it, the feeling of the medium in which, that June evening out-of-doors, I had had my first sight of Quint, and in which, too, at those other instants, I had, after seeing him through the window, looked for him in vain in the circle of shrubbery. I recognized the signs, the portents—I recognized the moment, the spot. But they remained unaccompanied and empty, and I continued unmolested; if unmolested one could call a young woman whose sensibility had, in the most extraordinary fashion, not declined but deepened. I had said in my talk with Mrs. Grose on that horrid scene of Flora's by the lake—and had perplexed her by so saying—that it would from that moment distress me much more to lose my power than to keep it. I had then expressed what was vividly in my mind: the truth that, whether the children really saw or not—since, that is, it was not yet definitely proved—I greatly preferred, as a safeguard, the fulness of my own exposure. I was ready to know the very worst that was to be known. What I had then had an ugly glimpse of was that my eyes might be sealed just while theirs were most opened. Well, my eyes *were* sealed, it appeared, at present—a consummation for which it seemed blasphemous not to thank God. There was, alas, a difficulty about that: I would have thanked him with all my soul had I not had in a proportionate measure this conviction of the secret of my pupils.

How can I retrace today the strange steps of my obsession? There were times of our being together when I would have been ready to swear that, literally, in my presence, but with my direct sense of it closed, they had visitors who were known and were welcome. Then it was that, had I not been deterred by the very chance that such an injury might prove greater than the injury to be averted, my exultation would have broken out. "They're here, they're here, you little wretches," I would have cried, "and you can't deny it now!" The little wretches denied it with all the added volume of their sociability and their tenderness, in just the crystal depths of which—like the flash of a fish in a stream—the mockery of their advantage peeped up. The shock, in truth, had sunk into me still deeper than I knew on the night when, looking out to see either Quint or Miss Jessel under the stars, I had beheld the boy over whose rest I watched and who had immediately brought in with him—had straightway, there, turned it on me—the lovely upward look with which, from the battlements above me, the hideous apparition of Quint had played. If it was a question of a scare, my discovery on this occasion had scared me more than any other, and it was in the condition of nerves produced by it that I made my actual inductions. They harassed me so that sometimes, at odd moments, I shut myself up audibly to rehearse—it was at once a fantastic relief and a renewed despair—the manner in which I might come to the point. I approached it from one side and the other while, in my room, I flung myself about, but I always broke down in the monstrous utterance of names. As they died away on my lips, I said to myself that I should indeed help them to represent something infamous if, by pronouncing them, I should violate as rare a little case of instinctive delicacy as any schoolroom, probably, had ever known. When I said to myself: "*They* have the manners to be silent, and you, trusted as you are, the baseness to speak!" I felt myself crimson and I covered my face with my hands. After these secret scenes I chattered more than ever, going on volubly enough till one of our prodigious, palpable hushes occurred—I can call them nothing else—the strange, dizzy lift or swim (I try for terms!) into a stillness, a pause of all life, that had nothing to do with the more or less noise that at the moment we might be engaged in making and that I could hear through any deepened exhilaration or quickened recitation or louder strum of the piano. Then it was that the others, the outsiders, were there. Though they were not angels, they "passed," as the French say, causing me, while they stayed, to tremble with the fear of their addressing to their younger victims some yet more infernal message or more vivid image than they had thought good enough for myself.

What it was most impossible to get rid of was the cruel idea that, whatever I had seen, Miles and Flora saw *more*— things terrible and unguessable and that sprang from dreadful passages of intercourse in the past. Such things naturally left on the surface, for the time, a chill which we vociferously denied that we felt; and we had, all three, with repetition, got into such splendid training that we went, each time, almost automatically, to mark the close of the incident, through the very same movements. It was striking of the children, at all events, to kiss me inveterately with a kind of wild irrelevance and never to fail—one or the other—of the precious question that had helped us through many a peril. "When do you think he *will* come? Don't you think we *ought* to write?"—there was nothing like that inquiry, we found by experience, for carrying off an awkwardness. "He" of course was their uncle in Harley Street; and we lived in much profusion of theory that he might at any moment arrive to mingle in our circle. It was impossible to have given less encouragement than he had done to such a doctrine, but if we had not had the doctrine to fall back upon we should have deprived each other of some of our first exhibitions. He never wrote to them—that may have been selfish, but it was part of the flattery of his trust of me; for the way in which a man pays his highest tribute to a woman is apt to be but the more festal celebration of one of the sacred laws of his comfort; and I held that I carried out the spirit of the pledge given not to appeal to him when I let my charges understand that their own letters were but charming literary exercises. They were too beautiful to be posted; I kept them myself; I have them all to this hour. This was a rule indeed which only added to the satiric effect of my being plied with the supposition that he might at any moment be among us. It was exactly as if my charges knew how almost more awkward than anything else that might be for me. There appears to me, moreover, as I look back, no note in all this more extraordinary than the mere fact that, in spite of my tension and of their triumph, I never lost patience with them. Adorable they must in truth have been, I now reflect, that I didn't in these days hate them! Would exasperation, however, if relief had longer been postponed, finally have betrayed me? It little matters, for relief arrived. I call it relief, though it was only the relief that a snap brings to a strain or the burst of a thunderstorm to a day of suffocation. It was at least change, and it came with a rush.

XIV

Walking to church a certain Sunday morning, I had little Miles at my side and his sister, in advance of us and at Mrs. Grose's, well in sight. It was a crisp, clear day, the first of its order for some time; the night had brought a touch of frost, and the autumn air, bright and sharp, made the church-bells almost gay. It was an odd accident of thought that I should have happened at such a moment to be particularly and very gratefully struck with the obedience of my little charges. Why did they never resent my inexorable, my perpetual society? Something or other had brought nearer home to me that I had all but pinned the boy to my shawl and that, in the way our companions were marshalled before me, I might have appeared to provide against some danger of rebellion. I was like a gaoler with an eye to possible surprises and escapes. But all this belonged—I mean their magnificent little surrender—just to the special array of the facts that were most abysmal. Turned out for Sunday by his uncle's tailor, who had had a free hand and a notion of pretty waistcoats and of his grand little air, Miles's whole title to independence, the rights of his sex and situation, were so stamped upon him that if he had suddenly struck for freedom I should have had nothing to say. I was by the strangest of chances wondering how I should meet him when the revolution unmistakably occurred. I call it a revolution because I now see how, with the word he spoke, the curtain rose on the last act of my dreadful drama and the catastrophe was precipitated. "Look here, my dear, you know," he charmingly said, "when in the world, please, am I going back to school?"

Transcribed here the speech sounds harmless enough, particularly as uttered in the sweet, high, casual pipe with which, at all interlocutors, but above all at his eternal governess, he threw off intonations as if he were tossing roses. There was something in them that always made one "catch," and I caught, at any rate, now so effectually that I stopped as short as if one of the trees of the park had fallen across the road. There was something new, on the spot, between us, and he was perfectly aware that I recognized it, though, to enable me to do so, he had no need to look a whit less candid and charming than usual. I could feel in him how he already, from my at first finding nothing to reply, perceived the advantage he had gained. I was so slow to find anything that he had plenty of time, after a minute, to continue with his suggestive but inconclusive smile: "You know, my dear, that for a fellow to be with a lady *always*—!" His "my dear" was constantly on his lips for me, and nothing could have expressed more the exact shade of the sentiment with which I desired to inspire my pupils than its fond familiarity. It was so respectfully easy.

But, oh, how I felt that at present I must pick my own phrases! I remember that, to gain time, I tried to laugh, and I seemed to see in the beautiful face with which he watched me how ugly and queer I looked. "And always with the same lady?" I returned.

He neither blenched nor winked. The whole thing was virtually out between us. "Ah, of course, she's a jolly, 'perfect' lady; but, after all, I'm a fellow, don't you see? that's—well, getting on."

I lingered there with him an instant ever so kindly. "Yes, you're getting on." Oh, but I felt helpless!

I have kept to this day the heartbreaking little idea of how he seemed to know that and to play with it. "And you can't say I've not been awfully good, can you?"

I laid my hand on his shoulder, for, though I felt how much better it would have been to walk on, I was not yet quite able. "No, I can't say that, Miles."

"Except just that one night, you know—!"

"That one night?" I couldn't look as straight as he.

"Why, when I went down—went out of the house."

"Oh, yes. But I forget what you did it for."

"You forget?"—he spoke with the sweet extravagance of childish reproach. "Why, it was to show you I could!"

"Oh, yes, you could."

"And I can again."

I felt that I might, perhaps, after all, succeed in keeping my wits about me. "Certainly. But you won't."

"No, not *that* again. It was nothing."

"It was nothing," I said. "But we must go on."

He resumed our walk with me, passing his hand into my arm. "Then when *am* I going back?"

I wore, in turning it over, my most responsible air. "Were you very happy at school?"

He just considered. "Oh, I'm happy enough anywhere!"

"Well, then," I quavered, "if you're just as happy here—!"

"Ah, but that isn't everything! Of course *you* know a lot—"

"But you hint that you know almost as much?" I risked as he paused.

"Not half I want to!" Miles honestly professed. "But it isn't so much that."

"What is it, then?"

"Well—I want to see more life."

"I see; I see." We had arrived within sight of the church and of various persons, including several of the household of Bly, on their way to it and clustered about the door to see us go in. I quickened our step; I wanted to get there before the question between us opened up much further; I reflected hungrily that, for more than an hour, he would have to be silent; and I thought with envy of the comparative dusk of the pew and the almost spiritual help of the hassock on which I might bend my knees. I seemed literally to be running a race with some confusion to which he was about to reduce me, but I felt that he had got in first when, before we had even entered the churchyard, he threw out—

"I want my own sort!"

It literally made me bound forward. "There are not many of your own sort, Miles!" I laughed. "Unless perhaps dear little Flora!"

"You really compare me to a baby girl?"

This found me singularly weak. "Don't you, then, *love* our sweet Flora?"

"If I didn't—and you too; if I didn't—!' he repeated as if retreating for a jump, yet leaving his thought so unfinished that, after we had come into the gate, another stop, which he imposed on me by the pressure of his arm, had become inevitable. Mrs. Grose and Flora had passed into the church, the other worshippers had followed, and we were, for the minute, alone among the old, thick graves. We had paused, on the path from the gate, by a low, oblong, table-like tomb.

"Yes, if you didn't—?"

He looked, while I waited, about at the graves. "Well, you know what!" But he didn't move, and he presently produced something that made me drop straight down on the stone slab, as if suddenly to rest. "Does my uncle think what *you* think?"

I markedly rested. "How do you know what I think?"

"Ah, well, of course I don't; for it strikes me you never tell me. But I mean does *he* know?"

"Know what, Miles?"

"Why, the way I'm going on."

I perceived quickly enough that I could make, to this inquiry, no answer that would not involve something of a sacrifice of my employer. Yet it appeared to me that we were all, at Bly, sufficiently sacrificed to make that venial. "I don't think your uncle much cares."

Miles, on this, stood looking at me. "Then don't you think he can be made to?"

"In what way?"

"Why, by his coming down."

"But who'll get him to come down?"

"*I* will!" the boy said with extraordinary brightness and emphasis. He gave me another look charged with that expression and then marched off alone into the church.

XV

The business was practically settled from the moment I never followed him. It was a pitiful surrender to agitation, but my being aware of this had somehow no power to restore me. I only sat there on my tomb and read into what my little friend had said to me the fulness of its meaning; by the time I had grasped the whole of which I had also embraced, for absence, the pretext that I was ashamed to offer my pupils and the rest of the congregation such an example of delay. What I said to myself above all was that Miles had got something out of me and that the proof of it, for him, would be just this awkward collapse. He had got out of me that there was something I was much afraid of and that he should probably be able to make use of my fear to gain, for his own purpose, more freedom. My fear was of having to deal with the intolerable question of the grounds of his dismissal from school, for that was really but the question of the horrors gathered behind. That his uncle should arrive to treat with me of these things was a solution that, strictly speaking, I ought now to have desired to bring on; but I could so little face that ugliness and the pain of it that I simply procrastinated and lived from hand to mouth. The boy, to my deep discomposure, was immensely in the right, was in a position to say to me: "Either you clear up with my guardian the mystery of this interruption of my studies, or you cease to expect me to lead with you a life that's so unnatural for a boy." What was so unnatural for the particular boy I was concerned with was this sudden revelation of a consciousness and a plan.

That was what really overcame me, what prevented my going in. I walked round the church, hesitating, hovering; I reflected that I had already, with him, hurt myself beyond repair. Therefore I could patch up nothing, and it was too extreme an effort to squeeze beside him into the pew: he would be so much more sure than ever to pass his arm into mine and make me sit there for an hour in close, silent contact with his commentary on our talk. For the first minute since his arrival I wanted to get away from him. As I paused beneath the high east window and listened to the sounds of worship, I was taken with an impulse that might master me, I felt, completely should I give it the least encouragement. I might easily put an end to my predicament by getting away altogether. Here was my chance; there was no one to stop me; I could give the whole thing up—turn my back and retreat. It was only a question of hurrying again, for a few preparations, to the house which the attendance at church of so many of the servants would practically have left unoccupied. No one, in short, could blame me if I should just drive desperately off. What was it to get away if I got away only till dinner? That would be in a couple of hours, at the end of which—I had the acute prevision—my little pupils would play at innocent wonder about my non-appearance in their train.

"What *did* you do, you naughty, bad thing? Why in the world, to worry us so—and take our thoughts off too, don't you know?—did you desert us at the very door?" I couldn't meet such questions nor, as they asked them, their false little lovely eyes; yet it was all so exactly what I should have to meet that, as the prospect grew sharp to me, I at last let myself go.

I got, so far as the immediate moment was concerned, away; I came straight out of the churchyard and, thinking hard, retraced my steps through the park. It seemed to me that by the time I reached the house I had made up my mind I would fly. The Sunday stillness both of the approaches and of the interior, in which I met no one, fairly excited me with a sense of opportunity. Were I to get off quickly, this way, I should get off without a scene, without a word. My quickness would have to be remarkable, however, and the question of a conveyance was the great one to settle. Tormented, in the hall, with difficulties and obstacles, I remember sinking down at the foot of the staircase—suddenly collapsing there on the lowest step and then, with a revulsion, recalling that it was exactly where more than a month before, in the darkness of night and just so bowed with evil things, I had seen the spectre of the most horrible of women. At this I was able to straighten myself; I went the rest of the way up; I made, in my bewilderment, for the schoolroom, where there were objects belonging to me that I should have to take. But I opened the door to find again, in a flash, my eyes unsealed. In the presence of what I saw I reeled straight back upon my resistance.

Seated at my own table in clear noonday light I saw a person whom, without my previous experience, I should have taken at the first blush for some housemaid who might have stayed at home to look after the place and who, availing herself of rare relief from observation and of the schoolroom table and my pens, ink, and paper, had applied herself to the considerable effort of a letter to her sweetheart. There was an effort in the way that, while her arms rested on the table, her hands with evident weariness supported her head; but at the moment I took this in I had already become aware that, in spite of my entrance, her attitude strangely persisted. Then it was—with the very act of its announcing itself—that her identity flared up in a change of posture. She rose, not as if she had heard me, but with an indescribable grand melancholy of indifference and detachment, and, within a dozen feet of me, stood there as my vile predecessor. Dishonoured and tragic, she was all before me; but even as I fixed and, for memory, secured it, the awful image passed away. Dark as midnight in her black dress, her haggard beauty and her unutterable woe, she had looked at me long enough to appear to say that her right to sit at my table was as good as mine to sit at hers. While these instants lasted indeed I had the extraordinary chill of a feeling that it was I who was the intruder. It was as a wild protest against it that, actually addressing her—"You terrible, miserable woman!"—I heard myself break into a sound that, by the open door, rang through the long passage and the empty house. She looked at me as if she heard me, but I had recovered myself and cleared the air. There was nothing in the room the next minute but the sunshine and a sense that I must stay.

XVI

I had so perfectly expected that the return of my pupils would be marked by a demonstration that I was freshly upset at having to take into account that they were dumb about my absence. Instead of gaily denouncing and caressing me, they made no allusion to my having failed them, and I was left, for the time, on perceiving that she too said nothing, to study Mrs. Grose's odd face. I did this to such purpose that I made sure they had in some way bribed her to silence; a silence that, however, I would engage to break down on the first private opportunity. This opportunity came before tea: I secured five minutes with her in the housekeeper's room, where, in the twilight, amid a smell of lately-baked bread, but with the place all swept and garnished, I found her sitting in pained placidity before the fire. So I see her still, so I see her best: facing the flame from her straight chair in the dusky, shining room, a large clean image of the "put away"—of drawers closed and locked and rest without a remedy.

"Oh, yes, they asked me to say nothing; and to please them—so long as they were there—of course I promised. But what had happened to you?"

"I only went with you for the walk," I said. "I had then to come back to meet a friend."

She showed her surprise. "A friend—*you?*"

"Oh, yes, I have a couple!" I laughed. "But did the children give you a reason?"

"For not alluding to your leaving us? Yes; they said you would like it better. Do you like it better?"

My face had made her rueful. "No, I like it worse!" But after an instant I added: "Did they say why I should like it better?"

"No; Master Miles only said, 'We must do nothing but what she likes!' "

"I wish indeed he would! And what did Flora say?"

"Miss Flora was too sweet. She said, 'Oh, of course, of course!'—and I said the same."

I thought a moment. "You were too sweet too—I can hear you all. But none the less, between Miles and me, it's now all out."

"All out?" My companion stared. "But what, miss?"

"Everything. It doesn't matter. I've made up my mind. I came home, my dear," I went on, "for a talk with Miss Jessel."

I had by this time formed the habit of having Mrs. Grose literally well in hand in advance of my sounding that note; so that even now, as she bravely blinked under the signal of my word, I could keep her comparatively firm. "A talk! Do you mean she spoke?"

"It came to that. I found her, on my return, in the schoolroom."

"And what did she say?" I can hear the good woman still, and the candour of her stupefaction.

"That she suffers the torments—!"

It was this, of a truth, that made her, as she filled out my picture, gape. "Do you mean," she faltered, "—of the lost?"

"Of the lost. Of the damned. And that's why, to share them—" I faltered myself with the horror of it.

But my companion, with less imagination, kept me up. "To share them—?"

"She wants Flora." Mrs. Grose might, as I gave it to her, fairly have fallen away from me had I not been prepared. I still held her there, to show I was. "As I've told you, however, it doesn't matter."

"Because you've made up your mind? But to what?"

"To everything."

"And what do you call 'everything'?"

"Why, sending for their uncle."

"Oh, miss, in pity do," my friend broke out.

"Ah, but I will, I *will!* I see it's the only way. What's 'out,' as I told you, with Miles is that if he thinks I'm afraid to—and has ideas of what he gains by that—he shall see he's mistaken. Yes, yes; his uncle shall have it here from me on the spot (and before the boy himself if necessary) that if I'm to be reproached with having done nothing again about more school—"

"Yes, miss—" my companion pressed me.

"Well, there's that awful reason."

There were now clearly so many of these for my poor colleague that she was excusable for being vague. "But—a—which?"

"Why, the letter from his old place."

"You'll show it to the master?"

"I ought to have done so on the instant."

"Oh no!" said Mrs. Grose with decision.

"I'll put it before him," I went on inexorably, "that I can't undertake to work the question on behalf of a child who has been expelled—"

"For we've never in the least known what!" Mrs. Grose declared.

"For wickedness. For what else—when he's so clever and beautiful and perfect? Is he stupid? Is he untidy? Is he infirm? Is he ill-natured? He's exquisite—so it can be only *that;* and that would open up the whole thing. After all," I said, "it's their uncle's fault. If he left here such people—!"

"He didn't really in the least know them. The fault's mine." She had turned quite pale.

"Well, you shan't suffer," I answered.

"The children shan't!" she emphatically returned.

I was silent awhile; we looked at each other. "Then what am I to tell him?"

"You needn't tell him anything. *I'll* tell him."

I measured this. "Do you mean you'll write—?" Remembering she couldn't, I caught myself up. "How do you communicate?"

"I tell the bailiff. *He* writes."

"And should you like him to write our story?"

My question had a sarcastic force that I had not fully intended, and it made her, after a moment, inconsequently break down. The tears were again in her eyes. "Ah, miss, *you* write!"

"Well—tonight," I at last answered; and on this we separated.

XVII

I went so far, in the evening, as to make a beginning. The weather had changed back, a great wind was abroad, and beneath the lamp, in my room, with Flora at peace beside me, I sat for a long time before a blank sheet of paper and listened to the lash of the rain and the batter of gusts. Finally I went out, taking a candle; I crossed the passage and listened a minute at Miles's door. What, under my endless obsession, I had been impelled to listen for was some betrayal of his not being at rest, and I presently caught one, but not in the form I had expected. His voice tinkled out. "I say, you there—come in." It was a gaiety in the gloom!

I went in with my light and found him, in bed, very wide awake, but very much at his ease. "Well, what are *you* up to?" he asked with a grace of sociability in which it occurred to me that Mrs. Grose, had she been present, might have looked in vain for proof that anything was "out."

I stood over him with my candle. "How did you know I was there?"

"Why, of course I heard you. Did you fancy you made no noise? You're like a troop of cavalry!" he beautifully laughed.

"Then you weren't asleep?"

"Not much! I lie awake and think."

I had put my candle, designedly, a short way off, and then, as he held out his friendly old hand to me, had sat down on the edge of his bed. "What is it," I asked, "that you think of?"

"What in the world, my dear, but *you?*"

"Ah, the pride I take in your appreciation doesn't insist on that! I had so far rather you slept."

"Well, I think also, you know, of this queer business of ours."

I marked the coolness of his firm little hand. "Of what queer business, Miles?"

"Why, the way you bring me up. And all the rest!"

I fairly held my breath a minute, and even from my glimmering taper there was light enough to show how he smiled up at me from his pillow. "What do you mean by all the rest?"

"Oh, you know, you know!"

I could say nothing for a minute, though I felt, as I held his hand and our eyes continued to meet, that my silence had all the air of admitting his charge and that nothing in the whole world of reality was perhaps at that moment so fabulous as our actual relation. "Certainly you shall go back to school," I said, "if it be that that troubles you. But not to the old place—we must find another, a better. How could I know it did trouble you, this question, when you never told me so, never spoke of it at all?" His clear, listening face, framed in its smooth whiteness, made him for the minute as appealing as some wistful patient in a children's hospital; and I would have given, as the resemblance came to me, all I possessed on earth really to be the nurse or the sister of charity who might have helped to cure him. Well, even as it was, I perhaps might help! "Do you know you've never said a word to me about your school—I mean the old one; never mentioned it in any way?"

He seemed to wonder; he smiled with the same loveliness. But he clearly gained time; he waited, he called for guidance. "Haven't I?" It wasn't for *me* to help him—it was for the thing I had met!

Something in his tone and the expression of his face, as I got this from him, set my heart aching with such a pang as it had never yet known; so unutterably touching was it to see his little brain puzzled and his little resources taxed to play, under the spell laid on him, a part of innocence and consistency. "No, never—from the hour you came back. You've never mentioned to me one of your masters, one of your comrades, nor the least little thing that ever happened to you at school. Never, little Miles—no, never—have you given me an inkling of anything that *may* have happened there. Therefore you can fancy how much I'm in the dark. Until you came out, that way, this morning, you had, since the first hour I saw you, scarce even made a reference to anything in your previous life. You seemed so perfectly to accept the present." It was extraordinary how my absolute conviction of his secret precocity (or whatever I might call the poison of an influence that I dared but half to phrase) made him, in spite of the faint breath of his inward trouble, appear as accessible as an older person—imposed him almost as an intellectual equal. "I thought you wanted to go on as you are."

It struck me that at this he just faintly coloured. He gave, at any rate, like a convalescent slightly fatigued, a languid shake of his head. "I don't—I don't. I want to get away."

"You're tired of Bly?"

"Oh, no, I like Bly."

"Well, then—?"

"Oh, *you* know what a boy wants!"

I felt that I didn't know so well as Miles, and I took temporary refuge. "You want to go to your uncle?"

Again, at this, with his sweet ironic face, he made a movement on the pillow. "Ah, you can't get off with that!"

I was silent a little, and it was I, now, I think, who changed colour. "My dear, I don't want to get off!"

"You can't, even if you do. You can't, you can't!"—he lay beautifully staring. "My uncle must come down, and you must completely settle things."

"If we do," I returned with some spirit, "you may be sure it will be to take you quite away."

"Well, don't you understand that that's exactly what I'm working for? You'll have to tell him—about the way you've let it all drop: you'll have to tell him a tremendous lot!"

The exultation with which he uttered this helped me somehow, for the instant, to meet him rather more. "And how much will *you*, Miles, have to tell him? There are things he'll ask you!"

He turned it over. "Very likely. But what things?"

"The things you've never told me. To make up his mind what to do with you. He can't send you back—"

"Oh, I don't want to go back!" he broke in. "I want a new field."

He said it with admirable serenity, with positive unimpeachable gaiety; and doubtless it was that very note that most evoked for me the poignancy, the unnatural childish tragedy, of his probable reappearance at the end of three months with all this bravado and still more dishonour. It overwhelmed me now that I should never be able to bear that, and it made me let myself go. I threw myself upon him and in the tenderness of my pity I embraced him. "Dear little Miles, dear little Miles—!"

My face was close to his, and he let me kiss him, simply taking it with indulgent good-humour. "Well, old lady?"

"Is there nothing—nothing at all that you want to tell me?"

He turned off a little, facing round toward the wall and holding up his hand to look at as one had seen sick children look. "I've told you—I told you this morning."

Oh, I was sorry for him! "That you just want me not to worry you?"

He looked round at me now, as if in recognition of my understanding him; then ever so gently, "To let me alone," he replied.

There was even a singular little dignity in it, something that made me release him, yet, when I had slowly risen, linger beside him. God knows I never wished to harass him, but I felt that merely, at this, to turn my back on him was to abandon or, to put it more truly, to lose him. "I've just begun a letter to your uncle," I said.

"Well, then, finish it!"

I waited a minute. "What happened before?"

He gazed up at me again. "Before what?"

"Before you came back. And before you went away."

For some time he was silent, but he continued to meet my eyes. "What happened?"

It made me, the sound of the words, in which it seemed to me that I caught for the very first time a small faint quaver of consenting consciousness—it made me drop on my knees beside the bed and seize once more the chance of possessing him. "Dear little Miles, dear little Miles, if you *knew* how I want to help you! It's only that, it's nothing but that, and I'd rather die than give you a pain or do you a wrong—I'd rather die than hurt a hair of you. Dear little Miles"—oh, I brought it out now even if I *should* go too far—"I just want you to help me to save you!" But I knew in a moment after this that I had gone too far. The answer to my appeal was instantaneous, but it came in the form of an extraordinary blast and chill, a gust of frozen air and a shake of the room as great as if, in the wild wind, the casement had crashed in. The boy gave a loud, high shriek, which, lost in the rest of the shock of sound, might have seemed, indistinctly, though I was so close to him, a note either of jubilation or of terror. I jumped to my feet again and was conscious of darkness. So for a moment we remained, while I stared about me and saw that the drawn curtains were unstirred and the window tight. "Why, the candle's out!" I then cried.

"It was I who blew it, dear!" said Miles.

XVIII

The next day, after lessons, Mrs. Grose found a moment to say to me quietly: "Have you written, miss?"

"Yes—I've written." But I didn't add—for the hour—that my letter, sealed and directed, was still in my pocket. There would be time enough to send it before the messenger should go to the village. Meanwhile there had been, on the part of my pupils, no more brilliant, more exemplary morning. It was exactly as if they had both had at heart to gloss over any recent little friction. They performed the dizziest feats of arithmetic, soaring quite out of *my* feeble range, and perpetrated, in higher spirits than ever, geographical and historical jokes. It was conspicuous of course in Miles in particular that he appeared to wish to show how easily he could let me down. This child, to my memory, really lives in a setting of beauty and misery that no words can translate; there was a distinction all his own in every impulse he revealed; never was a small natural creature, to the uninitiated eye all frankness and freedom, a more ingenious, a more extraordinary little gentleman. I had perpetually to guard against the wonder of contemplation into which my initiated view betrayed me; to check the irrelevant gaze and discouraged sigh in which I constantly both attacked and renounced the enigma of what such a little gentleman could have done that deserved a penalty. Say that, by the dark prodigy I knew, the imagination of all evil *had* been opened up to him: all the justice within me ached for the proof that it could ever have flowered into an act.

He had never, at any rate, been such a little gentleman as when, after our early dinner on this dreadful day, he came round to me and asked if I shouldn't like him, for half an hour, to play to me. David playing to Saul could never have shown a finer sense of the occasion. It was literally a charming exhibition of tact, of magnanimity, and quite tantamount to his saying outright: "The true knights we love to read about never push an advantage too far. I know what you mean now: you mean that—to be let alone yourself and not followed up—you'll cease to worry and spy upon me, won't keep me so close to you, will let me go and come. Well, I 'come,' you see—but I don't go! There'll be plenty of time for that. I do really delight in your society, and I only want to show you that I contended for a principle." It may be imagined whether I resisted this appeal or failed to accompany him again, hand in hand, to the schoolroom. He sat down at the old piano and played as he had never played; and if there are those who think he had better have been kicking a football I can only say that I wholly agree with them. For at the end of a time that under his influence I had quite ceased to measure I started up with a strange sense of having literally slept at my post. It was after luncheon, and by the schoolroom fire, and yet I hadn't really, in the least, slept: I had only done something much worse—I had forgotten. Where, all this time, was Flora? When I put the question to Miles he played on a minute before answering, and then could only say: "Why, my dear, how do *I* know?"—breaking moreover into a happy laugh which, immediately after, as if it were a vocal accompaniment, he prolonged into incoherent, extravagant song.

I went straight to my room, but his sister was not there; then, before going downstairs, I looked into several others. As she was nowhere about she would surely be with Mrs. Grose, whom, in the comfort of that theory, I accordingly proceeded in quest of. I found her where I had found her the evening before, but she met my quick challenge with blank, scared ignorance. She had only supposed that, after the repast, I had carried off both the children; as to which she was quite in her right, for it was the very first time I had allowed the little girl out of my sight without some special provision. Of course now indeed she might be with the maids, so that the immediate thing was to look for her without an air of alarm. This we promptly arranged between us; but when, ten minutes later and in pursuance of our arrangement, we met in the hall, it was only to report on either side that after guarded inquiries we had altogether failed to trace her. For a minute there, apart from observation, we exchanged mute alarms, and I could feel with what high interest my friend returned me all those I had from the first given her.

"She'll be above," she presently said—"in one of the rooms you haven't searched."

"No; she's at a distance." I had made up my mind. "She has gone out."

Mrs. Grose stared. "Without a hat?"

I naturally also looked volumes. "Isn't that woman always without one?"

"She's with *her?*"

"She's with *her!*" I declared. "We must find them."

My hand was on my friend's arm, but she failed for the moment, confronted with such an account of the matter, to respond to my pressure. She communed, on the contrary, on the spot, with her uneasiness. "And where's Master Miles?"

"Oh, *he's* with Quint. They're in the schoolroom."

"Lord, miss!" My view, I was myself aware—and therefore I suppose my tone—had never yet reached so calm an assurance.

"The trick's played," I went on; "they've successfully worked their plan. He found the most divine little way to keep me quiet while she went off."

" 'Divine'?" Mrs. Grose bewilderedly echoed.

"Infernal, then!" I almost cheerfully rejoined. "He has provided for himself as well. But come!"

She had helplessly gloomed at the upper regions. "You leave him—?"

"So long with Quint? Yes—I don't mind that now."

She always ended, at these moments, by getting possession of my hand, and in this manner she could at present still stay me. But after gasping an instant at my sudden resignation, "Because of your letter?" she eagerly brought out.

I quickly, by way of answer, felt for my letter, drew it forth, held it up, and then, freeing myself, went and laid it on the great hall-table. "Luke will take it," I said as I came back. I reached the house-door and opened it; I was already on the steps.

My companion still demurred: the storm of the night and the early morning had dropped, but the afternoon was damp and grey. I came down to the drive while she stood in the doorway. "You go with nothing on?"

"What do I care when the child has nothing? I can't wait to dress," I cried, "and if you must do so, I leave you. Try meanwhile, yourself, upstairs."

"With *them?*" Oh, on this, the poor woman promptly joined me!

XIX

We went straight to the lake, as it was called by Bly, and I dare say rightly called, though I reflect that it may in fact have been a sheet of water less remarkable than it appeared to my untravelled eyes. My acquaintance with sheets of water was small, and the pool of Bly, at all events on the few occasions of my consenting, under the protection of my pupils, to affront its surface in the old flat-bottomed boat moored there for our use, had impressed me both with its extent and its agitation. The usual place of embarkation was half a mile from the house, but I had an intimate conviction that, wherever Flora might be, she was not near home. She had not given me the slip for any small adventure, and, since the day of the very great one that I had shared with her by the pond, I had been aware, in our walks, of the quarter to which she most inclined. This was why I had now given to Mrs. Grose's steps so marked a direction—a direction that made her, when she perceived it, oppose a resistance that showed me she was freshly mystified. "You're going to the water, miss?—you think she's *in*—?"

"She may be, though the depth is, I believe, nowhere very great. But what I judge most likely is that she's on the spot from which, the other day, we saw together what I told you."

"When she pretended not to see—?"

"With that astounding self-possession! I've always been sure she wanted to go back alone. And now her brother has managed it for her."

Mrs. Grose still stood where she had stopped. "You suppose they really *talk* of them?"

I could meet this with a confidence! "They say things that, if we heard them, would simply appall us."

"And if she *is* there—?"

"Yes?"

"Then Miss Jessel is?"

"Beyond a doubt. You shall see."

"Oh, thank you!" my friend cried, planted so firm that, taking it in, I went straight on without her. By the time I reached the pool, however, she was close behind me, and I knew that, whatever, to her apprehension, might befall me, the exposure of my society struck her as her least danger. She exhaled a moan of relief as we at last came in sight of the greater part of the water without a sight of the child. There was no trace of Flora on that nearer side of the bank where my observation of her had been most startling, and none on the opposite edge, where, save for a margin of some twenty yards, a thick copse came down to the water. The pond, oblong in shape, had a width so scant compared to its length that, with its ends out of view, it might have been taken for a scant river. We looked at the empty expanse, and then I felt the suggestion of my friend's eyes. I knew what she meant and I replied with a negative headshake.

"No, no; wait! She has taken the boat."

My companion stared at the vacant mooring-place and then again across the lake. "Then where is it?"

"Our not seeing it is the strongest of proofs. She has used it to go over, and then has managed to hide it."

"All alone—that child?"

"She's not alone, and at such times she's not a child: she's an old, old woman." I scanned all the visible shore while Mrs. Grose took again, into the queer element I offered her, one of her plunges of submission; then I pointed out that the boat might perfectly be in a small refuge formed by one of the recesses of the pool, an indentation masked, for the hither side, by a projection of the bank and by a clump of trees growing close to the water.

"But if the boat's there, where on earth's *she?*" my colleague anxiously asked.

"That's exactly what we must learn." And I started to walk further.

"By going all the way round?"

"Certainly, far as it is. It will take us but ten minutes, but it's far enough to have made the child prefer not to walk. She went straight over."

"Laws!" cried my friend again; the chain of my logic was ever too much for her. It dragged her at my heels even now, and when we had got half-way round—a devious, tiresome process, on ground much broken and by a path choked with overgrowth—I paused to give her breath. I sustained her with a grateful arm, assuring her that she might hugely help me; and this started us afresh, so that in the course of but few minutes more we reached a point from which we found the boat to be where I had supposed it. It had been intentionally left as much as possible out of sight and was tied to one of the stakes of a fence that came, just there, down to the brink and that had been an assistance to disembarking. I recognized, as I looked at the pair of short, thick oars, quite safely drawn up, the prodigious character of the feat for a little girl; but I had lived, by this time, too long among wonders and had panted to too many livelier measures. There was a gate in the fence, through which we passed, and that brought us, after a trifling interval, more into the open. Then, "There she is!" we both exclaimed at once.

Flora, a short way off, stood before us on the grass and smiled as if her performance was now complete. The next thing she did, however, was to stoop straight down and pluck—quite as if it were all she was there for—a big, ugly spray of withered fern. I instantly became sure she had just come out of the copse. She waited for us, not herself taking a step, and I was conscious of the rare solemnity with which we presently approached her. She smiled and smiled, and we met; but it was all done in a silence by this time flagrantly ominous. Mrs. Grose was the first to break the spell: she threw herself on her knees and, drawing the child to her breast, clasped in a long embrace the little tender, yielding body. While this dumb convulsion lasted I could only watch it—which I did the more intently when I saw Flora's face peep at me over our companion's shoulder. It was serious now—the flicker had left it; but it strengthened the pang with which I at that moment envied Mrs. Grose the simplicity of *her* relation. Still, all this while, nothing more passed between us save that Flora had let her foolish fern again drop to the ground. What she and I had virtually said to each other was that pretexts were useless now. When Mrs. Grose finally got up she kept the child's hand, so that the two were still before me; and the singular reticence of our communion was even more marked in the frank look she launched me. "I'll be hanged," it said, "if *I'll* speak!"

It was Flora who, gazing all over me in candid wonder, was the first. She was struck with our bareheaded aspect. "Why, where are your things?"

"Where yours are, my dear!" I promptly returned.

She had already got back her gaiety, and appeared to take this as an answer quite sufficient. "And where's Miles?" she went on.

There was something in the small valour of it that quite finished me: these three words from her were, in a flash like the glitter of a drawn blade, the jostle of the cup that my hand, for weeks and weeks, had held high and full to the brim and that now, even before speaking, I felt overflow in a deluge. "I'll tell you if you'll tell *me*—" I heard myself say, then heard the tremor in which it broke.

"Well, what?"

Mrs. Grose's suspense blazed at me, but it was too late now, and I brought the thing out handsomely. "Where, my pet, is Miss Jessel?"

X X

Just as in the churchyard with Miles, the whole thing was upon us. Much as I had made of the fact that this name had never once, between us, been sounded, the quick, smitten glare with which the child's face now received it fairly likened my breach of the silence to the smash of a pane of glass. It added to the interposing cry, as if to stay the blow, that Mrs. Grose, at the same instant, uttered over my violence—the shriek of a creature scared, or rather wounded, which, in turn, within a few seconds, was completed by a gasp of my own. I seized my colleague's arm. "She's there, she's there!"

Miss Jessel stood before us on the opposite bank exactly as she had stood the other time, and I remember, strangely, as the first feeling now produced in me, my thrill of joy at having brought on a proof. She was there, and I was neither cruel nor mad. She was there for poor scared Mrs. Grose, but she was there most for Flora; and no moment of my monstrous time was perhaps so extraordinary as that in which I consciously threw out to her—with the sense that, pale and ravenous demon as she was, she would catch and understand it—an inarticulate message of gratitude. She rose erect on the spot my friend and I had lately quitted, and there was not, in all the long reach of her desire, an inch of her evil that fell short. This first vividness of vision and emotion were things of a few seconds, during which Mrs. Grose's dazed blink across to where I pointed struck me as a sovereign sign that she too at last saw, just as it carried my own eyes precipitately to the child. The revelation then of the manner in which Flora was affected startled me, in truth, far more than it would have done to find her also merely agitated, for direct dismay was of course not what I had expected. Prepared and on her guard as our pursuit had actually made her, she would repress every betrayal; and I was therefore shaken, on the spot, by my first glimpse of the particular one for which I had not allowed. To see her, without a convulsion of her small pink face, not even feign to glance in the direction of the prodigy I announced, but only, instead of that, turn at *me* an expression of hard, still gravity, an expression absolutely new and unprecedented and that appeared to read and accuse and judge me—this was a stroke that somehow converted the little girl herself into the very presence that could make me quail. I quailed even though my certitude that she thoroughly saw was never greater than at that instant, and in the immediate need to defend myself I called it passionately to witness. "She's there, you little unhappy thing—there, there, *there,* and you see her as well as you see me!" I had said shortly before to Mrs. Grose that she was not at these times a child, but an old, old woman, and that description of her could not have been more strikingly confirmed than in the way in which, for all answer to this, she simply showed me, without a concession, an admission, of her eyes, a countenance of deeper and deeper, of indeed suddenly quite fixed, reprobation. I was by this time—if I can put the whole thing at all together—more appalled at what I may properly call her manner than at anything else, though it was simultaneously with this that I became aware of having Mrs. Grose also, and very formidably, to reckon with. My elder companion, the next moment, at any rate, blotted out everything but her own flushed face and her loud, shocked protest, a burst of high disapproval. "What a dreadful turn, to be sure, miss! Where on earth do you see anything?"

I could only grasp her more quickly yet, for even while she spoke the hideous plain presence stood undimmed and undaunted. It had already lasted a minute, and it lasted while I continued, seizing my colleague, quite thrusting her at it and presenting her to it, to insist with my pointing hand. "You don't see her exactly as *we* see?—you mean to say you don't now—*now?* She's as big as a blazing fire! Only look, dearest woman, *look*—!" She looked, even as I did, and gave me, with her deep groan of negation, repulsion, compassion—the mixture with her pity of her relief at her exemption—a sense, touching to me even then, that she would have backed me up if she could. I might well have needed that, for with this hard blow of the proof that her eyes were hopelessly sealed I felt my own situation horribly crumble, I felt—I saw—my livid predecessor press, from her position, on my defeat, and I was conscious, more than all, of what I should have from this instant to deal with in the astounding little attitude of Flora. Into this attitude Mrs. Grose immediately and violently entered, breaking, even while there pierced through my sense of ruin a prodigious private triumph, into breathless reassurance.

"She isn't there, little lady, and nobody's there—and you never see nothing, my sweet! How can poor Miss Jessel—when poor Miss Jessel's dead and buried? *We* know, don't we, love?"—and she appealed, blundering in, to the child. "It's all a mere mistake and a worry and a joke—and we'll go home as fast as we can!"

Our companion, on this, had responded with a strange, quick primness of propriety, and they were again, with Mrs. Grose on her feet, united, as it were, in pained opposition to me. Flora continued to fix me with her small mask of reprobation, and even at that minute I prayed God to forgive me for seeming to see that, as she stood there holding tight to our friend's dress, her incomparable childish beauty had suddenly failed, and quite vanished. I've said it already—she was literally, she was hideously, hard; she had turned common and almost ugly. "I don't know what you mean. I see nobody. I see nothing. I never *have*. I think you're cruel. I don't like you!" Then, after this deliverance, which might have been that of a vulgarly pert little girl in the street, she hugged Mrs. Grose more closely and buried in her skirts the dreadful little face. In this position she produced an almost furious wail. "Take me away, take me away—oh, take me away from *her!*"

"From *me?*" I panted.

"From you—from you!" she cried.

Even Mrs. Grose looked across at me dismayed, while I had nothing to do but communicate again with the figure that, on the opposite bank, without a movement, as rigidly still as if catching, beyond the interval, our voices, was as vividly there for my disaster as it was not there for my service. The wretched child had spoken exactly as if she had got from some outside source each of her stabbing little words, and I could therefore, in the full despair of all I had to accept, but sadly shake my head at her. "If I had ever doubted, all my doubt would at present have gone. I've been living with the miserable truth, and now it has only too much closed round me. Of course I've lost you: I've interfered, and you've seen—under *her* dictation"—with which I faced, over the pool again, our infernal witness—"the easy and perfect way to meet it. I've done my best, but I've lost you. Good-bye." For Mrs. Grose I had an imperative, an almost frantic "Go, go!" before which, in infinite distress, but mutely possessed of the little girl and clearly convinced, in spite of her blindness, that something awful had occurred and some collapse engulfed us, she retreated, by the way we had come, as fast as she could move.

Of what first happened when I was left alone I had no subsequent memory. I only knew that at the end of, I sup-

pose, a quarter of an hour, an odorous dampness and rough-
ness, chilling and piercing my trouble, had made me
understand that I must have thrown myself, on my face, on
the ground and given way to a wildness of grief. I must have
lain there long and cried and sobbed, for when I raised my
head the day was almost done. I got up and looked a moment,
through the twilight, at the grey pool and its blank, haunted
edge, and then I took, back to the house, my dreary and
difficult course. When I reached the gate in the fence the
boat, to my surprise, was gone, so that I had a fresh reflection
to make on Flora's extraordinary command of the situation.
She passed that night, by the most tacit, and I should add,
were not the word so grotesque a false note, the happiest of
arrangements, with Mrs. Grose. I saw neither of them on my
return, but, on the other hand as by an ambiguous compen-
sation, I saw a great deal of Miles. I saw—I can use no other
phrase—so much of him that it was as if it were more than
it had ever been. No evening I had passed at Bly had the
portentous quality of this one; in spite of which—and in spite
also of the deeper depths of consternation that had opened
beneath my feet—there was literally, in the ebbing actual,
an extraordinarily sweet sadness. On reaching the house I
had never so much as looked for the boy; I had simply gone
straight to my room to change what I was wearing and to
take in, at a glance, much material testimony to Flora's rup-
ture. Her little belongings had all been removed. When later,
by the schoolroom fire, I was served with tea by the usual
maid, I indulged, on the article of my other pupil, in no
inquiry whatever. He had his freedom now—he might have
it to the end! Well, he did have it; and it consisted—in part
at least—of his coming in at about eight o'clock and sitting
down with me in silence. On the removal of the tea-things I
had blown out the candles and drawn my chair closer: I was

conscious of a mortal coldness and felt as if I should never again be warm. So, when he appeared, I was sitting in the glow with my thoughts. He paused a moment by the door as if to look at me; then—as if to share them—came to the other side of the hearth and sank into a chair. We sat there in absolute stillness; yet he wanted, I felt, to be with me.

XXI

Before a new day, in my room, had fully broken, my eyes opened to Mrs. Grose, who had come to my bedside with worse news. Flora was so markedly feverish that an illness was perhaps at hand; she had passed a night of extreme unrest, a night agitated above all by fears that had for their subject not in the least her former, but wholly her present, governess. It was not against the possible re-entrance of Miss Jessel on the scene that she protested—it was conspicuously and passionately against mine. I was promptly on my feet of course, and with an immense deal to ask; the more that my friend had discernibly now girded her loins to meet me once more. This I felt as soon as I had put to her the question of her sense of the child's sincerity as against my own. "She persists in denying to you that she saw, or has ever seen, anything?"

My visitor's trouble, truly, was great. "Ah, miss, it isn't a matter on which I can push her! Yet it isn't either, I must say, as if I much needed to. It has made her, every inch of her, quite old."

"Oh, I see her perfectly from here. She resents, for all the world like some high little personage, the imputation on her truthfulness and, as it were, her respectability. 'Miss Jessel indeed—*she!*' Ah, she's 'respectable,' the chit! The impression she gave me there yesterday was, I assure you, the very strangest of all; it was quite beyond any of the others. I *did* put my foot in it! She'll never speak to me again."

Hideous and obscure as it all was, it held Mrs. Grose briefly silent; then she granted my point with a frankness which, I made sure, had more behind it. "I think indeed, miss, she never will. She do have a grand manner about it!"

"And that manner"—I summed it up—"is practically what's the matter with her now!"

Oh, that manner, I could see in my visitor's face, and not a little else besides! "She asks me every three minutes if I think you're coming in."

"I see—I see." I too, on my side, had so much more than worked it out. "Has she said to you since yesterday—except to repudiate her familiarity with anything so dreadful—a single other word about Miss Jessel?"

"Not one, miss. And of course you know," my friend added, "I took it from her, by the lake, that, just then and there at least, there *was* nobody."

"Rather! And, naturally, you take it from her still."

"I don't contradict her. What else can I do?"

"Nothing in the world! You've the cleverest little person to deal with. They've made them—their two friends, I mean—still cleverer even than nature did; for it was wondrous material to play on! Flora has now her grievance, and she'll work it to the end."

"Yes, miss; but to *what* end?"

"Why, that of dealing with me to her uncle. She'll make me out to him the lowest creature—?"

I winched at the fair show of the scene in Mrs. Grose's face; she looked for a minute as if she sharply saw them together. "And him who thinks so well of you!"

"He has an odd way—it comes over me now," I laughed,

"—of proving it! But that doesn't matter. What Flora wants, of course, is to get rid of me."

My companion bravely concurred. "Never again to so much as look at you."

"So that what you've come to me now for," I asked, "is to speed me on my way?" Before she had time to reply, however, I had her in check. "I've a better idea—the result of my reflections. My going *would* seem the right thing, and on Sunday I was terribly near it. Yet that won't do. It's *you* who must go. You must take Flora."

My visitor, at this, did speculate. "But where in the world—?"

"Away from here. Away from *them.* Away, even most of all, now, from me. Straight to her uncle."

"Only to tell on you—?"

"No, not 'only'! To leave me, in addition, with my remedy."

She was still vague. "And what *is* your remedy?"

"Your loyalty, to begin with. And then Miles's."

She looked at me hard. "Do you think he—?"

"Won't if he has the chance, turn on me? Yes, I venture still to think it. At all events, I want to try. Get off with his sister as soon as possible and leave me with him alone." I was amazed, myself, at the spirit I had still in reserve, and therefore perhaps a trifle the more disconcerted at the way in which, in spite of this fine example of it, she hesitated. "There's one thing, of course," I went on: "they mustn't, before she goes, see each other for three seconds." Then it came over me that, in spite of Flora's presumable sequestration from the instant of her return from the pool, it might already be too late. "Do you mean," I anxiously asked, "that they *have* met?"

At this she quite flushed. "Ah, miss, I'm not such a fool

as that! If I've been obliged to leave her three or four times, it has been each time with one of the maids, and at present, though she's alone, she's locked in safe. And yet—and yet!" There were too many things.

"And yet what?"

"Well, are you so sure of the little gentleman?"

"I'm not sure of anything but *you*. But I have, since last evening, a new hope. I think he wants to give me an opening. I do believe that—poor little exquisite wretch!—he wants to speak. Last evening, in the firelight and the silence, he sat with me for two hours as if it were just coming."

Mrs. Grose looked hard, through the window, at the grey, gathering day. "And did it come?"

"No, though I waited and waited, I confess it didn't, and it was without a breach of the silence or so much as a faint allusion to his sister's condition and absence that we at last kissed for good-night. All the same," I continued, "I can't, if her uncle sees her, consent to his seeing her brother without my having given the boy—and most of all because things have got so bad—a little more time."

My friend appeared on this ground more reluctant than I could quite understand. "What do you mean by more time?"

"Well, a day or two—really to bring it out. He'll then be on *my* side—of which you see the importance. If nothing comes, I shall only fail, and you will, at the worst, have helped me by doing, on your arrival in town, whatever you may have found possible." So I put it before her, but she continued for a little so inscrutably embarrassed that I came again to her aid. "Unless, indeed," I wound up, "you really want *not* to go."

I could see it, in her face, at last clear itself; she put out her hand to me as a pledge. "I'll go—I'll go. I'll go this morning."

I wanted to be very just. "If you *should* wish still to wait, I would engage she shouldn't see me."

"No, no: it's the place itself. She must leave it." She held me a moment with heavy eyes, then brought out the rest. "Your idea's the right one. I myself, miss—"

"Well?"

"I can't stay."

The look she gave me with it made me jump at possibilities. "You mean that, since yesterday, you *have* seen—?"

She shook her head with dignity. "I've *heard*—!"

"Heard?"

"From that child—horrors! There!" she sighed with tragic relief. "On my honour, miss, she says things—!" But at this evocation she broke down; she dropped, with a sudden sob, upon my sofa and, as I had seen her do before, gave way to all the grief of it.

It was quite in another manner that I, for my part, let myself go. "Oh, thank God!"

She sprang up again at this, drying her eyes with a groan. " 'Thank God'?"

"It so justifies me!"

"It does that, miss!"

I couldn't have desired more emphasis, but I just hesitated. "She's so horrible?"

I saw my colleague scarce knew how to put it. "Really shocking."

"And about me?"

"About you, miss—since you must have it. It's beyond everything, for a young lady; and I can't think wherever she must have picked up—"

"The appalling language she applied to me? I can, then!" I broke in with a laugh that was doubtless significant enough.

It only, in truth, left my friend still more grave. "Well,

perhaps I ought to also—since I've heard some of it before! Yet I can't bear it," the poor woman went on while, with the same movement, she glanced, on my dressing-table, at the face of my watch. "But I must go back."

I kept her, however. "Ah, if you can't bear it—!"

"How can I stop with her, you mean? Why, just *for* that: to get her away. Far from this," she pursued, "far from *them*—"

"She may be different? she may be free?" I seized her almost with joy. "Then, in spite of yesterday, you *believe*—"

"In such doings?" Her simple description of them required, in the light of her expression, to be carried no further, and she gave me the whole thing as she had never done. "I believe."

Yes, it was a joy, and we were still shoulder to shoulder: if I might continue sure of that I should care but little what else happened. My support in the presence of disaster would be the same as it had been in my early need of confidence, and if my friend would answer for my honesty, I would answer for all the rest. On the point of taking leave of her, none the less, I was to some extent embarrassed. "There's one thing of course—it occurs to me—to remember. My letter, giving the alarm, will have reached town before you."

I now perceived still more how she had been beating about the bush and how weary at last it had made her. "Your letter won't have got there. Your letter never went."

"What then became of it?"

"Goodness knows! Master Miles—"

"Do you mean *he* took it?" I gasped.

She hung fire, but she overcame her reluctance. "I mean that I saw yesterday, when I came back with Miss Flora, that it wasn't where you had put it. Later in the evening I had the chance to question Luke, and he declared that he had neither noticed nor touched it." We could only exchange, on this, one of our deeper mutual soundings, and it was Mrs. Grose who first brought up the plump with an almost elate "You see!"

"Yes, I see that if Miles took it instead he probably will have read it and destroyed it."

"And don't you see anything else?"

I faced her a moment with a sad smile. "It strikes me that by this time your eyes are open even wider than mine."

They proved to be so indeed, but she could still blush, almost, to show it. "I make out now what he must have done at school." And she gave, in her simple sharpness, an almost droll disillusioned nod. "He stole!"

I turned it over—I tried to be more judicial. "Well—perhaps."

She looked as if she found me unexpectedly calm. "He stole *letters!*"

She couldn't know my reasons for a calmness after all pretty shallow; so I showed them off as I might. "I hope then it was to more purpose than in this case! The note, at any rate, that I put on the table yesterday," I pursued, "will have given him so scant an advantage—for it contained only the bare demand for an interview—that he is already much ashamed of having gone so far for so little, and that what he had on his mind last evening was precisely the need of confession." I seemed to myself, for the instant, to have mastered it, to see it all. "Leave us, leave us"—I was already, at the door, hurrying her off. "I'll get it out of him. He'll meet me—he'll confess. If he confesses, he's saved. And if he's saved—"

"Then *you* are?" The dear woman kissed me on this, and I took her farewell. "I'll save you without him!" she cried as she went.

XXII

Yet it was when she had got off—and I missed her on the spot—that the great pinch really came. If I had counted on what it would give me to find myself alone with Miles, I speedily perceived, at least, that it would give me a measure. No hour of my stay in fact was so assailed with apprehensions as that of my coming down to learn that the carriage containing Mrs. Grose and my younger pupil had already rolled out of the gates. Now I *was,* I said to myself, face to face with the elements, and for much of the rest of the day, while I fought my weakness, I could consider that I had been supremely rash. It was a tighter place still than I had yet turned round in; all the more that, for the first time, I could see in the aspect of others a confused reflection of the crisis. What had happened naturally caused them all to stare; there was too little of the explained, throw out whatever we might, in the suddenness of my colleague's act. The maids and the men looked blank; the effect of which on my nerves was an aggravation until I saw the necessity of making it a positive aid. It was precisely, in short, by just clutching the helm that I avoided total wreck; and I dare say that, to bear up at all, I became, that morning, very grand and very dry. I welcomed the consciousness that I was charged with much to do, and I caused it to be known as well that, left thus to myself, I was quite remarkably firm. I wandered with that manner, for the next hour or two, all over the place and looked, I have no doubt, as if I were ready for any onset. So, for the benefit of whom it might concern, I paraded with a sick heart.

The person it appeared least to concern proved to be, till dinner, little Miles himself. My perambulations had given me, meanwhile, no glimpse of him, but they had tended to make more public the change taking place in our relation as a consequence of his having at the piano, the day before, kept me, in Flora's interest, so beguiled and befooled. The stamp of publicity had of course been fully given by her confinement and departure, and the change itself was now ushered in by our non-observance of the regular custom of the schoolroom. He had already disappeared when, on my way down, I pushed open his door, and I learned below that he had breakfasted—in the presence of a couple of the maids—with Mrs. Grose and his sister. He had then gone out, as he said, for a stroll; than which nothing, I reflected, could better have expressed his frank view of the abrupt transformation of my office. What he would now permit this office to consist of was yet to be settled: there was a queer relief, at all events—I mean for myself in especial—in the renouncement of one pretension. If so much had sprung to the surface, I scarce put it too strongly in saying that what had perhaps sprung highest was the absurdity of our prolonging the fiction that I had anything more to teach him. It sufficiently stuck out that, by tacit little tricks in which even more than myself he carried out the care for my dignity, I had had to appeal to him to let me off straining to meet him on the ground of his true capacity. He had at any rate his freedom now; I was never to touch it again; as I had amply shown, moreover, when, on his joining me in the schoolroom the previous night, I had uttered, on the subject of the interval just concluded, neither challenge nor hint. I had too much, from this moment, my other ideas. Yet when he at last arrived the difficulty of applying them, the accumulations of my problem, were brought straight home to me by the beautiful little presence on which what had occurred had as yet, for the eye, dropped neither stain nor shadow.

To mark, for the house, the high state I cultivated I de-
creed that my meals with the boy should be served, as we
called it, downstairs; so that I had been awaiting him in the
ponderous pomp of the room outside of the window of which
I had had from Mrs. Grose, that first scared Sunday, my flash
of something it would scarce have done to call light. Here at
present I felt afresh—for I had felt it again and again—how
my equilibrium depended on the success of my rigid will,
the will to shut my eyes as tight as possible to the truth that
what I had to deal with was, revoltingly, against nature. I
could only get on at all by taking "nature" into my confidence
and my account, by treating my monstrous ordeal as a push
in a direction unusual, of course, and unpleasant, but de-
manding, after all, for a fair front, only another turn of the
screw of ordinary human virtue. No attempt, none the less,
could well require more tact than just this attempt to supply,
one's self, *all* the nature. How could I put even a little of
that article into a suppression of reference to what had occurred? How, on the other hand, could I make a reference
without a new plunge into the hideous obscure? Well, a sort
of answer, after a time, had come to me, and it was so far
confirmed as that I was met, incontestably, by the quickened
vision of what was rare in my little companion. It was indeed
as if he had found even now—as he had so often found at
lessons—still some other delicate way to ease me off. Wasn't
there light in the fact which, as we shared our solitude, broke
out with a specious glitter it had never yet quite worn?—the
fact that (opportunity aiding, precious opportunity which had
now come) it would be preposterous, with a child so en-
dowed, to forgo the help one might wrest from absolute
intelligence? What had his intelligence been given him for
but to save him? Mightn't one, to reach his mind, risk the
stretch of an angular arm over his character? It was as if, when

we were face to face in the dining-room, he had literally shown me the way. The roast mutton was on the table, and I had dispensed with attendance. Miles, before he sat down, stood a moment with his hands in his pockets and looked at the joint, on which he seemed on the point of passing some humorous judgment. But what he presently produced was: "I say, my dear, is she really very awfully ill?"

"Little Flora? Not so bad but that she'll presently be better. London will set her up. Bly had ceased to agree with her. Come here and take your mutton."

He alertly obeyed me, carried the plate carefully to his seat, and, when he was established, went on. "Did Bly disagree with her so terribly suddenly?"

"Not so suddenly as you might think. One had seen it coming on."

"Then why didn't you get her off before?"

"Before what?"

"Before she became too ill to travel."

I found myself prompt. "She's *not* too ill to travel: she only might have become so if she had stayed. This was just the moment to seize. The journey will dissipate the influence"—oh, I was grand!—"and carry it off."

"I see, I see"—Miles, for that matter, was grand too. He settled to his repast with the charming little "table manner" that, from the day of his arrival, had relieved me of all grossness of admonition. Whatever he had been driven from school for, it was not for ugly feeding. He was irreproachable, as always, today; but he was unmistakably more conscious. He was discernibly trying to take for granted more things than he found, without assistance, quite easy; and he dropped into peaceful silence while he felt his situation. Our meal was of the briefest—mine a vain pretence, and I had the things immediately removed. While this was done Miles stood again with his hands in his little pockets and his back to me—stood and looked out of the wide window through which, that other day, I had seen what pulled me up. We continued silent while the maid was with us—as silent, it whimsically occurred to me, as some young couple who, on their wedding-journey, at the inn, feel shy in the presence of the waiter. He turned round only when the waiter had left us. "Well—so we're alone!"

XXIII

"Oh, more or less." I fancy my smile was pale. "Not absolutely. We shouldn't like that!" I went on.

"No—I suppose we shouldn't. Of course we have the others."

"We have the others—we have indeed the others," I concurred.

"Yet even though we have them," he returned, still with his hands in his pockets and planted there in front of me, "they don't much count, do they?"

I made the best of it, but I felt wan. "It depends on what you call 'much'!"

"Yes"—with all accommodation—"everything depends!" On this, however, he faced to the window again and presently reached it with his vague, restless, cogitating step. He remained there awhile, with his forehead against the glass, in contemplation of the stupid shrubs I knew and the dull things of November. I had always my hypocrisy of "work," behind which, now, I gained the sofa. Steadying myself with it there as I had repeatedly done at those moments of torment that I have described as the moments of my knowing the children to be given to something from which I was barred, I sufficiently obeyed my habit of being prepared for the worst. But an extraordinary impression dropped on me as I extracted a meaning from the boy's embarrassed back—none other than the impression that I was not barred now. This inference grew in a few minutes to sharp intensity and seemed bound up with the direct perception that it was positively *he* who was. The frames and squares of the great window were a kind of image, for him, of a kind of failure. I felt that I saw him, at any rate, shut in or shut out. He was admirable, but not comfortable: I took it in with a throb of hope. Wasn't he looking, through the haunted pane, for something he couldn't see?—and wasn't it the first time in the whole business that he had known such a lapse? The first, the very first: I found it a splendid portent. It made him anxious, though he watched himself; he had been anxious all day and, even while in his usual sweet little manner he sat at table, had needed all his small strange genius to give it a gloss. When he at last turned round to meet me, it was almost as if this genius had succumbed. "Well, I think I'm glad Bly agrees with *me!*"

"You would certainly seem to have seen, these twenty-four hours, a good deal more of it than for some time before. I hope," I went on bravely, "that you've been enjoying yourself."

"Oh, yes, I've been ever so far; all round about—miles and miles away. I've never been so free."

He had really a manner of his own, and I could only try to keep up with him. "Well, do you like it?"

He stood there smiling; then at last he put into two words—"Do *you?*"—more discrimination than I had ever heard two words contain. Before I had time to deal with that, however, he continued as if with the sense that this was an impertinence to be softened. "Nothing could be more charming than the way you take it, for of course if we're alone together now it's you that are alone most. But I hope," he threw in, "you don't particularly mind!"

"Having to do with you?" I asked. "My dear child, how can I help minding? Though I've renounced all claim to your company—you're so beyond me—I at least greatly enjoy it. What else should I stay on for?"

He looked at me more directly, and the expression of his face, graver now, struck me as the most beautiful I had ever found in it. "You stay on just for *that?*"

"Certainly. I stay on as your friend and from the tremendous interest I take in you till something can be done for you that may be more worth your while. That needn't surprise you." My voice trembled so that I felt it impossible to suppress the shake. "Don't you remember how I told you, when I came and sat on your bed the night of the storm, that there was nothing in the world I wouldn't do for you?"

"Yes, yes!" He, on his side, more and more visibly nervous, had a tone to master; but he was so much more successful than I that, laughing out through his gravity, he could pretend we were pleasantly jesting. "Only that, I think, was to get me to do something for *you!*"

"It was partly to get you to do something," I conceded. "But, you know, you didn't do it."

"Oh, yes," he said with the brightest superficial eagerness, "you wanted me to tell you something."

"That's it. Out, straight out. What you have on your mind, you know."

"Ah, then, is *that* what you've stayed for?"

He spoke with a gaiety through which I could still catch the finest little quiver of resentful passion; but I can't begin to express the effect upon me of an implication of surrender even so faint. It was as if what I had yearned for had come at last only to astonish me. "Well, yes—I may as well make a clean breast of it. It was precisely for that."

He waited so long that I supposed it for the purpose of repudiating the assumption on which my action had been founded; but what he finally said was: "Do you mean now—here?"

"There couldn't be a better place or time." He looked round him uneasily, and I had the rare—oh, the queer!—impression of the very first symptom I had seen in him of the approach of immediate fear. It was as if he were suddenly afraid of me—which struck me indeed as perhaps the best thing to make him. Yet in the very pang of the effort I felt it vain to try sternness, and I heard myself the next instant so gentle as to be almost grotesque. "You want so to go out again?"

"Awfully!" He smiled at me heroically, and the touching little bravery of it was enhanced by his actually flushing with pain. He had picked up his hat, which he had brought in, and stood twirling it in a way that gave me, even as I was just nearly reaching port, a perverse horror of what I was doing. To do it in *any* way was an act of violence, for what did it consist of but the obtrusion of the idea of grossness and guilt on a small helpless creature who had been for me a revelation of the possibilities of beautiful intercourse? Wasn't it base to create for a being so exquisite a mere alien awkwardness? I suppose I now read into our situation a clearness it couldn't have had at the time, for I seem to see our poor eyes already lighted with some spark of a prevision of the anguish that was to come. So we circled about, with terrors and scruples, like fighters not daring to close. But it was for each other we feared! That kept us a little longer suspended and unbruised. "I'll tell you everything," Miles said—"I mean I'll tell you anything you like. You'll stay on

with me, and we shall both be all right and I *will* tell you—
I *will*. But not now."

"Why not now?"

My insistence turned him from me and kept him once
more at his window in a silence during which, between us,
you might have heard a pin drop. Then he was before me
again with the air of a person for whom, outside, someone
who had frankly to be reckoned with was waiting. "I have to
see Luke."

I had not yet reduced him to quite so vulgar a lie, and I
felt proportionately ashamed. But, horrible as it was, his lies
made up my truth. I achieved thoughtfully a few loops of my
knitting. "Well, then, go to Luke, and I'll wait for what you
promise. Only, in return for that, satisfy, before you leave
me, one very much smaller request."

He looked as if he felt he had succeeded enough to be
able still a little to bargain. "Very much smaller—?"

"Yes, a mere fraction of the whole. Tell me"—oh, my
work preoccupied me, and I was offhand!—"if, yesterday
afternoon, from the table in the hall, you took, you know,
my letter."

XXIV

My sense of how he received this suffered for a minute from
something that I can describe only as a fierce split of my
attention—a stroke that at first, as I sprang straight up, reduced me to the mere blind movement of getting hold of
him, drawing him close, and, while I just fell for support
against the nearest piece of furniture, instinctively keeping
him with his back to the window. The appearance was full
upon us that I had already had to deal with here: Peter Quint

had come into view like a sentinel before a prison. The next thing I saw was that, from outside, he had reached the window, and then I knew that, close to the glass and glaring in through it, he offered once more to room his white face of damnation. It represents but grossly what took place within me at the sight to say that on the second my decision was made; yet I believe that no woman so overwhelmed ever in so short a time recovered her grasp of the *act*. It came to me in the very horror of the immediate presence that the act would be, seeing and facing what I saw and faced, to keep the boy himself unaware. The inspiration—I can call it by no other name—was that I felt how voluntarily, how transcendently, I *might*. It was like fighting with a demon for a human soul, and when I had fairly so appraised it I saw how the human soul—held out, in the tremor of my hands, at arm's length—had a perfect dew of sweat on a lovely childish forehead. The face that was close to mine was as white as the face against the glass, and out of it presently came a sound, not low nor weak, but as if from much farther away, that I drank like a waft of fragrance.

"Yes—I took it."

At this, with a moan of joy, I enfolded, I drew him close; and while I held him to my breast, where I could feel in the sudden fever of his little body the tremendous pulse of his little heart, I kept my eyes on the thing at the window and saw it move and shift its posture. I have likened it to a sentinel, but its slow wheel, for a moment, was rather the prowl of a baffled beast. My present quickened courage, however, was such that, not too much to let it through, I had to shade, as it were, my flame. Meanwhile the glare of the face was again at the window, the scoundrel fixed as if to watch and wait. It was the very confidence that I might now defy him, as well as the positive certitude, by this time, of the child's unconsciousness, that made me go on. "What did you take it for?"

"To see what you said about me."

"You opened the letter?"

"I opened it."

My eyes were now, as I held him off a little again, on Miles's own face, in which the collapse of mockery showed me how complete was the ravage of uneasiness. What was prodigious was that at last, by my success, his sense was sealed and his communication stopped: he knew that he was in presence, but knew not of what, and knew still less that I also was and that I did know. And what did this strain of trouble matter when my eyes went back to the window only to see that the air was clear again and—by my personal triumph— the influence quenched? There was nothing there. I felt that the cause was mine and that I should surely get *all*. "And you found nothing!"—I let my elation out.

He gave the most mournful, thoughtful little headshake. "Nothing."

"Nothing, nothing!" I almost shouted in my joy.

"Nothing, nothing," he sadly repeated.

I kissed his forehead; it was drenched. "So what have you done with it?"

"I've burnt it."

"Burnt it?" It was now or never. "Is that what you did at school?"

Oh, what this brought up! "At school?"

"Did you take letters—or other things?"

"Other things?" He appeared now to be thinking of something far off and that reached him only through the pressure of his anxiety. Yet it did reach him. "Did I *steal?*"

I felt myself redden to the roots of my hair as well as wonder if it were more strange to put to a gentleman such a question or to see him take it with allowances that gave the very distance of his fall in the world. "Was it for that you mightn't go back?"

The only thing he felt was rather a dreary little surprise. "Did you know I mightn't go back?"

"I know everything."

He gave me at this the longest and strangest look. "Everything?"

"Everything. Therefore *did* you—?" But I couldn't say it again.

Miles could, very simply. "No. I didn't steal."

My face must have shown him I believed him utterly; yet my hands—but it was for pure tenderness—shook him as if to ask him why, if it was all for nothing, he had condemned me to months of torment. "What then did you do?"

He looked in vague pain all round the top of the room and drew his breath, two or three times over, as if with difficulty. He might have been standing at the bottom of the sea and raising his eyes to some faint green twilight. "Well— I said things."

"Only that?"

"They thought it was enough!"

"To turn you out for?"

Never, truly, had a person "turned out" shown so little to explain it as this little person! He appeared to weigh my question, but in a manner quite detached and almost helpless. "Well, I suppose I oughtn't."

"But to whom did you say them?"

He evidently tried to remember, but it dropped—he had lost it. "I don't know!"

He almost smiled at me in the desolation of his surrender, which was indeed practically, by this time, so complete that I ought to have left it there. But I was infatuated—I was blind with victory, though even then the very effect that was to have brought him so much nearer was already that of added separation. "Was it to everyone?" I asked.

"No; it was only to—" But he gave a sick little headshake. "I don't remember their names."

"Were they then so many?"

"No—only a few. Those I liked."

Those he liked? I seemed to float not into clearness, but into a darker obscure, and within a minute there had come to me out of my very pity the appalling alarm of his being perhaps innocent. It was for the instant confounding and bottomless, for if he *were* innocent, what then on earth was *I*? Paralyzed, while it lasted, by the mere brush of the question, I let him go a little, so that, with a deep-drawn sigh, he turned away from me again; which, as he faced toward the clear window, I suffered, feeling that I had nothing now there to keep him from. "And did they repeat what you said?" I went on after a moment.

He was soon at some distance from me, still breathing hard and again with the air, though now without anger for it, of being confined against his will. Once more, as he had done before, he looked up at the dim day as if, of what had hitherto sustained him, nothing was left but an unspeakable anxiety. "Oh, yes," he nevertheless replied—"they must have repeated them. To those *they* liked," he added.

There was, somehow, less of it than I had expected; but I turned it over. "And these things came round—?"

"To the masters? Oh, yes!" he answered very simply. "But I didn't know they'd tell."

"The masters? They didn't—they've never told. That's why I ask you."

He turned to me again his little beautiful fevered face. "Yes, it was too bad."

"Too bad?"

"What I suppose I sometimes said. To write home."

I can't name the exquisite pathos of the contradiction given to such a speech by such a speaker; I only know that the next instant I heard myself throw off with homely force: "Stuff and nonsense!" But the next after that I must have sounded stern enough. "What *were* these things?"

My sternness was all for his judge, his executioner; yet it made him avert himself again, and that movement made *me,* with a single bound and an irrepressible cry, spring straight upon him. For there again, against the glass, as if to blight his confession and stay his answer, was the hideous author of our woe—the white face of damnation. I felt a sick swim at the drop of my victory and all the return of my battle, so that the wildness of my veritable leap only served as a great betrayal. I saw him, from the midst of my act, meet it with a divination, and on the perception that even now he only guessed, and that the window was still to his own eyes free, I let the impulse flame up to convert the climax of his dismay into the very proof of his liberation. "No more, no more, no more!" I shrieked, as I tried to press him against me, to my visitant.

"Is she *here?*" Miles panted as he caught with his sealed eyes the direction of my words. Then as his strange "she" staggered me and, with a gasp, I echoed it, "Miss Jessel, Miss Jessel!" he with a sudden fury gave me back.

I seized, stupefied, his supposition—some sequel to what he had done to Flora, but this made me only want to show him that it was better still than that. "It's not Miss Jessel! But it's at the window—straight before us. It's *there*—the coward horror, there for the last time!"

At this, after a second in which his head made the movement of a baffled dog's on a scent and then gave a frantic little shake for air and light, he was at me in a white rage, bewildered, glaring vainly over the place and missing wholly, though it now, to my sense, filled the room like the taste of poison, the wide, overwhelming presence. "It's *he?*"

I was so determined to have all my proof that I flashed into ice to challenge him. "Whom do you mean by 'he'?"

"Peter Quint—you devil!" His face gave again, round the room, its convulsed supplication. *"Where?"*

They are in my ears still, his supreme surrender of the name and his tribute to my devotion. "What does he matter now, my own?—what will he *ever* matter? *I* have you," I launched at the beast, "but he has lost you for ever!" Then, for the demonstration of my work, "There, *there!*" I said to Miles.

But he had already jerked straight round, stared, glared again, and seen but the quiet day. With the stroke of the loss I was so proud of, he uttered the cry of a creature hurled over an abyss, and the grasp with which I recovered him might have been that of catching him in his fall. I caught him, yes, I held him—it may be imagined with what a passion; but at the end of a minute I began to feel what it truly was that I held. We were alone with the quiet day, and his little heart, dispossessed, had stopped.

OWEN
WINGRAVE

I

U pon my honour, you must be off your head!" cried
Spencer Coyle, as the young man, with a white face,
stood there panting a little, and repeating, "Really, I've
quite decided," and "I assure you I've thought it all out."
They were both pale, but Owen Wingrave smiled in a manner
exasperating to his interlocutor, who, however, still discrim-
inated sufficiently to see that his grimace (it was like an irrelevant leer) was the result of extreme and conceivable
nervousness.

"It was certainly a mistake to have gone so far; but that
is exactly why I feel I mustn't go further," poor Owen said,
waiting mechanically, almost humbly (he wished not to swagger, and indeed he had nothing to swagger about), and carrying through the window to the stupid opposite houses the
dry glitter of his eyes.

"I'm unspeakably disgusted. You've made me dreadfully
ill," Mr. Coyle went on, looking thoroughly upset.

"I'm very sorry. It was the fear of the effect on you that
kept me from speaking sooner."

"You should have spoken three months ago. Don't you know your mind from one day to the other?"

The young man for a moment said nothing. Then he replied, with a little tremor: "You're very angry with me, and I expected it. I'm awfully obliged to you for all you've done for me. I'll do anything else for you in return, but I can't do that. Every one else will let me have it, of course. I'm prepared for it—I'm prepared for everything. That's what has taken the time: to be sure I was prepared. I think it's your displeasure I feel most and regret most. But, little by little, you'll get over it."

"*You'll* get over it rather faster, I suppose!" Spencer Coyle satirically exclaimed. He was quite as agitated as his young friend, and they were evidently in no condition to prolong an encounter in which they each drew blood. Mr. Coyle was a professional "coach"; he prepared young men for the army, taking only three or four at a time, to whom he applied the irresistible stimulus of which the possession was both his secret and his fortune. He had not a great establishment; he would have said himself that it was not a wholesale business. Neither his system, his health, nor his temper could have accommodated itself to numbers; so he weighed and measured his pupils, and turned away more applicants than he passed. He was an artist in his line, caring only for picked subjects, and capable of sacrifices almost passionate for the individual. He liked ardent young men (there were kinds of capacity to which he was indifferent), and he had taken a particular fancy to Owen Wingrave. This young man's facility really fascinated him. His candidates usually did wonders, and he might have sent up a multitude. He was a person of exactly the stature of the great Napoleon, with a certain flicker of genius in his light blue eye: it had been said of him that he looked like a pianist. The tone of his favourite pupil now expressed (without intention, indeed) a superior wisdom, which irritated him. He had not especially suffered before from Wingrave's high opinion of himself, which had seemed justified by remarkable parts; but today it struck him as intolerable. He cut short the discussion, declining absolutely to regard their relations as terminated, and remarked to his pupil that he had better go off somewhere (down to Eastbourne, say; the sea would bring him round) and take a few days to find his feet and come to his senses. He could afford the time, he was so well up—when Spencer Coyle remembered how well up he was he could have boxed his ears. The tall, athletic young man was not physically a subject for simplified reasoning; but there was a troubled gentleness in his handsome face, the index of compunction mixed with pertinacity, which signified that if it could have done any good he would have turned both cheeks. He evidently didn't pretend that his wisdom was superior; he only presented it as his own. It was his own career, after all, that was in question. He couldn't refuse to go through the form of trying Eastbourne, or at least of holding his tongue, though there was that in his manner which implied that if he should do so it would be really to give Mr. Coyle a chance to recuperate. He didn't feel a bit overworked, but there was nothing more natural than that, with their tremendous pressure, Mr. Coyle should be. Mr. Coyle's own intellect would derive an advantage from his pupil's holiday. Mr. Coyle saw what he meant, but he controlled himself; he only demanded, as his right, a truce of three days. Owen Wingrave granted it, though, as fostering sad illusions, this went visibly against his conscience; but before they separated the famous crammer remarked:

"All the same, I feel as if I ought to see some one. I think you mentioned to me that your aunt had come to town?"

"Oh yes; she's in Baker Street. Do go and see her," the boy said, comfortingly.

Mr. Coyle looked at him an instant. "Have you broached this folly to her?"

"Not yet—to no one. I thought it right to speak to you first."

"Oh, what you 'think right!' " cried Spencer Coyle, outraged by his young friend's standards. He added that he would probably call on Miss Wingrave; after which the recreant youth got out of the house.

Owen Wingrave didn't however start punctually for Eastbourne; he only directed his steps to Kensington Gardens, from which Mr. Coyle's desirable residence (he was terribly expensive and had a big house) was not far removed. The famous coach "put up" his pupils, and Owen had mentioned to the butler that he would be back to dinner. The spring day was warm to his young blood, and he had a book in his pocket which, when he had passed into the gardens, and, after a short stroll, dropped into a chair, he took out with the slow, soft sigh that finally ushers in a pleasure postponed. He stretched his long legs and began to read it; it was a volume of Goethe's poems. He had been for days in a state of the highest tension, and now that the cord had snapped the relief was proportionate; only it was characteristic of him that this deliverance should take the form of an intellectual pleasure. If he had thrown up the probability of a magnificent career, it was not to dawdle along Bond Street nor parade his indifference in the window of a club. At any rate, he had in a few moments forgotten everything—the tremendous pressure, Mr. Coyle's disappointment, and even his formidable aunt in Baker Street. If these watchers had overtaken him there would surely have been some excuse for their exasperation. There was no doubt he was perverse, for his very choice of a pastime only showed how he had got up his German.

"What the devil's the matter with him, do *you* know?" Spencer Coyle asked that afternoon of young Lechmere, who had never before observed the head of the establishment to set a fellow such an example of bad language. Young Lechmere was not only Wingrave's fellow-pupil, he was supposed to be his intimate, indeed quite his best friend, and had unconsciously performed for Mr. Coyle the office of making the promise of his great gifts more vivid by contrast. He was short and sturdy, and, as a general thing, uninspired, and Mr. Coyle, who found no amusement in believing in him, had never thought him less exciting than as he stared now out of a face from which you could never guess whether he had caught an idea. Young Lechmere concealed such achievements as if they had been youthful indiscretions. At any rate he could evidently conceive no reason why it should be thought there was anything more than usual the matter with the companion of his studies; so Mr. Coyle had to continue:

"He declines to go up. He chucks the whole thing!"

The first thing that struck young Lechmere in the case was the freshness it had imparted to the governor's vocabulary.

"He doesn't want to go to Sandhurst?"

"He doesn't want to go anywhere. He gives up the army altogether. He objects," said Mr. Coyle, in a tone that made young Lechmere almost hold his breath, "to the military profession."

"Why, it has been the profession of all his family!"

"Their profession? It has been their religion! Do you know Miss Wingrave?"

"Oh yes. Isn't she awful?" young Lechmere candidly ejaculated.

His instructor demurred.

"She's formidable, if you mean that, and it's right she should be; because somehow in her very person, good maiden lady as she is, she represents the might, she represents the traditions and the exploits of the British army. She represents the expansive property of the English name. I think his family can be trusted to come down on him, but every influence should be set in motion. I want to know what yours is. Can *you* do anything in the matter?"

"I can try a couple of rounds with him," said young Lechmere, reflectively. "But he knows a fearful lot. He has the most extraordinary ideas."

"Then he has told you some of them—he has taken you into his confidence?"

"I've heard him jaw by the yard," smiled the honest youth. "He has told me he despises it."

"What *is* it he despises? I can't make out."

The most consecutive of Mr. Coyle's nurslings considered a moment, as if he were conscious of a responsibility.

"Why, I think, military glory. He says we take the wrong view of it."

"He oughtn't to talk to *you* that way. It's corrupting the youth of Athens. It's sowing sedition."

"Oh, I'm all right!" said young Lechmere. "And he never told me he meant to chuck it. I always thought he meant to see it through, simply because he had to. He'll argue on any side you like. It's a tremendous pity—I'm sure he'd have a big career."

"Tell him so, then; plead with him; struggle with him—for God's sake!"

"I'll do what I can—I'll tell him it's a regular shame."

"Yes, strike *that* note—insist on the disgrace of it."

The young man gave Mr. Coyle a more perceptive glance. "I'm sure he wouldn't do anything dishonourable."

"Well—it won't look right. He must be made to feel *that*—work it up. Give him a comrade's point of view—that of a brother-in-arms."

"That's what I thought we were going to be!" young Lechmere mused, romantically, much uplifted by the nature of the mission imposed on him. "He's an awfully good sort."

"No one will think so if he backs out!" said Spencer Coyle.

"They mustn't say it to *me!*" his pupil rejoined, with a flush.

Mr. Coyle hesitated a moment, noting his tone and aware that in the perversity of things, though this young man was a born soldier, no excitement would ever attach to *his* alternatives save, perhaps, on the part of the nice girl to whom at an early day he was sure to be placidly united. "Do you like him very much—do you believe in him?"

Young Lechmere's life in these days was spent in answering terrible questions; but he had never been subjected to so queer an interrogation as this. "Believe in him? Rather!"

"Then *save* him!"

The poor boy was puzzled, as if it were forced upon him by this intensity that there was more in such an appeal than could appear on the surface; and he doubtless felt that he was only entering into a complex situation when, after another moment, with his hands in his pockets, he replied hopefully but not pompously: "I dare say I can bring him round!"

II

Before seeing young Lechmere, Mr. Coyle had determined to telegraph an inquiry to Miss Wingrave. He had prepaid the answer, which, being promptly put into his hand, brought the interview we have just related to a close. He immediately drove off to Baker Street, where the lady had said she awaited him, and five minutes after he got there, as he sat with Owen Wingrave's remarkable aunt, he repeated over several times, in his angry sadness and with the infallibility of his experience: "He's so intelligent—he's so intelligent!" He had declared it had been a luxury to put such a fellow through.

"Of course he's intelligent, what else could he be? We've never, that I know of, had but *one* idiot in the family!" said Jane Wingrave. This was an allusion that Mr. Coyle could understand, and it brought home to him another of the reasons for the disappointment, the humiliation as it were, of the good people at Paramore, at the same time that it gave an example of the conscientious coarseness he had on former occasions observed in his interlocutress. Poor Philip Wingrave, her late brother's eldest son, was literally imbecile and banished from view; deformed, unsocial, irretrievable, he had been relegated to a private asylum and had become among the friends of the family only a little hushed lugubrious legend. All the hopes of the house, picturesque Paramore, now unintermittently old Sir Philip's rather melancholy home (his infirmities would keep him there to the last), were therefore collected on the second boy's head, which nature, as if in compunction for her previous botch, had, in addition to making it strikingly handsome, filled with marked originalities and talents. These two had been the only children of the old man's only son, who, like so many of his ancestors, had given up a gallant young life to the service of his country. Owen Wingrave the elder had received his death-cut, in close-quarters, from an Afghan sabre; the blow had come crashing across his skull. His wife, at that time in India, was about to give birth to her third child; and when the event took place, in darkness and anguish, the baby came lifeless into the world and the mother sank under the multiplication of her woes.

The second of the little boys in England, who was at Paramore with his grandfather, became the peculiar charge of his aunt, the only unmarried one, and during the interesting Sunday that, by urgent invitation, Spencer Coyle, busy as he was, had, after consenting to put Owen through, spent under that roof, the celebrated crammer received a vivid impression of the influence exerted at least in intention by Miss Wingrave. Indeed, the picture of this short visit remained with the observant little man a curious one—the vision of an impoverished Jacobean house, shabby and remarkably "creepy," but full of character still and full of felicity as a setting for the distinguished figure of the peaceful old soldier. Sir Philip Wingrave, a relic rather than a celebrity, was a small, brown, erect octogenarian, with smouldering eyes and a studied courtesy. He liked to do the diminished honours of his house, but even when with a shaky hand he lighted a bedroom candle for a deprecating guest, it was impossible not to feel that beneath the surface he was a merciless old warrior. The eye of the imagination could glance back into his crowded Eastern past—back at episodes in which his scrupulous forms would only have made him more terrible.

Mr. Coyle remembered also two other figures—a faded, inoffensive Mrs. Julian, domesticated there by a system of frequent visits as the widow of an officer and a particular friend of Miss Wingrave, and a remarkably clever little girl of eighteen, who was this lady's daughter, and who struck the speculative visitor as already formed for other relations. She was very impertinent to Owen, and in the course of a long walk that he had taken with the young man, and the effect of which, in much talk, had been to clinch his high opinion of him, he had learned (for Owen chattered confidentially) that Mrs. Julian was the sister of a very gallant gentleman, Captain Hume-Walker, of the Artillery, who had fallen in the Indian Mutiny, and between whom and Miss Wingrave (it had been that lady's one known concession) a passage of some delicacy, taking a tragic turn, was believed to have been enacted. They had been engaged to be married, but she had given way to the jealousy of her nature—had broken with him and sent him off to his fate, which had been horrible. A passionate sense of having wronged him, a hard eternal remorse had thereupon taken possession of her, and when his poor sister, linked also to a soldier, had by a still heavier blow been left almost without resources, she had devoted herself charitably to a long expiation. She had sought comfort in taking Mrs. Julian to live much of the time at Paramore, where she became an unremunerated though not uncriticized housekeeper, and Spencer Coyle suspected that it was a part of this comfort that she could at her leisure trample on her. The impression of Jane Wingrave was not the faintest he had gathered on that intensifying Sunday— an occasion singularly tinged for him with the sense of be- reavement and mourning and memory, of names never men- tioned, of the far-away plaint of widows and the echoes of battles and bad news. It was all military indeed, and Mr. Coyle was made to shudder a little at the profession of which he helped to open the door to harmless young men. Miss Win- grave, moreover, might have made such a bad conscience worse—so cold and clear a good one looked at him out of her hard, fine eyes, and trumpeted in her sonorous voice.

She was a high, distinguished person; angular but not awkward, with a large forehead and abundant black hair, ar- ranged like that of a woman conceiving, perhaps excusably, of her head as "noble," and irregularly streaked today with white. If, however, she represented for Spencer Coyle the genius of a military race, it was not that she had the step of a grenadier or the vocabulary of a camp-follower; it was only

that such sympathies were vividly implied in the general fact
to which her very presence and each of her actions and glances
and tones were a constant and direct allusion—the paramount
valour of her family. If she was military, it was because she
sprang from a military house and because she wouldn't for
the world have been anything but what the Wingraves had
been. She was almost vulgar about her ancestors; and if one
had been tempted to quarrel with her, one would have found
a fair pretext in her defective sense of proportion. This temptation, however, said nothing to Spencer Coyle, for whom,
as a strong character revealing itself in colour and sound, she
was as a spectacle, and who was glad to regard her as a force
exerted on his own side. He wished her nephew had more
of her narrowness instead of being almost cursed with the
tendency to look at things in their relations. He wondered
why, when she came up to town, she always resorted to Baker
Street for lodgings. He had never known nor heard of Baker
Street as a residence—he associated it only with bazaars and
photographers. He divined in her a rigid indifference to
everything that was not the passion of her life. Nothing really
mattered to her but that, and she would have occupied apartments in Whitechapel if they had been a feature in her tactics.
She had received her visitor in a large, cold, faded room,
furnished with slippery seats and decorated with alabaster
vases and wax-flowers. The only little personal comfort for
which she appeared to have looked out was a fat catalogue
of the Army and Navy Stores, which reposed on a vast, des-
olate table-cover of false blue. Her clear forehead—it was,
like a porcelain slate, a receptacle for addresses and sums—
had flushed when her nephew's crammer told her the extraordinary news; but he saw she was fortunately more angry
than frightened. She had essentially, she would always have,
too little imagination for fear, and the healthy habit moreover

of facing everything had taught her that the occasion usually found her a quantity to reckon with. Mr. Coyle saw that her only fear at present could have been that of not being able to prevent her nephew from being absurd, and that to such an apprehension as this she was in fact inaccessible. Practically, too, she was not troubled by surprise; she recognized none of the futile, none of the subtle sentiments. If Philip had for an hour made a fool of himself, she was angry—disconcerted as she would have been on learning that he had confessed to debts or fallen in love with a low girl. But there remained in any annoyance the saving fact that no one could make a fool of *her*.

"I don't know when I've taken such an interest in a young man—I think I never have, since I began to handle them," Mr. Coyle said. "I like him, I believe in him—it's been a delight to see how he was going."

"Oh, I know how they go!" Miss Wingrave threw back her head with a familiar briskness, as if a rapid procession of the generations had flashed before her, rattling their scabbards and spurs. Spencer Coyle recognized the intimation that she had nothing to learn from anybody about the natural carriage of a Wingrave, and he even felt convicted by her next words of being, in her eyes, with the troubled story of his check, his weak complaint of his pupil, rather a poor creature. "If you like him," she exclaimed, "for mercy's sake, keep him quiet!"

Mr. Coyle began to explain to her that this was less easy than she appeared to imagine; but he perceived that she understood very little of what he said. The more he insisted that the boy had a kind of intellectual independence, the more this struck her as a conclusive proof that her nephew was a Wingrave and a soldier. It was not till he mentioned to her that Owen had spoken of the profession of arms as of something that would be "beneath" him, it was not till her attention was arrested by this intenser light on the complexity of the problem, that Miss Wingrave broke out, after a moment's stupefied reflection: "Send him to see me immediately!"

"That's exactly what I wanted to ask your leave to do. But I've wanted also to prepare you for the worst, to make you understand that he strikes me as really obstinate, and to suggest to you that the most powerful arguments at your command—especially if you should be able to put your hand on some intensely practical one—will be none too effective."

"I think I've got a powerful argument." Miss Wingrave looked very hard at her visitor. He didn't know in the least what it was, but he begged her to put it forward without delay. He promised that their young man should come to Baker Street that evening, mentioning, however, that he had already urged him to spend without delay a couple of days at Eastbourne. This lead Jane Wingrave to inquire with surprise what virtue there might be in *that* expensive remedy, and to reply, with decision, when Mr. Coyle had said, "The virtue of a little rest, a little change, a little relief to overwrought nerves," "Ah, don't coddle him—he's costing us a great deal of money! I'll talk to him, and I'll take him down to Paramore; then I'll send him back to you straightened out."

Spencer Coyle hailed this pledge superficially with satisfaction, but before he quitted Miss Wingrave he became conscious that he had really taken on a new anxiety—a restlessness that made him say to himself, groaning inwardly: "Oh, she *is* a grenadier at bottom, and she'll have no tact. I don't know what her powerful argument is; I'm only afraid she'll be stupid and make him worse. The old man's better—*he's* capable of tact, though he's not quite an extinct volcano. Owen will probably put him in a rage. In short, the difficulty is that the boy's the best of them."

Spencer Coyle felt afresh that evening at dinner that the

boy was the best of them. Young Wingrave (who, he was
pleased to observe, had not yet proceeded to the seaside)
appeared at the repast as usual, looking inevitably a little self-
conscious, but not too original for Bayswater. He talked very
naturally to Mrs. Coyle, who had thought him from the first
the most beautiful young man they had ever received; so that
the person most ill at ease was poor Lechmere, who took
great trouble, as if from the deepest delicacy, not to meet
the eye of his misguided mate. Spencer Coyle, however, paid
the penalty of his own profundity in feeling more and more
worried; he could so easily see that there were all sorts of
things in his young friend that the people of Paramore
wouldn't understand. He began even already to react against
the notion of his being harassed—to reflect that, after all, he
had a right to his ideas—to remember that he was of a substance too fine to be in fairness roughly used. It was in this
way that the ardent little crammer, with his whimsical perceptions and complicated sympathies, was generally condemned not to settle down comfortably either into his
displeasures or into his enthusiasms. His love of the real truth
never gave him a chance to enjoy them. He mentioned to
Wingrave after dinner the propriety of an immediate visit to
Baker Street, and the young man, looking "queer," as he
thought—that is, smiling again with the exaggerated glory he
had shown in their recent interview—went off to face the
ordeal. Spencer Coyle noted that he was scared—he was
afraid of his aunt; but somehow this didn't strike him as a
sign of pusillanimity. *He* should have been scared, he was
well aware, in the poor boy's place, and the sight of his pupil
marching up to the battery in spite of his terrors was a positive
suggestion of the temperament of the soldier. Many a plucky
youth would have shirked this particular peril.

"He *has* got ideas!" young Lechmere broke out to his

instructor after his comrade had quitted the house. He was evidently bewildered and agitated—he had an emotion to work off. He had before dinner gone straight at his friend, as Mr. Coyle had requested, and had elicited from him that his scruples were founded on an overwhelming conviction of the stupidity—the "crass barbarism" he called it—of war. His great complaint was that people hadn't invented anything cleverer, and he was determined to show, the only way he could, that *he* wasn't such an ass.

"And he thinks all the great generals ought to have been shot, and that Napoleon Bonaparte in particular, the greatest, was a criminal, a monster for whom language has no adequate name!" Mr. Coyle rejoined, completing young Lechmere's picture. "He favoured you, I see, with exactly the same pearls of wisdom that he produced for me. But I want to know what *you* said."

"I said they were awful rot!" Young Lechmere spoke with emphasis, and he was slightly surprised to hear Mr. Coyle laugh incongruously at this just declaration, and then after a moment continue:

"It's all very curious—I dare say there's something in it. But it's a pity!"

"He told me when it was that the question began to strike him in that light. Four or five years ago, when he did a lot of reading about all the great swells and their campaigns— Hannibal and Julius Caesar, Marlborough and Frederick and Bonaparte. He *has* done a lot of reading, and he says it opened his eyes. He says that a wave of disgust rolled over him. He talked about the 'immeasurable misery' of wars, and asked me why nations don't tear to pieces the governments, the rulers that go in for them. He hates poor old Bonaparte worst of all."

"Well, poor old Bonaparte *was* a brute. He was a frightful

HENRY JAMES

ruffian," Mr. Coyle unexpectedly declared. "But I suppose
you didn't admit that."

"Oh, I dare say he was objectionable, and I'm very glad
we laid him on his back. But the point I made to Wingrave
was that his own behaviour would excite no end of remark."
Young Lechmere hesitated an instant, then he added: "I told
him he must be prepared for the worst."

"Of course he asked you what you meant by the 'worst,'"
said Spencer Coyle.

"Yes, he asked me that; and do you know what I said? I
said people would say that his conscientious scruples and his
wave of disgust are only a pretext. Then he asked, 'A pretext
for what?'"

"Ah, he rather had you there!" Mr. Coyle exclaimed, with
a little laugh that was mystifying to his pupil.

"Not a bit—for I told him."

"What did you tell him?"

Once more, for a few seconds, with his conscious eyes
in his instructor's, the young man hung fire.

"Why, what we spoke of a few hours ago. The appearance
he'd present of not having—" The honest youth faltered a
moment, then brought it out: "The military temperament,
don't you know? But do you know what he said to that?"
young Lechmere went on.

"Damn the military temperament!" the crammer
promptly replied.

Young Lechmere stared. Mr. Coyle's tone left him un-
certain if he were attributing the phrase to Wingrave or ut-
tering his own opinion, but he exclaimed:

"Those were exactly his words!"

"He doesn't care," said Mr. Coyle.

"Perhaps not. But it isn't fair for him to abuse *us* fellows.
I told him it's the finest temperament in the world, and that
there's nothing so splendid as pluck and heroism."

"Ah! there you had *him*."

"I told him it was unworthy of him to abuse a gallant, a magnificent profession. I told him there's no type so fine as that of the soldier doing his duty."

"That's essentially *your* type, my dear boy." Young Lechmere blushed; he couldn't make out (and the danger was naturally unexpected to him) whether at that moment he didn't exist mainly for the recreation of his friend. But he was partly reassured by the genial way this friend continued, laying a hand on his shoulder: "Keep *at* him that way! We may do something. I'm extremely obliged to you." Another doubt, however, remained unassuaged—a doubt which led him to exclaim to Mr. Coyle, before they dropped the painful subject.

"He *doesn't* care! But it's awfully odd he shouldn't!"

"So it is; but remember what you said this afternoon—I mean about your not advising people to make insinuations to *you*."

"I believe I should knock a fellow down!" said young Lechmere. Mr. Coyle had got up; the conversation had taken place while they sat together after Mrs. Coyle's withdrawal from the dinner-table, and the head of the establishment administered to his disciple, on principles that were a part of his thoroughness, a glass of excellent claret. The disciple, also on his feet, lingered an instant, not for another "go," as he would have called it, at the decanter, but to wipe his microscopic mustache with prolonged and unusual care. His companion saw he had something to bring out which required a final effort, and waited for him an instant with a hand on the knob of the door. Then, as young Lechmere approached him, Spencer Coyle grew conscious of an unwonted intensity in the round and ingenuous face. The boy was nervous, but he tried to behave like a man of the world. "Of course, it's between ourselves," he stammered, "and I wouldn't breathe

such a word to any one who wasn't interested in poor Wingrave as you are. But do you think he funks it?"

Mr. Coyle looked at him so hard for an instant that he
was visibly frightened at what he had said.

"Funks it! Funks what?"

"Why, what we're talking about—the service." Young
Lechmere gave a little gulp, and added, with a naivete almost
pathetic to Spencer Coyle, "The dangers, you know!"

"Do you mean he's thinking of his skin?"

Young Lechmere's eyes expanded appealingly, and what
his instructor saw in his pink face—he even thought he saw
a tear—was the dread of a disappointment shocking in the
degree in which the loyalty of admiration had been great.

"Is he—is he *afraid?*" repeated the honest lad, with a
quaver of suspense.

"Dear no!" said Spencer Coyle, turning his back.

Young Lechmere felt a little snubbed and even a little
ashamed; but he felt still more relieved.

III

Less than a week after this Spencer Coyle received a note
from Miss Wingrave, who had immediately quitted London
with her nephew. She proposed that he should come down
to Paramore for the following Sunday—Owen was really so
tiresome. On the spot, in that house of examples and memories, and in combination with her poor dear father, who was
"dreadfully annoyed," it might be worth their while to make
a last stand. Mr. Coyle read between the lines of this letter
that the party at Paramore had got over a good deal of ground
since Miss Wingrave, in Baker Street, had treated his despair
as superficial. She was not an insinuating woman, but she

went so far as to put the question on the ground of his conferring a particular favour on an afflicted family; and she expressed the pleasure it would give them if he should be accompanied by Mrs. Coyle, for whom she enclosed a separate invitation. She mentioned that she was also writing, subject to Mr. Coyle's approval, to young Lechmere. She thought such a nice, manly boy might do her wretched nephew some good. The celebrated crammer determined to embrace this opportunity; and now it was the case not so much that he was angry as that he was anxious. As he directed his answer to Miss Wingrave's letter he caught himself smiling at the thought that at bottom he was going to defend his young friend rather than to attack him. He said to his wife, who was a fair, fresh, slow woman—a person of much more presence than himself—that she had better take Miss Wingrave at her word: it was such an extraordinary, such a fascinating specimen of an old English home. This last allusion was amicably sarcastic; he had already accused the good lady more than once of being in love with Owen Wingrave. She admitted that she was, she even gloried in her passion; which shows that the subject, between them, was treated in a liberal spirit. She carried out the joke by accepting the invitation with eagerness. Young Lechmere was delighted to do the same; his instructor had good-naturedly taken the view that the little break would freshen him up for his last spurt.

It was the fact that the occupants of Paramore did indeed take their trouble hard that struck Spencer Coyle after he had been an hour or two in that fine old house. This very short second visit, beginning on the Saturday evening, was to constitute the strangest episode of his life. As soon as he found himself in private with his wife—they had retired to dress for dinner—they called each other's attention, with effusion and almost with alarm, to the sinister gloom that was stamped on the place. The house was admirable with its old grey front, which came forward in wings so as to form three sides of a square; but Mrs. Coyle made no scruple to declare that if she had known in advance the sort of impression she was going to receive she would never have put her foot in it. She characterized it as "uncanny," she accused her husband of not having warned her properly. He had mentioned to her in advance certain facts, but while she almost feverishly dressed she had innumerable questions to ask. He hadn't told her about the girl, the extraordinary girl, Miss Julian—that is, he hadn't told her that this young lady, who in plain terms was a mere dependent, would be in effect, and as a consequence of the way she carried herself, the most important person in the house. Mrs. Coyle was already prepared to announce that she hated Miss Julian's affectations. Her husband, above all, hadn't told her that they should find their young charge looking five years older.

"I couldn't imagine that," said Mr. Coyle, "nor that the character of the crisis here would be quite so perceptible. But I suggested to Miss Wingrave the other day that they should press her nephew in real earnest, and she has taken me at my word. They've cut off his supplies—they're trying to starve him out. That's not what I meant—but, indeed, I don't quite *know* today what I meant. Owen feels the pressure, but he won't yield." The strange thing was that, now that he was there, the versatile little coach felt still more that his own spirit had been caught up by a wave of reaction. If he was there it was because he was on poor Owen's side. His whole impression, his whole apprehension, had on the spot become much deeper. There was something in the dear boy's very resistance that began to charm him. When his wife, in the intimacy of the conference I have mentioned, threw off the mask and commended even with extravagance the stand his pupil had taken (he was too good to be a horrid soldier, and it was noble of him to suffer for his convictions—wasn't he as upright as a young hero, even though as pale as a Christian martyr?) the good lady only expressed the sympathy which, under cover of regarding his young friend as a rare exception, he had already recognized in his own soul.

For, half an hour ago, after they had had superficial tea in the brown old hall of the house, his young friend had proposed to him, before going to dress, to take a turn outside, and had even, on the terrace, as they walked together to one of the far ends of it, passed his hand entreatingly into his companion's arm, permitting himself thus a familiarity unusual between pupil and master, and calculated to show that he had guessed whom he could most depend on to be kind to him. Spencer Coyle on his own side had guessed something, so that he was not surprised at the boy's having a particular confidence to make. He had felt on arriving that each member of the party had wished to get hold of him first, and he knew that at that moment Jane Wingrave was peering through the ancient blur of one of the windows (the house had been modernized so little that the thick dim panes were three centuries old) to see if her nephew looked as if he were poisoning the visitor's mind. Mr. Coyle lost no time therefore in reminding the youth (and he took care to laugh as he did so) that he had not come down to Paramore to be corrupted. He had come down to make, face to face, a last appeal to him—he hoped it wouldn't be utterly vain. Owen smiled sadly as they went, asking him if he thought he had the general air of a fellow who was going to knock under.

"I think you look strange—I think you look ill," Spencer Coyle said, very honestly. They had paused at the end of the terrace.

"I've had to exercise a great power of resistance, and it rather takes it out of one."

"Ah, my dear boy, I wish your great power—for you evidently possess it—were exerted in a better cause!"

Owen Wingrave smiled down at his small instructor. "I don't believe that!" Then he added, to explain why: "Isn't what you want, if you're so good as to think well of my character, to see me exert *most* power, in whatever direction? Well, *this* is the way I exert most." Owen Wingrave went on to relate that he had had some terrible hours with his grandfather, who had denounced him in a way to make one's hair stand up on one's head. He had expected them not to like it, not a bit, but he had had no idea they would make such a row. His aunt was different, but she was equally insulting. Oh, they had made him feel they were ashamed of him; they accused him of putting a public dishonour on their name. He was the only one who had ever backed out—he was the first for three hundred years. Every one had known he was to go up, and now every one would know he was a young hypocrite who suddenly pretended to have scruples. They talked of his scruples as you wouldn't talk of a cannibal's god. His grandfather had called him outrageous names. "He called me—he called me—" Here the young man faltered, his voice failed him. He looked as haggard as was possible to a young man in such magnificent health.

"I probably know!" said Spencer Coyle, with a nervous laugh.

Owen Wingrave's clouded eyes, as if they were following the far-off consequences of things, rested for an instant on a distant object. Then they met his companion's, and for another moment sounded them deeply. "It isn't true—no, it isn't. It's not *that!*"

"I don't suppose it is! But what *do* you propose instead of it?"

"Instead of what?"

"Instead of the stupid solution of war. If you take that away, you should suggest at least a substitute."

"That's for the people in charge, for governments and cabinets," said Owen Wingrave. "*They'll* arrive soon enough at a substitute, in the particular case, if they're made to understand that they'll be hung if they don't find one. Make it a capital crime—that'll quicken the wits of ministers!" His eyes brightened as he spoke, and he looked assured and exalted. Mr. Coyle gave a sigh of perplexed resignation—it was a monomania. He fancied after this for a moment that Owen was going to ask him if he too thought he was a coward; but he was relieved to observe that he either didn't suspect him of it or shrank uncomfortably from putting the question to the test. Spencer Coyle wished to show confidence, but somehow a direct assurance that he didn't doubt of his courage appeared too gross a compliment—it would be like saying he didn't doubt of his honesty. The difficulty was presently averted by Owen's continuing: "My grandfather can't break the entail; but I shall have nothing but this place, which, as you know, is small and, with the way rents are going, has quite ceased to yield an income. He has some money—not much, but such as it is he cuts me off. My aunt does the same—she has let me know her intentions. She was to have left me her six hundred a year. It was all settled; but now what's settled is that I don't get a penny of it if I give up the army. I must add, in fairness, that I have from my mother three hundred a year of my own. And I tell you the simple truth when I say that I don't care a rap for the loss of the money." The young man drew a long, slow breath, like a creature in pain; then he subjoined: "*That's* not what worries me!"

"What are you going to do?" asked Spencer Coyle.

"I don't know; perhaps nothing. Nothing great, at all events. Only something peaceful!"

Owen gave a weary smile, as if, worried as he was, he could yet appreciate the humorous effect of such a declaration from a Wingrave; but what it suggested to his companion, who looked up at him with a sense that he was after all not a Wingrave for nothing, and had a military steadiness under fire, was the exasperation that such a programme, uttered in such a way and striking them as the last word of the inglorious, might well have engendered on the part of his grandfather and his aunt. "Perhaps nothing"—when he might carry on the great tradition! Yes, he wasn't weak, and he was interesting; but there *was* a point of view from which he was provoking. "What *is* it, then, that worries you?" Mr. Coyle demanded.

"Oh, the house—the very air and feeling of it. There are strange voices in it that seem to mutter at me—to say dreadful things as I pass. I mean the general consciousness and responsibility of what I'm doing. Of course it hasn't been easy for me—not a bit. I assure you I don't enjoy it." With a light in them that was like a longing for justice, Owen again bent his eyes on those of the little coach; then he pursued: "I've started up all the old ghosts. The very portraits glower at me on the walls. There's one of my great-great-grandfather (the one the extraordinary story you know is about—the old fellow who hangs on the second landing of the big staircase) that fairly stirs on the canvas—just heaves a little—when I come near it. I have to go up and down stairs—it's rather awkward! It's what my aunt calls the family circle. It's all constituted here, it's a kind of indestructible presence, it stretches away into the past, and when I came back with her the other day Miss Wingrave told me I wouldn't have the impudence to stand in the midst of it and say such things. I *had* to say them to my grandfather; but now that I've said them, it seems to me that the question's ended. I want to go away—I don't care if I never come back again."

"Oh, you *are* a soldier; you must fight it out!" Mr. Coyle laughed.

The young man seemed discouraged at his levity, but as they turned round, strolling back in the direction from which they had come, he himself smiled faintly after an instant and replied:

"Why, we're tainted—all!"

They walked in silence part of the way to the old portico; then Spencer Coyle, stopping short after having assured himself that he was at a sufficient distance from the house not to be heard, suddenly put the question: "What does Miss Julian say?"

"Miss Julian?" Owen had perceptibly coloured.

"I'm sure *she* hasn't concealed her opinion."

"Oh, it's the opinion of the family circle, for she's a member of it, of course. And then she has her own as well."

"Her own opinion?"

"Her own family circle."

"Do you mean her mother—that patient lady?"

"I mean more particularly her father, who fell in battle. And her grandfather, and *his* father, and her uncles and great-uncles—they all fell in battle."

"Hasn't the sacrifice of so many lives been sufficient? Why should she sacrifice *you?*"

"Oh, she *hates* me!" Owen declared, as they resumed their walk.

"Ah, the hatred of pretty girls for fine young men!" exclaimed Spencer Coyle.

He didn't believe in it, but his wife did, it appeared perfectly, when he mentioned this conversation while, in the fashion that has been described, the visitors dressed for dinner. Mrs. Coyle had already discovered that nothing could have been nastier than Miss Julian's manner to the disgraced youth during the half-hour the party had spent in the hall;

HENRY JAMES

and it was this lady's judgment that one must have had no
eyes in one's head not to see that she was already trying
outrageously to flirt with young Lechmere. It was a pity they
had brought that silly boy; he was down in the hall with her
at that moment. Spencer Coyle's version was different; he
thought there were finer elements involved. The girl's footing
in the house was inexplicable on any ground save that of her
being predestined to Miss Wingrave's nephew. As the niece
of Miss Wingrave's own unhappy intended she had been ded-
icated early by this lady to the office of healing, by a union
with Owen, the tragic breach that had separated their elders;
and if, in reply to this, it was to be said that a girl of spirit
couldn't enjoy in such a matter having her duty cut out for
her, Owen's enlightened friend was ready with the argument
that a young person in Miss Julian's position would never be
such a fool as really to quarrel with a capital chance. She was
familiar at Paramore, and she felt safe; therefore she might
trust herself to the amusement of pretending that she had
her option. But it was all innocent coquetry. She had a curious
charm, and it was vain to pretend that the heir of that house
wouldn't seem good enough to a girl, clever as she might be,
of eighteen. Mrs. Coyle reminded her husband that the poor
young man was precisely now *not* of that house; this problem
was among the questions that exercised their wits after the
two men had taken the turn on the terrace. Spencer Coyle
told his wife that Owen was afraid of the portrait of his great-
great-grandfather. He would show it to her, since she hadn't
noticed it, on their way down-stairs.

"Why of his great-great-grandfather more than of any of
the others?"

"Oh, because he's the most formidable. He's the one
who's sometimes seen."

"Seen where?" Mrs. Coyle had turned round with a jerk.

"In the room he was found dead in—the White Room they've always called it."

"Do you mean to say the house has a *ghost?*" Mrs. Coyle almost shrieked. "You brought me here without telling me?"

"Didn't I mention it after my other visit?"

"Not a word. You only talked about Miss Wingrave."

"Oh, I was full of the story—you have simply forgotten."

"Then you should have reminded me!"

"If I had thought of it I would have held my peace, for you wouldn't have come."

"I wish, indeed, I hadn't!" cried Mrs. Coyle. "What *is* the story?"

"Oh, a deed of violence that took place here ages ago. I think it was in George the First's time. Colonel Wingrave, one of their ancestors, struck in a fit of passion one of his children, a lad just growing up, a blow on the head, of which the unhappy child died. The matter was hushed up for the hour—some other explanation was put about. The poor boy was laid out in one of those rooms on the other side of the house, and amid strange, smothered rumours the funeral was hurried on. The next morning, when the household assembled, Colonel Wingrave was missing; he was looked for vainly, and at last it occurred to some one that he might perhaps be in the room from which his child had been carried to burial. The seeker knocked without an answer—then opened the door. Colonel Wingrave lay dead on the floor, in his clothes, as if he had reeled and fallen back, without a wound, without a mark, without anything in his appearance to indicate that he had either struggled or suffered. He was a strong, sound man—there was nothing to account for such a catastrophe. He is supposed to have gone to the room during the night, just before going to bed, in some fit of compunction or some fascination of dread. It was only after this that the truth about the boy came out. But no one ever sleeps in the room."

Mrs. Coyle had fairly turned pale. "I hope not! Thank heaven they haven't put *us* there!"

"We're at a comfortable distance; but I've seen the grewsome chamber."

"Do you mean you've been *in* it?"

"For a few moments. They're rather proud of it, and my young friend showed it to me when I was here before."

Mrs. Coyle stared. "And what is it like?"

"Simply like an empty, dull, old-fashioned bedroom, rather big, with the things of the 'period' in it. It's panelled from floor to ceiling, and the panels evidently, years and years ago, were painted white. But the paint has darkened with time, and there are three or four quaint little ancient 'samplers,' framed and glazed, hung on the walls."

Mrs. Coyle looked round with a shudder. "I'm glad there are no samplers here! I never heard anything so jumpy! Come down to dinner."

On the staircase, as they went down, her husband showed her the portrait of Colonel Wingrave—rather a vigorous representation, for the place and period, of a gentleman with a hard, handsome face, in a red coat and a peruke. Mrs. Coyle declared that his descendant Sir Philip was wonderfully like him; and her husband could fancy, though he kept it to himself, that if one should have the courage to walk about the old corridors of Paramore at night one might meet a figure that resembled him roaming, with the restlessness of a ghost, hand in hand with the figure of a tall boy. As he proceeded to the drawing-room with his wife he found himself suddenly wishing that he had made more of a point of his pupil's going to Eastbourne. The evening, however, seemed to have taken upon itself to dissipate any such whimsical forebodings, for

the grimness of the family circle, as Spencer Coyle had pre-
conceived its composition, was mitigated by an infusion of
the "neighbourhood." The company at dinner was recruited
by two cheerful couples—one of them the vicar and his wife,
and by a silent young man who had come down to fish. This
was a relief to Mr. Coyle, who had begun to wonder what
was after all expected of him, and why he had been such a
fool as to come, and who now felt that for the first hours at
least the situation would not have directly to be dealt with.
Indeed, he found, as he had found before, sufficient occupation for his ingenuity in reading the various symptoms of
which the picture before him was an expression. He should
probably have an irritating day on the morrow; he foresaw
the difficulty of the long, decorous Sunday, and how dry Jane
Wingrave's ideas, elicited in a strenuous conference, would
taste. She and her father would make him feel that they
depended upon him for the impossible, and if they should
try to associate him with a merely stupid policy he might end
by telling them what he thought of it—an accident not required to make his visit a sensible mistake. The old man's
actual design was evidently to let their friends see in it a
positive mark of their being all right. The presence of the
great London coach was tantamount to a profession of faith
in the results of the impending examination. It had clearly
been obtained from Owen, rather to Spencer Coyle's surprise, that he would do nothing to interfere with the apparent
harmony. He let the allusions to his hard work pass and,
holding his tongue about his affairs, talked to the ladies as
amicably as if he had not been "cut off." When Spencer Coyle
looked at him once or twice across the table, catching his
eye, which showed an indefinable passion, he saw a puzzling
pathos in his laughing face; one couldn't resist a pang for a
young lamb so visibly marked for sacrifice. "Hang him—what

a pity he's such a fighter!" he privately sighed, with a want of logic that was only superficial.

This idea, however, would have absorbed him more if so much of his attention had not been given to Kate Julian, who, now that he had her well before him, struck him as a remarkable and even as a possibly fascinating young woman. The fascination resided not in any extraordinary prettiness, for if she was handsome, with her long Eastern eyes, her magnificent hair, and her general unabashed originality, he had seen complexions rosier and features that pleased him more; it resided in a strange impression that she gave of being exactly the sort of person whom, in her position, common considerations, those of prudence, and perhaps even a little those of decorum, would have enjoined on her not to be. She was what was vulgarly termed a dependent—penniless, patronized, tolerated; but something in her aspect and manner signified that, if her situation was inferior, her spirit, to make up for it, was above precautions or submissions. It was not in the least that she was aggressive, she was too indifferent for that; it was only as if, having nothing either to gain or to lose, she could afford to do as she liked. It occurred to Spencer Coyle that she might really have had more at stake than her imagination appeared to take account of; whatever it was, at any rate, he had never seen a young woman at less pains to be on the safe side. He wondered inevitably how the peace was kept between Jane Wingrave and such an inmate as this; but those questions of course were unfathomable deeps. Perhaps Kate Julian lorded it even over her protectress. The other time he was at Paramore he had received an impression that, with Sir Philip beside her, the girl could fight with her back to the wall. She amused Sir Philip, she charmed him, and he liked people who weren't afraid; between him and his daughter, moreover, there was no doubt which was the higher in command. Miss Wingrave took many things for granted, and most of all the rigour of discipline and the fate of the vanquished and the captive.

But between their clever boy and so original a companion of his childhood what odd relation would have grown up? It couldn't be indifference, and yet on the part of happy, handsome, youthful creatures it was still less likely to be aversion. They weren't Paul and Virginia, but they must have had their common summer and their idyll; no nice girl could have disliked such a nice fellow for anything but not liking *her,* and no nice fellow could have resisted such propinquity. Mr. Coyle remembered indeed that Mrs. Julian had spoken to him as if the propinquity had been by no means constant, owing to her daughter's absences at school, to say nothing of Owen's; her visits to a few friends who were so kind as to "take her" from time to time; her sojourns in London—so difficult to manage, but still managed by God's help—for "advantages," for drawing and singing, especially drawing, or rather painting in oils, in which she had had immense success. But the good lady had also mentioned that the young people were quite brother and sister, which *was* a little, after all, like Paul and Virginia. Mrs. Coyle had been right, and it was apparent that Virginia was doing her best to make the time pass agreeably for young Lechmere. There was no such whirl of conversation as to render it an effort for Mr. Coyle to reflect on these things, for the tone of the occasion, thanks principally to the other guests, was not disposed to stray— it tended to the repetition of anecdote and the discussion of rents, topics that huddled together like uneasy animals. He could judge how intensely his hosts wished the evening to pass off as if nothing had happened; and this gave him the measure of their private resentment. Before dinner was over he found himself fidgety about his second pupil. Young

Lechmere, since he began to cram, had done all that might have been expected of him; but this couldn't blind his instructor to a present perception of his being in moments of relaxation as innocent as a babe. Mr. Coyle had considered that the amusements of Paramore would probably give him a fillip, and the poor fellow's manner testified to the soundness of the forecast. The fillip had been unmistakably administered; it had come in the form of a revelation. The light on young Lechmere's brow announced with a candour that was almost an appeal for compassion, or at least a deprecation of ridicule, that he had never seen anything like Miss Julian.

IV

In the drawing-room after dinner the girl found an occasion to approach Spencer Coyle. She stood before him a moment, smiling while she opened and shut her fan, and then she said, abruptly, raising her strange eyes: "I know what you've come for; but it isn't any use."

"I've come to look after *you* a little. Isn't *that* any use?"

"It's very kind. But I'm not the question of the hour. You won't do anything with Owen."

Spencer Coyle hesitated a moment. "What will *you* do with his young friend?"

She stared, looked round her.

"Mr. Lechmere? Oh, poor little lad! We've been talking about Owen. He admires him so."

"So do I. I should tell you that."

"So do we all. That's why we're in such despair."

"Personally, then, you'd *like* him to be a soldier?" Spencer Coyle inquired.

"I've quite set my heart on it. I adore the army, and I'm awfully fond of my old playmate," said Miss Julian.

Her interlocutor remembered the young man's own different version of her attitude; but he judged it loyal not to challenge the girl.

"It's not conceivable that your old playmate shouldn't be fond of you. He must therefore wish to please you; and I don't see why—between you—you don't set the matter right."

"Wish to please me!" Miss Julian exclaimed. "I'm sorry to say he shows no such desire. He thinks me an impudent wretch. I've told him what I think of *him,* and he simply hates me."

"But you think so highly! You just told me you admire him."

"His talents, his possibilities, yes; even his appearance, if I may allude to such a matter. But I don't admire his present behaviour."

"Have you had the question out with him?" Spencer Coyle asked.

"Oh yes; I've ventured to be frank—the occasion seemed to excuse it. He couldn't like what I said."

"What did you say?"

Miss Julian, thinking a moment, opened and shut her fan again.

"Why, that such conduct isn't that of a gentleman!"

After she had spoken her eyes met Spencer Coyle's, who looked into their charming depths.

"Do you want, then, so much to send him off to be killed?"

"How odd for *you* to ask that—in such a way!" she replied, with a laugh. "I don't understand your position; I thought your line was to *make* soldiers!"

"You should take my little joke. But, as regards Owen Wingrave, there's no 'making' needed," Mr. Coyle added. "To my sense"—the little crammer paused a moment, as if with a consciousness of responsibility for his paradox—"to my sense he *is,* in a high sense of the term, a fighting man."

"Ah, let him prove it!" the girl exclaimed, turning away.

Spencer Coyle let her go; there was something in her tone that annoyed and even a little shocked him. There had evidently been a violent passage between these young people, and the reflection that such a matter was, after all, none of his business only made him more sore. It was indeed a military house, and she was, at any rate, a person who placed her ideal of manhood (young persons doubtless always had their ideals of manhood) in the type of the belted warrior. It was a taste like another; but, even a quarter of an hour later, finding himself near young Lechmere, in whom this type was embodied, Spencer Coyle was still so ruffled that he addressed the innocent lad with a certain magisterial dryness. "You're not to sit up late, you know. That's not what I brought you down for." The dinner-guests were taking leave and the bedroom candles twinkled in a monitory row. Young Lechmere, however, was too agreeably agitated to be accessible to a snub: he had a happy preoccupation which almost engendered a grin.

"I'm only too eager for bedtime. Do you know there's an awfully jolly room?"

"Surely they haven't put you there?"

"No, indeed; no one has passed a night in it for ages. But that's exactly what I want to do—it would be tremendous fun."

"And have you been trying to get Miss Julian's permission?"

"Oh, *she* can't give leave, she says. But she believes in it, and she maintains that no man dare."

"No man *shall!* A man in your critical position in particular must have a quiet night," said Spencer Coyle.

Young Lechmere gave a disappointed but reasonable sigh. "Oh, all right. But mayn't I sit up for a little go at Wingrave? I haven't had any yet."

Mr. Coyle looked at his watch.

"You may smoke *one* cigarette."

He felt a hand on his shoulder, and he turned round to see his wife tilting candle-grease upon his coat. The ladies were going to bed, and it was Sir Philip's inveterate hour; but Mrs. Coyle confided to her husband that after the dreadful things he had told her she positively declined to be left alone, for no matter how short an interval, in any part of the house. He promised to follow her within three minutes, and after the orthodox hand-shakes the ladies rustled away. The forms were kept up at Paramore as bravely as if the old house had no present heartache. The only one of which Spencer Coyle noticed the omission was some salutation to himself from Kate Julian. She gave him neither a word nor a glance, but he saw her look hard at Owen Wingrave. Her mother, timid and pitying, was apparently the only person from whom this young man caught an inclination of the head. Miss Wingrave marshalled the three ladies—her little procession of twinkling tapers—up the wide oaken stairs and past the watching portrait of her ill-fated ancestor. Sir Philip's servant appeared and offered his arm to the old man, who turned a perpendicular back on poor Owen when the boy made a vague movement to anticipate this office. Spencer Coyle learned afterwards that before Owen had forfeited favour it had always, when he was at home, been his privilege at bedtime to conduct his grandfather ceremoniously to rest. Sir Philip's habits were contemptuously different now. His apartments were on the lower floor, and he shuffled stiffly off to them with his valet's help, after fixing for a moment significantly on the most responsible of his visitors the thick red ray, like the glow of stirred embers, that always made his eyes conflict oddly with his mild manners. They seemed to say to Spencer Coyle, "We'll let the young scoundrel have it tomorrow!" One might have gathered from them that the young scoundrel, who had now strolled to the other end of the hall, had at least forged a check. Mr. Coyle watched him an instant, saw him drop nervously into a chair, and then with a restless movement get up. The same movement brought him back to where his late instructor stood addressing a last injunction to young Lechmere.

"I'm going to bed, and I should like you particularly to conform to what I said to you a short time ago. Smoke a single cigarette with your friend here, and then go to your room. You'll have me down on you if I hear of your having, during the night, tried any preposterous games." Young Lechmere, looking down with his hands in his pockets, said nothing—he only poked at the corner of a rug with his toe; so that Spencer Coyle, dissatisfied with so tacit a pledge, presently went on, to Owen: "I must request you, Wingrave, not to keep this sensitive subject sitting up—and, indeed, to put him to bed and turn his key in the door." As Owen stared an instant, apparently not understanding the motive of so much solicitude, he added: "Lechmere has a morbid curiosity about one of your legends—of your historic rooms. Nip it in the bud."

"Oh, the legend's rather good, but I'm afraid the room's an awful sell!" Owen laughed.

"You know you don't *believe* that, my boy!" young Lechmere exclaimed.

"I don't think he does," said Mr. Coyle, noticing Owen's mottled flush.

"He wouldn't try a night there himself!" young Lechmere pursued.

"I know who told you that," rejoined Owen, lighting a cigarette in an embarrassed way at the candle, without offering one to either of his companions.

"Well, what if she did?" asked the younger of these gentlemen, rather red. "Do you want them *all* yourself?" he continued, facetiously, fumbling in the cigarette-box.

Owen Wingrave only smoked quietly; then he exclaimed: "Yes—what if she did? But she doesn't know," he added.

"She doesn't know what?"

"She doesn't know anything!—I'll tuck him in!" Owen went on gayly, to Mr. Coyle, who saw that his presence, now that a certain note had been struck, made the young men uncomfortable. He was curious, but there was a kind of discretion, with his pupils, that he had always pretended to practise; a discretion that, however, didn't prevent him as he took his way upstairs from recommending them not to be donkeys.

At the top of the staircase, to his surprise, he met Miss Julian, who was apparently going down again. She had not begun to undress, nor was she perceptibly disconcerted at seeing him. She nevertheless, in a manner slightly at variance with the rigour with which she had overlooked him ten minutes before, dropped the words, "I'm going down to look for something. I've lost a jewel."

"A jewel?"

"A rather good turquoise, out of my locket. As it's the only ornament I have the honour to possess—" And she passed down.

"Shall I go with you and help you?" asked Spencer Coyle.

The girl paused a few steps below him, looking back with her Oriental eyes.

"Don't I hear voices in the hall?"

"Those remarkable young men are there."

"*They'll* help me." And Kate Julian descended.

Spencer Coyle was tempted to follow her, but remembering his standard of tact, he rejoined his wife in their apartment. He delayed, however, to go to bed, and though he went into his dressing-room, he couldn't bring himself even to take off his coat. He pretended for half an hour to read a novel; after which, quietly, or perhaps I should say agitatedly, he passed from the dressing-room into the corridor. He followed this passage to the door of the room which he knew to have been assigned to young Lechmere, and was comforted to see that it was closed. Half an hour earlier he had seen it standing open; therefore he could take for granted that the bewildered boy had come to bed. It was of this he had wished to assure himself, and having done so, he was on the point of retreating. But at the same instant he heard a sound in the room—the occupant was doing to the window something which showed him that he might knock without the reproach of waking his pupil up. Young Lechmere came in fact to the door in his shirt and trousers. He admitted his visitor in some surprise, and when the door was closed again Spencer Coyle said:

"I don't want to make your life a burden to you, but I had it on my conscience to see for myself that you're not exposed to undue excitement."

"Oh, there's plenty of that!" said the ingenuous youth. "Miss Julian came down again."

"To look for a turquoise?"

"So she said."

"Did she find it?"

"I don't know. I came up. I left her with poor Wingrave."

"Quite the right thing," said Spencer Coyle.

"I don't know," young Lechmere repeated, uneasily. "I left them quarrelling."

"What about?"

"I don't understand. They're a quaint pair!"

Spencer Coyle hesitated. He had, fundamentally, principles and scruples, but what he had in particular just now was a curiosity, or rather, to recognize it for what it was, a sympathy, which brushed them away.

"Does it strike you that *she's* down on him?" he permitted himself to inquire.

"Rather!—when she tells him he lies!"

"What do you mean?"

"Why, before *me.* It made me leave them; it was getting too hot. I stupidly brought up the question of the haunted room again, and said how sorry I was that I had had to promise you not to try my luck with it."

"You can't pry about in that gross way in other people's houses—you can't take such liberties, you know!" Mr. Coyle interjected.

"I'm all right—see how good I am. I don't want to go *near* the place!" said young Lechmere, confidingly. "Miss Julian said to me, 'Oh, I dare say *you'd* risk it, but'—and she turned and laughed at poor Owen—'that's more than we can expect of a gentleman who has taken *his* extraordinary line.' I could see that something had already passed between them on the subject—some teasing or challenging of hers. It may have been only chaff, but his chucking the profession had evidently brought up the question of his pluck."

"And what did Owen say?"

"Nothing at first; but presently he brought out very quietly: 'I spent all last night in the confounded place.' We both stared and cried out at this, and I asked him what he had seen there. He said he had seen nothing, and Miss Julian replied that he ought to tell his story better than that—he ought to make something good of it. 'It's not a story—it's a simple fact,' said he; on which she jeered at him and wanted to know why, if he had done it, he hadn't told her in the morning, since he knew what she thought of him. 'I know, but I don't care,' said Wingrave. This made her angry, and she asked him, quite seriously, whether he would care if he should know she believed him to be trying to deceive us."

"Ah, what a brute!" cried Spencer Coyle.

"She's a most extraordinary girl—I don't know what she's up to."

"Extraordinary indeed—to be romping and bandying words at that hour of the night with fast young men!"

Young Lechmere reflected a moment. "I mean because I think she likes him."

Spencer Coyle was so struck with this unwonted symptom of subtlety that he flashed out: "And do you think he likes *her?*"

But his interlocutor only replied with a puzzled sigh and a plaintive "I don't know—I give it up!—I'm sure he *did* see something or hear something," young Lechmere added.

"In that ridiculous place? What makes you sure?"

"I don't know—he looks as if he had. He behaves as if he had."

"Why, then, shouldn't he mention it?"

Young Lechmere thought a moment. "Perhaps it's too grewsome!"

Spencer Coyle gave a laugh. "Aren't you glad, then, *you're* not in it?"

"Uncommonly!"

"Go to bed, you goose," said Spencer Coyle, with another laugh. "But, before you go, tell me what he said when she told him he was trying to deceive you."

" 'Take me there yourself, then, and lock me in!' "

"And *did* she take him?"

"I don't know—I came up."

Spencer Coyle exchanged a long look with his pupil.

"I don't think they're in the hall now. Where's Owen's own room?"

"I haven't the least idea."

Mr. Coyle was perplexed; he was in equal ignorance, and he couldn't go about trying doors. He bade young Lechmere sink to slumber, and came out into the passage. He asked himself if he should be able to find his way to the room Owen had formerly shown him, remembering that, in common with many of the others, it had its ancient name painted upon it. But the corridors of Paramore were intricate; moreover, some of the servants would still be up, and he didn't wish to have the appearance of roaming over the house. He went back to his own quarters, where Mrs. Coyle soon perceived that his inability to rest had not subsided. As she confessed for her own part, in the dreadful place, to an increased sense of "creepiness," they spent the early part of the night in conversation, so that a portion of their vigil was inevitably beguiled by her husband's account of his colloquy with little Lechmere, and by their exchange of opinions upon it. Towards two o'clock Mrs. Coyle became so nervous about their persecuted young friend, and so possessed by the fear that that wicked girl had availed herself of his invitation to put him to an abominable test, that she begged her husband to go and look into the matter, at whatever cost to his own equilibrium. But Spencer Coyle, perversely, had ended, as the perfect stillness of the night settled upon them, by charming himself into a tremulous acquiescence in Owen's readiness to face a formidable ordeal—an ordeal the more formidable to an excited imagination, as the poor boy now knew from the experience of the previous night how resolute an effort he should have to make. "I hope he *is* there," he said to his wife; "it puts them all so in the wrong!" At any rate, he couldn't take upon himself to explore a house he knew so little. He was inconsequent—he didn't prepare for bed. He sat in the dressing-room with his light and his novel, waiting to find himself nodding. At last, however, Mrs. Coyle turned over and ceased to talk, and at last, too, he fell asleep in his chair. How long he slept he only knew afterwards by computation; what he knew, to begin with, was that he had started up, in confusion, with the sense of a sudden appalling sound. His sense cleared itself quickly, helped doubtless by a confirmatory cry of horror from his wife's room. But he gave no heed to his wife; he had already bounded into the passage. There the sound was repeated—it was the "Help! help!" of a woman in agonized terror. It came from a distant quarter of the house, but the quarter was sufficiently indicated. Spencer Coyle rushed straight before him, with the sound of opening doors and alarmed voices in his ears, and the faintness of the early dawn in his eyes. At a turn of one of the passages he came upon the white figure of a girl in a swoon on a bench, and in the vividness of the revelation he read as he went that Kate Julian, stricken in her pride too late with a chill of compunction for what she had mockingly done, had, after coming to release the victim of her derision, reeled away, overwhelmed, from the catastrophe that was her work—the catastrophe that the next moment he found himself aghast at on the threshold of an open door. Owen Wingrave, dressed as he had last seen him, lay dead on the spot on which his ancestor had been found. He looked like a young soldier on a battle-field.

SIR DOMINICK
FERRAND

I

There are several objections to it, but I'll take it if you'll alter it," Mr. Locket's rather curt note had said; and there was no waste of words in the postscript in which he had added: "If you'll come in and see me, I'll show you what I mean." This communication had reached Jersey Villas by the first post, and Peter Baron had scarcely swallowed his leathery muffin before he got into motion to obey the editorial behest. He knew that such precipitation looked eager, and he had no desire to look eager—it was not in his interest; but how could he maintain a god-like calm, principled though he was in favour of it, the first time one of the great magazines had accepted, even with a cruel reservation, a specimen of his ardent young genius?

It was not till, like a child with a sea-shell at his ear, he began to be aware of the great roar of the "underground," that, in his third-class carriage, the cruelty of the reservation penetrated, with the taste of acrid smoke, to his inner sense. It was really degrading to be eager in the face of having to "alter." Peter Baron tried to figure to himself at that moment that he was not flying to betray the extremity of his need, but hurrying to fight for some of those passages of superior boldness which were exactly what the conductor of the "Promiscuous Review" would be sure to be down upon. He made believe—as if to the greasy fellow-passenger oppo-site—that he felt indignant; but he saw that to the small round eye of this still more downtrodden brother he represented selfish success. He would have liked to linger in the concep-tion that he had been "approached" by the Promiscuous; but whatever might be thought in the office of that periodical of some of his flights of fancy, there was no want of vividness in his occasional suspicion that he passed there for a familiar bore. The only thing that was clearly flattering was the fact that the Promiscuous rarely published fiction. He should therefore be associated with a deviation from a solemn habit, and that would more than make up to him for a phrase in one of Mr. Locket's inexorable earlier notes, a phrase which still rankled, about his showing no symptom of the faculty really creative. "You don't seem able to keep a character together," this pitiless monitor had somewhere else re-marked. Peter Baron, as he sat in his corner while the train stopped, considered, in the befogged gaslight, the bookstall standard of literature and asked himself whose character had fallen to pieces now. Tormenting indeed had always seemed to him such a fate as to have the creative head without the creative hand.

It should be mentioned, however, that before he started on his mission to Mr. Locket his attention had been briefly engaged by an incident occurring at Jersey Villas. On leaving the house (he lived at No. 3, the door of which stood open to a small front garden), he encountered the lady who, a week before, had taken possession of the rooms on the ground floor, the "parlours" of Mrs. Bundy's terminology. He had heard her, and from his window, two or three times, had even seen her pass in and out, and this observation had created in his mind a vague prejudice in her favour. Such a prejudice, it was true, had been subjected to a violent test; it had been fairly apparent that she had a light step, but it was still less to be overlooked that she had a cottage piano. She had furthermore a little boy and a very sweet voice, of which Peter Baron had caught the accent, not from her singing (for she only played), but from her gay admonitions to her child, whom she occasionally allowed to amuse himself—under restrictions very publicly enforced—in the tiny black patch which, as a forecourt to each house, was held, in the humble row, to be a feature. Jersey Villas stood in pairs, semi-detached, and Mrs. Ryves—such was the name under which the new lodger presented herself—had been admitted to the house as confessedly musical. Mrs. Bundy, the earnest proprietress of No. 3, who considered her "parlours" (they were a dozen feet square), even more attractive, if possible, than the second floor with which Baron had had to content himself—Mrs. Bundy, who reserved the drawing-room for a casual dressmaking business, had threshed out the subject of the new lodger in advance with our young man, reminding him that her affection for his own person was a proof that, other things being equal, she positively preferred tenants who were clever.

This was the case with Mrs. Ryves; she had satisfied Mrs. Bundy that she was not a simple strummer. Mrs. Bundy admitted to Peter Baron that, for herself, she had a weakness for a pretty tune, and Peter could honestly reply that his ear was equally sensitive. Everything would depend on the "touch" of their inmate. Mrs. Ryves's piano would blight his existence if her hand should prove heavy or her selections vulgar; but if she played agreeable things and played them in an agreeable way she would render him rather a service while he smoked the pipe of "form." Mrs. Bundy, who wanted to let her rooms, guaranteed on the part of the stranger a first-class talent, and Mrs. Ryves, who evidently knew thoroughly what she was about, had not falsified this somewhat rash prediction. She never played in the morning, which was Baron's working-time, and he found himself listening with pleasure at other hours to her discreet and melancholy strains. He really knew little about music, and the only criticism he would have made of Mrs. Ryves's conception of it was that she seemed devoted to the dismal. It was not, however, that these strains were not pleasant to him; they floated up, on the contrary, as a sort of conscious response to some of his broodings and doubts. Harmony, therefore, would have reigned supreme had it not been for the singularly bad taste of No. 4. Mrs. Ryves's piano was on the free side of the house and was regarded by Mrs. Bundy as open to no objection but that of their own gentleman, who was so reasonable. As much, however, could not be said of the gentleman of No. 4, who had not even Mr. Baron's excuse of being "littery" (he kept a bull-terrier and had five hats—the street could count them), and whom, if you had listened to Mrs. Bundy, you would have supposed to be divided from the obnoxious instrument by walls and corridors, obstacles and intervals, of massive structure and fabulous extent. This gentleman had taken up an attitude which had now passed into the phase of correspondence and compromise; but it was the opinion of the immediate neighbourhood that he had not a leg to stand upon, and on whatever subject the sentiment of Jersey Villas might have been vague, it was not so on the rights and the wrongs of landladies.

Mrs. Ryves's little boy was in the garden as Peter Baron

issued from the house, and his mother appeared to have come out for a moment, bareheaded, to see that he was doing no harm. She was discussing with him the responsibility that he might incur by passing a piece of string round one of the iron palings and pretending he was in command of a "geegee"; but it happened that at the sight of the other lodger the child was seized with a finer perception of the drivable. He rushed at Baron with a flourish of the bridle, shouting, "Ou geegee!" in a manner productive of some refined embarrassment to his mother. Baron met his advance by mounting him on a shoulder and feigning to prance an instant, so that by the time this performance was over—it took but a few seconds— the young man felt introduced to Mrs. Ryves. Her smile struck him as charming, and such an impression shortens many steps. She said, "Oh, thank you—you mustn't let him worry you"; and then as, having put down the child and raised his hat, he was turning away, she added: "It's very good of you not to complain of my piano."

"I particularly enjoy it—you play beautifully," said Peter Baron.

"I have to play, you see—it's all I can do. But the people next door don't like it, though my room, you know, is not against their wall. Therefore I thank you for letting me tell them that you, in the house, don't find me a nuisance."

She looked gentle and bright as she spoke, and as the young man's eyes rested on her the tolerance for which she expressed herself indebted seemed to him the least indulgence she might count upon. But he only laughed and said "Oh, no, you're not a nuisance!" and felt more and more introduced.

The little boy, who was handsome, hereupon clamoured for another ride, and she took him up herself, to moderate his transports. She stood a moment with the child in her arms, and he put his fingers exuberantly into her hair, so that while she smiled at Baron she slowly, permittingly shook her head to get rid of them.

"If they really make a fuss I'm afraid I shall have to go," she went on.

"Oh, don't go!" Baron broke out, with a sudden expressiveness which made his voice, as it fell upon his ear, strike him as the voice of another. She gave a vague exclamation and, nodding slightly but not unsociably, passed back into the house. She had made an impression which remained till the other party to the conversation reached the railway-station, when it was superseded by the thought of his prospective discussion with Mr. Locket. This was a proof of the intensity of that interest.

The aftertaste of the later conference was also intense for Peter Baron, who quitted his editor with his manuscript under his arm. He had had the question out with Mr. Locket, and he was in a flutter which ought to have been a sense of triumph and which indeed at first he succeeded in regarding in this light. Mr. Locket had had to admit that there was an idea in his story, and that was a tribute which Baron was in a position to make the most of. But there was also a scene which scandalised the editorial conscience and which the young man had promised to rewrite. The idea that Mr. Locket had been so good as to disengage depended for clearness mainly on this scene; so it was easy to see his objection was perverse. This inference was probably a part of the joy in which Peter Baron walked as he carried home a contribution it pleased him to classify as accepted. He walked to work off his excitement and to think in what manner he should reconstruct. He went some distance without settling that point, and then, as it began to worry him, he looked vaguely into shop-windows for solutions and hints. Mr. Locket lived in the depths of Chelsea, in a little panelled, amiable house, and Baron took his way homeward along the King's Road. There was a new amusement for him, a fresher bustle, in a London walk in the morning; these were hours that he habitually spent at his table, in the awkward attitude engendered by the poor piece of furniture, one of the rickety features of Mrs. Bundy's second floor, which had to serve as his altar of literary sacrifice. If by exception he went out when the day was young he noticed that life seemed younger with it; there were livelier industries to profit by and shop-girls, often rosy, to look at; a different air was in the streets and a chaff of traffic for the observer of manners to catch. Above all, it was the time when poor Baron made his purchases, which were wholly of the wandering mind; his extravagances, for some mysterious reason, were all matutinal, and he had a foreknowledge that if ever he should ruin himself it would be well before noon. He felt lavish this morning, on the strength of what the Promiscuous would do for him; he had lost sight for the moment of what he should have to do for the Promiscuous. Before the old bookshops and printshops, the crowded panes of the curiosity-mongers and the desirable exhibitions of mahogany "done up," he used, by an innocent process, to commit luxurious follies. He refurnished Mrs. Bundy with a freedom that cost her nothing, and lost himself in pictures of a transfigured second floor.

On this particular occasion the King's Road proved almost unprecedentedly expensive, and indeed this occasion differed from most others in containing the germ of real danger. For once in a way he had a bad conscience—he felt himself tempted to pick his own pocket. He never saw a commodious writing-table, with elbow-room and drawers and a fair expanse of leather stamped neatly at the edge with gilt, without being freshly reminded of Mrs. Bundy's dilapidations. There were several such tables in the King's Road—they seemed indeed particularly numerous today. Peter Baron glanced at them all through the fronts of the shops, but there was one that detained him in supreme contemplation. There was a fine assurance about it which seemed a guarantee of masterpieces; but when at last he went in and, just to help himself on his way, asked the impossible price, the sum mentioned by the voluble vendor mocked at him even more than he had feared. It was far too expensive, as he hinted, and he was on the point of completing his comedy by a pensive retreat when the shopman bespoke his attention for another article of the same general character, which he described as remarkably cheap for what it was. It was an old piece, from a sale in the country, and it had been in stock some time; but it had got pushed out of sight in one of the upper rooms—they contained such a wilderness of treasures—and happened to have but just come to light. Peter suffered himself to be conducted into an interminable dusky rear, where he presently found himself bending over one of those square substantial desks of old mahogany, raised, with the aid of front legs, on a sort of retreating pedestal which is fitted with small drawers, contracted conveniences known immemorially to the knowing as davenports. This specimen had visibly seen service, but it had an old-time solidity and to Peter Baron it unexpectedly appealed.

He would have said in advance that such an article was exactly what he didn't want, but as the shopman pushed up a chair for him and he sat down with his elbows on the gentle slope of the large, firm lid, he felt that such a basis for literature would be half the battle. He raised the lid and looked lovingly into the deep interior; he sat ominously silent while his companion dropped the striking words: "Now that's an article I personally covet!" Then when the man mentioned

the ridiculous price (they were literally giving it away), he
reflected on the economy of having a literary altar on which
one could really kindle a fire. A davenport was a compromise,
but what was all life but a compromise? He could beat down
the dealer, and at Mrs. Bundy's he had to write on an insincere
cardtable. After he had sat for a minute with his nose in the
friendly desk he had a queer impression that it might tell him
a secret or two—one of the secrets of form, one of the sac-
rificial mysteries—though no doubt its career had been literary only in the sense of its helping some old lady to write
invitations to dull dinners. There was a strange, faint odour
in the receptacle, as if fragrant, hallowed things had once
been put away there. When he took his head out of it he said
to the shopman: "I don't mind meeting you halfway." He had
been told by knowing people that that was the right thing.
He felt rather vulgar, but the davenport arrived that evening
at Jersey Villas.

II

"I daresay it will be all right; he seems quiet now," said the
poor lady of the "parlours" a few days later, in reference to
their litigious neighbour and the precarious piano. The two
lodgers had grown regularly acquainted, and the piano had
had much to do with it. Just as this instrument served, with
the gentleman at No. 4, as a theme for discussion, so between
Peter Baron and the lady of the parlours it had become a
basis of peculiar agreement, a topic, at any rate, of conversation frequently renewed. Mrs. Ryves was so prepossessing
that Peter was sure that even if they had not had the piano
he would have found something else to thresh out with her.
Fortunately however they did have it, and he, at least, made

the most of it, knowing more now about his new friend, who
when, widowed and fatigued, she held her beautiful child in
her arms, looked dimly like a modern Madonna. Mrs. Bundy,
as a letter of furnished lodgings, was characterised in general
by a familiar domestic severity in respect to picturesque
young women, but she had the highest confidence in Mrs.
Ryves. She was luminous about her being a lady, and a lady
who could bring Mrs. Bundy back to a gratified recognition
of one of those manifestations of mind for which she had an
independent esteem. She was professional, but Jersey Villas
could be proud of a profession that didn't happen to be the
wrong one—they had seen something of that. Mrs. Ryves
had a hundred a year (Baron wondered how Mrs. Bundy
knew this; he thought it unlikely Mrs. Ryves had told her),
and for the rest she depended on her lovely music. Baron
judged that her music, even though lovely, was a frail dependence; it would hardly help to fill a concert-room, and he
asked himself at first whether she played country-dances at
children's parties or gave lessons to young ladies who studied
above their station.

Very soon, indeed, he was sufficiently enlightened; it all
went fast, for the little boy had been almost as great a help
as the piano. Sidney haunted the doorstep of No. 3; he was
eminently sociable, and had established independent relations with Peter, a frequent feature of which was an adven-
turous visit, upstairs, to picture books criticised for not being
all geegees and walking sticks happily more conformable. The
young man's window, too, looked out on their acquaintance;
through a starched muslin curtain it kept his neighbour before
him, made him almost more aware of her comings and goings
than he felt he had a right to be. He was capable of a shyness
of curiosity about her and of dumb little delicacies of consideration. She did give a few lessons; they were essentially
local, and he ended by knowing more or less what she went

out for and what she came in from. She had almost no visitors, only a decent old lady or two, and, every day, poor dingy Miss Teagle, who was also ancient and who came humbly enough to governess the infant of the parlours. Peter Baron's window had always, to his sense, looked out on a good deal of life, and one of the things it had most shown him was that there is nobody so bereft of joy as not to be able to command for twopence the services of somebody less joyous. Mrs. Ryves was a struggler (Baron scarcely liked to think of it), but she occupied a pinnacle for Miss Teagle, who had lived on—and from a noble nursery—into a period of diplomas and humiliation.

Mrs. Ryves sometimes went out, like Baron himself, with manuscripts under her arm, and, still more like Baron, she almost always came back with them. Her vain approaches were to the music-sellers; she tried to compose—to produce songs that would make a hit. A successful song was an income, she confided to Peter one of the first times he took Sidney, blasé and drowsy, back to his mother. It was not on one of these occasions, but once when he had come in on no better pretext than that of simply wanting to (she had after all virtually invited him), that she mentioned how only one song in a thousand was successful and that the terrible difficulty was in getting the right words. This rightness was just a vulgar "fluke"—there were lots of words really clever that were of no use at all. Peter said, laughing, that he supposed any words he should try to produce would be sure to be too clever; yet only three weeks after his first encounter with Mrs. Ryves he sat at his delightful davenport (well aware that he had duties more pressing), trying to string together rhymes idiotic enough to make his neighbour's fortune. He was satisfied of the fineness of her musical gift—it had the touching note. The touching note was in her person as well.

The davenport was delightful, after six months of its

tottering predecessor, and such a reënforcement to the young man's style was not impaired by his sense of something lawless in the way it had been gained. He had made the purchase in anticipation of the money he expected from Mr. Locket, but Mr. Locket's liberality was to depend on the ingenuity of his contributor, who now found himself confronted with the consequence of a frivolous optimism. The fruit of his labour presented, as he stared at it with his elbows on his desk, an aspect uncompromising and incorruptible. It seemed to look up at him reproachfully and to say, with its essential finish: "How could you promise anything so base; how could you pass your word to mutilate and dishonour me?" The alterations demanded by Mr. Locket were impossible, the concessions to the platitude of his conception of the public mind were degrading. The public mind!—as if the public *had* a mind, or any principle of perception more discoverable than the stare of huddled sheep! Peter Baron felt that it concerned him to determine if he were only not clever enough or if he were simply not abject enough to rewrite his story. He might in truth have had less pride if he had had more skill, and more discretion if he had had more practice. Humility, in the profession of letters, was half of practice, and resignation was half of success. Poor Peter actually flushed with pain as he recognised that this was not success, the production of gelid prose which his editor could do nothing with on the one side and he himself could do nothing with on the other. The truth about his luckless tale was now the more bitter from his having managed, for some days, to taste it as sweet.

As he sat there, baffled and sombre, biting his pen and wondering what was meant by the "rewards" of literature, he generally ended by tossing away the composition deflowered by Mr. Locket and trying his hand at the sort of twaddle that Mrs. Ryves might be able to set to music. Success in these experiments wouldn't be a reward of literature, but it might very well become a labour of love. The experiments would be pleasant enough for him if they were pleasant for his inscrutable neighbour. That was the way he thought of her now, for he had learned enough about her, little by little, to guess how much there was still to learn. To spend his mornings over cheap rhymes for her was certainly to shirk the immediate question; but there were hours when he judged this question to be altogether too arduous, reflecting that he might quite as well perish by the sword as by famine. Besides, he did meet it obliquely when he considered that he shouldn't be an utter failure if he were to produce some songs to which Mrs. Ryves's accompaniments would give a circulation. He had not ventured to show her anything yet, but one morning, at a moment when her little boy was in his room, it seemed to him that, by an inspiration, he had arrived at the happy middle course (it was an art by itself), between sound and sense. If the sense was not confused it was because the sound was so familiar.

He had said to the child, to whom he had sacrificed barley-sugar (it had no attraction for his own lips, yet in these days there was always some of it about), he had confided to the small Sidney that if he would wait a little he should be intrusted with something nice to take down to his parent. Sidney had absorbing occupation and, while Peter copied off the song in a pretty hand, roamed, gurgling and sticky, about the room. In this manner he lurched like a little toper into the rear of the davenport, which stood a few steps out from the recess of the window, and, as he was fond of beating time to his intensest joys, began to bang on the surface of it with a paper-knife which at that spot had chanced to fall upon the floor. At the moment Sidney committed this violence his kind friend had happened to raise the lid of the desk and, with his head beneath it, was rummaging among a mass of papers for a proper envelope. "I say, I say, my boy!" he exclaimed, solicitous for the ancient glaze of his most cherished possession. Sidney paused an instant; then, while Peter still hunted for the envelope, he administered another, and this time a distinctly disobedient, rap. Peter heard it from within and was struck with its oddity of sound—so much so that, leaving the child for a moment under a demoralising impression of impunity, he waited with quick curiosity for a repetition of the stroke. It came of course immediately, and then the young man, who had at the same instant found his envelope and ejaculated "Hallo, this thing has a false back!" jumped up and secured his visitor, whom with his left arm he held in durance on his knee while with his free hand he addressed the missive to Mrs. Ryves.

As Sidney was fond of errands he was easily got rid of, and after he had gone Baron stood a moment at the window chinking pennies and keys in pockets and wondering if the charming composer would think his song as good, or in other words as bad, as he thought it. His eyes as he turned away fell on the wooden back of the davenport, where, to his regret, the traces of Sidney's assault were visible in three or four ugly scratches. "Confound the little brute!" he exclaimed, feeling as if an altar had been desecrated. He was reminded, however, of the observation this outrage had led him to make, and, for further assurance, he knocked on the wood with his knuckle. It sounded from that position commonplace enough, but his suspicion was strongly confirmed when, again standing beside the desk, he put his head beneath the lifted lid and gave ear while with an extended arm he tapped sharply in the same place. The back was distinctly hollow; there was a space between the inner and the outer pieces (he could measure it), so wide that he was a fool not to have noticed it before. The depth of the receptacle from front to rear was so great that it could sacrifice a certain quantity of room without detection. The sacrifice could of course only be for a purpose, and the purpose could only be the creation of a secret compartment. Peter Baron was still boy enough to be thrilled by the idea of such a feature, the more so as every indication of it had been cleverly concealed. The people at the shop had never noticed it, else they would have called his attention to it as an enhancement of value. His legendary lore instructed him that where there was a hiding-place there was always a hidden spring, and he pried and pressed and fumbled in an eager search for the sensitive spot. The article was really a wonder of neat construction; everything fitted with a closeness that completely saved appearances.

It took Baron some minutes to pursue his inquiry, during which he reflected that the people of the shop were not such fools after all. They had admitted moreover that they had accidentally neglected this relic of gentility—it had been overlooked in the multiplicity of their treasures. He now recalled that the man had wanted to polish it up before sending it home, and that, satisfied for his own part with its honourable appearance and averse in general to shiny furniture, he had in his impatience declined to wait for such an operation, so that the object had left the place for Jersey Villas, carrying presumably its secret with it, two or three hours after his visit. This secret it seemed indeed capable of keeping; there was an absurdity in being baffled, but Peter couldn't find the spring. He thumped and sounded, he listened and measured again; he inspected every joint and crevice, with the effect of becoming surer still of the existence of a chamber and of making up his mind that his davenport was a rarity. Not only was there a compartment between the two backs, but there was distinctly something *in* the compartment! Perhaps it was a lost manuscript—a nice, safe, old-fashioned story that Mr. Locket wouldn't object to. Peter returned to the charge, for it had occurred to him that he had perhaps not sufficiently visited the small drawers, of which, in two vertical rows, there were six in number, of different sizes, inserted sideways into that portion of the structure which formed part of the support of the desk. He took them out again and examined more minutely the condition of their sockets, with the happy result of discovering at last, in the place into which the third on the left-hand row was fitted, a small sliding panel. Behind the panel was a spring, like a flat button, which yielded with a click when he pressed it and which instantly produced a loosening of one of the pieces of the shelf forming the highest part of the davenport—pieces adjusted to each other with the most deceptive closeness.

This particular piece proved to be, in its turn, a sliding panel, which, when pushed, revealed the existence of a smaller receptacle, a narrow, oblong box, in the false back. Its capacity was limited, but if it couldn't hold many things it might hold precious ones. Baron, in presence of the ingenuity with which it had been dissimulated, immediately felt that, but for the odd chance of little Sidney Ryves's having hammered on the outside at the moment he himself happened to have his head in the desk, he might have remained for years without suspicion of it. This apparently would have been a loss, for he had been right in guessing that the chamber was not empty. It contained objects which, whether precious or not, had at any rate been worth somebody's hiding. These objects were a collection of small flat parcels, of the shape of packets of letters, wrapped in white paper and neatly sealed. The seals, mechanically figured, bore the impress neither of arms nor of initials; the paper looked old—it had turned faintly sallow; the packets might have been there for ages. Baron counted them—there were nine in all, of different sizes; he turned them over and over, felt them curiously and snuffed in their vague, musty smell, which affected him with the melancholy of some smothered human accent. The little bundles were neither named nor numbered—there was not a word of writing on any of the covers; but they plainly contained old letters, sorted and matched according to dates or to authorship. They told some old, dead story— they were the ashes of fires burned out.

As Peter Baron held his discoveries successively in his hands he became conscious of a queer emotion which was not altogether elation and yet was still less pure pain. He had made a find, but it somehow added to his responsibility; he was in the presence of something interesting, but (in a manner he couldn't have defined) this circumstance suddenly constituted a danger. It was the perception of the danger, for instance, which caused to remain in abeyance any impulse he might have felt to break one of the seals. He looked at them all narrowly, but he was careful not to loosen them, and he wondered uncomfortably whether the contents of the secret compartment would be held in equity to be the property of the people in the King's Road. He had given money for the davenport, but had he given money for these buried papers? He paid by a growing consciousness that a nameless chill had stolen into the air the penalty, which he had many a time paid before, of being made of sensitive stuff. It was as if an occasion had insidiously arisen for a sacrifice—a sacrifice for the sake of a fine superstition, something like honour or kindness or justice, something indeed perhaps even finer still—a difficult deciphering of duty, an impossible tantalising wisdom. Standing there before his ambiguous treasure and losing himself for the moment in the sense of a dawning complication, he was startled by a light, quick tap at the door of his sitting-room. Instinctively, before answering, he listened an instant—he was in the attitude of a miser surprised while counting his hoard. Then he answered "One moment, please!" and slipped the little heap of packets into the biggest of the drawers of the davenport, which happened to be open. The aperture of the false back was still gaping, and he had not time to work back the spring. He hastily laid a big book over the place and then went and opened his door.

It offered him a sight none the less agreeable for being unexpected—the graceful and agitated figure of Mrs. Ryves. Her agitation was so visible that he thought at first that something dreadful had happened to her child—that she had rushed up to ask for help, to beg him to go for the doctor. Then he perceived that it was probably connected with the desperate verses he had transmitted to her a quarter of an hour before; for she had his open manuscript in one hand and was nervously pulling it about with the other. She looked frightened and pretty, and if, in invading the privacy of a fellow-lodger, she had been guilty of a departure from rigid custom, she was at least conscious of the enormity of the step and incapable of treating it with levity. The levity was for Peter Baron, who endeavoured, however, to clothe his familiarity with respect, pushing forward the seat of honour and repeating that he rejoiced in such a visit. The visitor came in, leaving the door ajar, and after a minute during which, to help her, he charged her with the purpose of telling him that he ought to be ashamed to send her down such rubbish, she recovered herself sufficiently to stammer out that his song was exactly what she had been looking for and that after reading it she had been seized with an extraordinary, irresistible impulse—that of thanking him for it in person and without delay.

"It was the impulse of a kind nature," he said, "and I can't tell you what pleasure you give me."

She declined to sit down, and evidently wished to appear to have come but for a few seconds. She looked confusedly at the place in which she found herself, and when her eyes met his own they struck him as anxious and appealing. She was evidently not thinking of his song, though she said three or four times over that it was beautiful. "Well, I only wanted you to know, and now I must go," she added; but on his hearthrug she lingered with such an odd helplessness that he felt almost sorry for her.

"Perhaps I can improve it if you find it doesn't go," said Baron. "I'm so delighted to do anything for you I can."

"There may be a word or two that might be changed," she answered, rather absently. "I shall have to think it over, to live with it a little. But I like it, and that's all I wanted to say."

"Charming of you. I'm not a bit busy," said Baron.

Again she looked at him with a troubled intensity, then suddenly she demanded: "Is there anything the matter with you?"

"The matter with me?"

"I mean like being ill or worried. I wondered if there might be; I had a sudden fancy; and that, I think, is really why I came up."

"There isn't, indeed; I'm all right. But your sudden fancies are inspirations."

"It's absurd. You must excuse me. Good-by!" said Mrs. Ryves.

"What are the words you want changed?" Baron asked.

"I don't want any—if you're all right. Good-by," his visitor repeated, fixing her eyes an instant on an object on his desk that had caught them. His own glanced in the same direction and he saw that in his hurry to shuffle away the packets found in the davenport he had overlooked one of them, which lay with its seals exposed. For an instant he felt found out, as if he had been concerned in something to be ashamed of, and it was only his quick second thought that told him how little the incident of which the packet was a sequel was an affair of Mrs. Ryves's. Her conscious eyes came back to his as if they were sounding them, and suddenly this instinct of keeping his discovery to himself was succeeded by a really startled inference that, with the rarest alertness, she had guessed something and that her guess (it seemed almost supernatural), had been her real motive. Some secret sympathy had made her vibrate—had touched her with the knowledge that he had brought something to light. After an instant he saw that she also divined the very reflection he was then making, and this gave him a lively desire, a grateful, happy desire, to appear to have nothing to conceal. For herself, it determined her still more to put an end to her momentary visit. But before she had passed to the door he exclaimed:

"All right? How can a fellow be anything else who has just had such a find?"

She paused at this, still looking earnest and asking: "What have you found?"

"Some ancient family papers, in a secret compartment of my writing-table." And he took up the packet he had left out, holding it before her eyes. "A lot of other things like that."

"What are they?" murmured Mrs. Ryves.

"I haven't the least idea. They're sealed."

"You haven't broken the seals?" She had come further back.

"I haven't had time; it only happened ten minutes ago."

"I knew it," said Mrs. Ryves, more gaily now.

"What did you know?"

"That you were in some predicament."

"You're extraordinary. I never heard of anything so miraculous; down two flights of stairs."

"*Are* you in a quandary?" the visitor asked.

"Yes, about giving them back." Peter Baron stood smiling at her and rapping his packet on the palm of his hand. "What do you advise?"

She herself smiled now, with her eyes on the sealed parcel. "Back to whom?"

"The man of whom I bought the table."

"Ah then, they're not from *your* family?"

"No indeed, the piece of furniture in which they were hidden is not an ancestral possession. I bought it at second hand—you see it's old—the other day in the King's Road. Obviously the man who sold it to me sold me more than he meant; he had no idea (from his own point of view it was stupid of him), that there was a hidden chamber or that mysterious documents were buried there. Ought I to go and tell him? It's rather a nice question."

"Are the papers of value?" Mrs. Ryves inquired.

"I haven't the least idea. But I can ascertain by breaking a seal."

"Don't!" said Mrs. Ryves, with much expression. She looked grave again.

"It's rather tantalising—it's a bit of a problem," Baron went on, turning his packet over.

Mrs. Ryves hesitated. "Will you show me what you have in your hand?"

He gave her the packet, and she looked at it and held it for an instant to her nose. "It has a queer, charming old fragrance," he said.

"Charming? It's horrid." She handed him back the packet, saying again more emphatically "Don't!"

"Don't break a seal?"

"Don't give back the papers."

"Is it honest to keep them?"

"Certainly. They're yours as much as the people's of the shop. They were in the hidden chamber when the table came to the shop, and the people had every opportunity to find them out. They didn't—therefore let them take the consequences."

Peter Baron reflected, diverted by her intensity. She was pale, with eyes almost ardent. "The table had been in the place for years."

"That proves the things haven't been missed."

"Let me show you how they were concealed," he rejoined; and he exhibited the ingenious recess and the working of the curious spring. She was greatly interested, she grew excited and became familiar; she appealed to him again not to do anything so foolish as to give up the papers, the rest of which, in their little blank, impenetrable covers, he placed in a row before her. "They might be traced—their history, their ownership," he argued; to which she replied that this was exactly why he ought to be quiet. He declared that women had not the smallest sense of honour, and she retorted that at any rate they have other perceptions more delicate than those of men. He admitted that the papers might be rubbish, and she conceded that nothing was more probable; yet when he offered to settle the point off-hand she caught him by the wrist, acknowledging that, absurd as it was, she was nervous. Finally she put the whole thing on the ground of his just doing her a favour. She asked him to retain the papers, to be silent about them, simply because it would please her. That would be reason enough. Baron's acquaintance, his agreeable relations with her, advanced many steps in the treatment of this question; an element of friendly candour made its way into their discussion of it.

"I can't make out why it matters to you, one way or the other, nor why you should think it worth talking about," the young man reasoned.

"Neither can I. It's just a whim."

"Certainly, if it will give you any pleasure, I'll say nothing at the shop."

"That's charming of you, and I'm very grateful. I see now that this was why the spirit moved me to come up—to save them," Mrs. Ryves went on. She added, moving away, that now she had saved them she must really go.

"To save them for what, if I mayn't break the seals?" Baron asked.

"I don't know—for a generous sacrifice."

"Why should it be generous? What's at stake?" Peter demanded, leaning against the doorpost as she stood on the landing.

"I don't know what, but I feel as if something or other were in peril. Burn them up!" she exclaimed with shining eyes.

"Ah, you ask too much—I'm so curious about them!"

Well, I won't ask more than I ought, and I'm much obliged to you for your promise to be quiet. I trust to your discretion. Good-by."

"You ought to *reward* my discretion," said Baron, coming out to the landing.

She had partly descended the staircase and she stopped, leaning against the baluster and smiling up at him. "Surely you've had your reward in the honour of my visit."

"That's delightful as far as it goes. But what will you do for me if I burn the papers?"

Mrs. Ryves considered a moment. "Burn them first and you'll see!"

On this she went rapidly downstairs, and Baron, to whom

the answer appeared inadequate and the proposition indeed
in that form grossly unfair, returned to his room. The vivacity
of her interest in a question in which she had discoverably
nothing at stake mystified, amused and, in addition, irresist-
ibly charmed him. She was delicate, imaginative, inflammable,
quick to feel, quick to act. He didn't complain of it, it was
the way he liked women to be; but he was not impelled for
the hour to commit the sealed packets to the flames. He
dropped them again into their secret well, and after that he
went out. He felt restless and excited; another day was lost
for work—the dreadful job to be performed for Mr. Locket
was still further off.

III

Ten days after Mrs. Ryves's visit he paid by appointment
another call on the editor of the Promiscuous. He found him
in the little wainscoted Chelsea house, which had to Peter's
sense the smoky brownness of an old pipebowl, surrounded
with all the emblems of his office—a litter of papers, a hedge
of encyclopædias, a photographic gallery of popular contrib-
utors—and he promised at first to consume very few of the
moments for which so many claims competed. It was Mr.
Locket himself however who presently made the interview
spacious, gave it air after discovering that poor Baron had
come to tell him something more interesting than that he
couldn't after all patch up his tale. Peter had begun with this,
had intimated respectfully that it was a case in which both
practice and principle rebelled, and then, perceiving how
little Mr. Locket was affected by his audacity, had felt weak
and slightly silly, left with his heroism on his hands. He had
armed himself for a struggle, but the Promiscuous didn't even

protest, and there would have been nothing for him but to go away with the prospect of never coming again had he not chanced to say abruptly, irrelevantly, as he got up from his chair:

"Do you happen to be at all interested in Sir Dominick Ferrand?"

Mr. Locket, who had also got up, looked over his glasses. "The late Sir Dominick?"

"The only one; you know the family's extinct."

Mr. Locket shot his young friend another sharp glance, a silent retort to the glibness of this information. "Very extinct indeed. I'm afraid the subject today would scarcely be regarded as attractive."

"Are you very sure?" Baron asked.

Mr. Locket leaned forward a little, with his finger-tips on his table, in the attitude of giving permission to retire. "I might consider the question in a special connection." He was silent a minute, in a way that relegated poor Peter to the general; but meeting the young man's eyes again he asked: "Are you—a—thinking of proposing an article upon him?"

"Not exactly proposing it—because I don't yet quite see my way; but the idea rather appeals to me."

Mr. Locket emitted the safe assertion that this eminent statesman had been a striking figure in his day; then he added: "Have you been studying him?"

"I've been dipping into him."

"I'm afraid he's scarcely a question of the hour," said Mr. Locket, shuffling papers together.

"I think I could make him one," Peter Baron declared.

Mr. Locket stared again; he was unable to repress an unattenuated "You?"

"I have some new material," said the young man, colouring a little. "That often freshens up an old story."

"It buries it sometimes. It's often only another tomb-stone."

"That depends upon what it is. However," Peter added, "the documents I speak of would be a crushing monument."

Mr. Locket, hesitating, shot another glance under his glasses. "Do you allude to—a—revelations?"

"Very curious ones."

Mr. Locket, still on his feet, had kept his body at the bowing angle; it was therefore easy for him after an instant to bend a little further and to sink into his chair with a move-ment of his hand toward the seat Baron had occupied. Baron resumed possession of this convenience, and the conversa-tion took a fresh start on a basis which such an extension of privilege could render but little less humiliating to our young man. He had matured no plan of confiding his secret to Mr. Locket, and he had really come out to make him conscien-tiously that other announcement as to which it appeared that so much artistic agitation had been wasted. He had indeed during the past days—days of painful indecision—appealed in imagination to the editor of the Promiscuous, as he had appealed to other sources of comfort; but his scruples turned their face upon him from quarters high as well as low, and if on the one hand he had by no means made up his mind not to mention his strange knowledge, he had still more left to the determination of the moment the question of how he should introduce the subject. He was in fact too nervous to decide; he only felt that he needed for his peace of mind to communicate his discovery. He wanted an opinion, the impression of somebody else, and even in this intensely professional presence, five minutes after he had begun to tell his queer story, he felt relieved of half his burden. His story was very queer; he could take the measure of that himself as he spoke; but wouldn't this very circumstance qualify it for the Promiscuous?

"Of course the letters may be forgeries," said Mr. Locket at last.

"I've no doubt that's what many people will say."

"Have they been seen by any expert?"

"No indeed; they've been seen by nobody."

"Have you got any of them with you?"

"No; I felt nervous about bringing them out."

"That's a pity. I should have liked the testimony of my eyes."

"You may have it if you'll come to my rooms. If you don't care to do that without a further guarantee I'll copy you out some passages."

"Select a few of the worst!" Mr. Locket laughed. Over Baron's distressing information he had become quite human and genial. But he added in a moment more dryly: "You know they ought to be seen by an expert."

"That's exactly what I dread," said Peter.

"They'll be worth nothing to me if they're not."

Peter communed with his innermost spirit. "How much will they be worth to *me* if they *are?*"

Mr. Locket turned in his study-chair. "I should require to look at them before answering that question."

"I've been to the British museum—there are many of his letters there. I've obtained permission to see them, and I've compared everything carefully. I repudiate the possibility of forgery. No sign of genuineness is wanting; there are details, down to the very postmarks, that no forger could have invented. Besides, whose interest could it conceivably have been? A labor of unspeakable difficulty, and all for what advantage? There are so many letters, too—twenty-seven in all."

"Lord, what an ass!" Mr. Locket exclaimed.

"It will be one of the strangest post-mortem revelations of which history preserves the record."

Mr. Locket, grave now, worried with a paper-knife the crevice of a drawer. "It's very odd. But to be worth anything such documents should be subjected to a searching criticism—I mean of the historical kind."

"Certainly; that would be the task of the writer introducing them to the public."

Again Mr. Locket considered; then with a smile he looked up. "You had better give up original composition and take to buying old furniture."

"Do you mean because it will pay better?"

"For you, I should think, original composition couldn't pay worse. The creative faculty's so rare."

"I do feel tempted to turn my attention to real heroes," Peter replied.

"I'm bound to declare that Sir Dominick Ferrand was never one of mine. Flashy, crafty, second-rate—that's how I've always read him. It was never a secret, moreover, that his private life had its weak spots. He was a mere flash in the pan."

"He speaks to the people of this country," said Baron.

"He did; but his voice—the voice, I mean, of his prestige—is scarcely audible now."

"They're still proud of some of the things he did at the Foreign Office—the famous 'exchange' with Spain, in the Mediterranean, which took Europe so by surprise and by which she felt injured, especially when it became apparent how much we had the best of the bargain. Then the sudden, unexpected show of force by which he imposed on the United States our interpretation of that tiresome treaty—I could never make out what it was about. These were both matters that no one really cared a straw about, but he made every one feel as if they cared; the nation rose to the way he played his trumps—it was uncommon. He was one of the few men we've had, in our period, who took Europe, or took America, by surprise, made them jump a bit; and the country liked his doing it—it was a pleasant change. The rest of the world considered that they knew in any case exactly what we would do, which was usually nothing at all. Say what you like, he's still a high name; partly also, no doubt, on account of other things—his early success and early death, his political 'cheek' and wit; his very appearance—he certainly was handsome—and the possibilities (of future personal supremacy) which it was the fashion at the time, which it's the fashion still, to say had passed away with him. He had been twice at the Foreign Office; that alone was remarkable for a man dying at forty-four. What therefore will the country think when it learns he was venal?"

Peter Baron himself was not angry with Sir Dominick Ferrand, who had simply become to him (he had been "reading up" feverishly for a week) a very curious subject of psychological study; but he could easily put himself in the place of that portion of the public whose memory was long enough for their patriotism to receive a shock. It was some time fortunately since the conduct of public affairs had wanted for men of disinterested ability, but the extraordinary documents concealed (of all places in the world—it was as fantastic as a nightmare) in a "bargain" picked up at second-hand by an obscure scribbler, would be a calculable blow to the retrospective mind. Baron saw vividly that if these relics should be made public the scandal, the horror, the chatter would be immense. Immense would be also the contribution to truth, the rectification of history. He had felt for several days (and it was exactly what had made him so nervous) as if he held in his hand the key to public attention.

"There are too many things to explain," Mr. Locket went

on, "and the singular *provenance* of your papers would count almost overwhelmingly against them even if the other objections were met. There would be a perfect and probably a very complicated pedigree to trace. How did they get into your davenport, as you call it, and how long had they been there? What hands secreted them? What hands had, so incredibly, clung to them and preserved them? Who are the persons mentioned in them? Who are the correspondents, the parties to the nefarious transactions? You say the transactions appear to be of two distinct kinds—some of them connected with public business and others involving obscure personal relations."

"They all have this in common," said Peter Baron, "that they constitute evidence of uneasiness, in some instances of painful alarm, on the writer's part, in relation to exposure— the exposure in the one case, as I gather, of the fact that he had availed himself of official opportunities to promote enterprises (public works and that sort of thing) in which he had a pecuniary stake. The dread of the light in the other connection is evidently different, and these letters are the earliest in date. They are addressed to a woman, from whom he had evidently received money."

Mr. Locket wiped his glasses. "What woman?"

"I haven't the least idea. There are lots of questions I can't answer, of course; lots of identities I can't establish; lots of gaps I can't fill. But as to two points I'm clear, and they are the essential ones. In the first place the papers in my possession are genuine; in the second place they're compromising."

With this Peter Baron rose again, rather vexed with himself for having been led on to advertise his treasure (it was his interlocutor's perfectly natural scepticism that produced this effect), for he felt that he was putting himself in a false position. He detected in Mr. Locket's studied detachment the fermentation of impulses from which, unsuccessful as he was, he himself prayed to be delivered.

Mr. Locket remained seated; he watched Baron go across the room for his hat and umbrella. "Of course, the question would come up of whose property today such documents would legally be. There are heirs, descendants, executors to consider."

"In some degree perhaps; but I've gone into that a little. Sir Dominick Ferrand had no children, and he left no brothers and no sisters. His wife survived him, but she died ten years ago. He can have had no heirs and no executors to speak of, for he left no property."

"That's to his honour and against your theory," said Mr. Locket.

"I *have* no theory. He left a largeish mass of debt," Peter Baron added. At this Mr. Locket got up, while his visitor pursued: "So far as I can ascertain, though of course my inquiries have had to be very rapid and superficial, there is no one now living, directly or indirectly related to the personage in question, who would be likely to suffer from any steps in the direction of publicity. It happens to be a rare instance of a life that had, as it were, no loose ends. At least there are none perceptible at present."

"I see, I see," said Mr. Locket. "But I don't think I should care much for your article."

"What article?"

"The one you seem to wish to write, embodying this new matter."

"Oh, I don't wish to write it!" Peter exclaimed. And then he bade his host good-by.

"Good-by," said Mr. Locket. "Mind you, I don't say that I think there's nothing in it."

"You would think there was something in it if you were to see my documents."

"I should like to see the secret compartment," the caustic editor rejoined. "Copy me out some extracts."

"To what end, if there's no question of their being of use to you?"

"I don't say that—I might like the letters themselves."

"Themselves?"

"Not as the basis of a paper, but just to publish—for a sensation."

"They'd sell your number!" Baron laughed.

"I daresay I should like to look at them," Mr. Locket conceded after a moment. "When should I find you at home?"

"Don't come," said the young man. "I make you no offer."

"I might make *you* one," the editor hinted.

"Don't trouble yourself; I shall probably destroy them." With this Peter Baron took his departure, waiting however just afterwards, in the street near the house, as if he had been looking out for a stray hansom, to which he would not have signalled had it appeared. He thought Mr. Locket might hurry after him, but Mr. Locket seemed to have other things to do, and Peter Baron returned on foot to Jersey Villas.

IV

On the evening that succeeded this apparently pointless encounter he had an interview more conclusive with Mrs. Bundy, for whose shrewd and philosophic view of life he had several times expressed, even to the good woman herself, a considerable relish. The situation at Jersey Villas (Mrs. Ryves had suddenly flown off to Dover) was such as to create in him a desire for moral support, and there was a kind of domestic determination in Mrs. Bundy which seemed, in general, to advertise it. He had asked for her on coming in, but had been told she was absent for the hour; upon which he had addressed himself mechanically to the task of doing up his dishonoured manuscript—the ingenious fiction about which Mr. Locket had been so stupid—for further adventures and not improbable defeats. He passed a restless, ineffective afternoon, asking himself if his genius were a horrid delusion, looking out of his window for something that didn't happen, something that seemed now to be the advent of a persuasive Mr. Locket and now the return, from an absence more disappointing even than Mrs. Bundy's, of his interesting neighbour of the parlours. He was so nervous and so depressed that he was unable even to fix his mind on the composition of the note with which, on its next peregrination, it was necessary that his manuscript should be accompanied. He was too nervous to eat, and he forgot even to dine; he forgot to light his candles, he let his fire go out, and it was in the melancholy chill of the late dusk that Mrs. Bundy, arriving at last with his lamp, found him extended moodily upon his sofa. She had been informed that he wished to speak to her, and as she placed on the malodorous luminary an oily shade of green pasteboard she expressed the friendly hope that there was nothing wrong with his 'ealth.

The young man rose from his couch, pulling himself together sufficiently to reply that his health was well enough but that his spirits were down in his boots. He had a strong disposition to "draw" his landlady on the subject of Mrs. Ryves, as well as a vivid conviction that she constituted a theme as to which Mrs. Bundy would require little pressure to tell him even more than she knew. At the same time he hated to appear to pry into the secrets of his absent friend; to discuss her with their bustling hostess resembled too much

for his taste a gossip with a tattling servant about an uncon-
scious employer. He left out of account however Mrs. Bundy's knowledge of the human heart, for it was this fine
principle that broke down the barriers after he had reflected
reassuringly that it was not meddling with Mrs. Ryves's affairs
to try and find out if she struck such an observer as happy.
Crudely, abruptly, even a little blushingly, he put the direct
question to Mrs. Bundy, and this led tolerably straight to
another question, which, on his spirit, sat equally heavy (they
were indeed but different phases of the same), and which the
good woman answered with expression when she ejaculated:
"Think it a liberty for you to run down for a few hours? If
she do, my dear sir, just send her to me to talk to!" As regards
happiness indeed she warned Baron against imposing too high
a standard on a young thing who had been through so much,
and before he knew it he found himself, without the responsibility of choice, in submissive receipt of Mrs. Bundy's
version of this experience. It was an interesting picture,
though it had its infirmities, one of them congenital and con-
sisting of the fact that it had sprung essentially from the
virginal brain of Miss Teagle. Amplified, edited, embellished
by the richer genius of Mrs. Bundy, who had incorporated
with it and now liberally introduced copious interleavings of
Miss Teagle's own romance, it gave Peter Baron much food
for meditation, at the same time that it only half relieved his
curiosity about the causes of the charming woman's under-
lying strangeness. He sounded this note experimentally in
Mrs. Bundy's ear, but it was easy to see that it didn't rever-
berate in her fancy. She had no idea of the picture it would
have been natural for him to desire that Mrs. Ryves should
present to him, and she was therefore unable to estimate the
points in respect in which his actual impression was irritating.
She had indeed no adequate conception of the intellectual

requirements of a young man in love. She couldn't tell him why their faultless friend was so isolated, so unrelated, so nervously, shrinkingly proud. On the other hand she could tell him (he knew it already) that she had passed many years of her life in the acquisition of accomplishments at a seat of learning no less remote than Boulogne, and that Miss Teagle had been intimately acquainted with the late Mr. Everard Ryves, who was a "most rising" young man in the city, not making any year less than his clear twelve hundred. "Now that he isn't there to make them, his mourning widow can't live as she had then, can she?" Mrs. Bundy asked.

Baron was not prepared to say that she could, but he thought of another way she might live as he sat, the next day, in the train which rattled him down to Dover. The place, as he approached it, seemed bright and breezy to him; his roamings had been neither far enough nor frequent enough to make the cockneyfied coast insipid. Mrs. Bundy had of course given him the address he needed, and on emerging from the station he was on the point of asking what direction he should take. His attention however at this moment was drawn away by the bustle of the departing boat. He had been long enough shut up in London to be conscious of refreshment in the mere act of turning his face to Paris. He wandered off to the pier in company with happier tourists and, leaning on a rail, watched enviously the preparation, the agitation of foreign travel. It was for some minutes a foretaste of adventure; but, ah, when was he to have the very draught? He turned away as he dropped this interrogative sigh, and in doing so perceived that in another part of the pier two ladies and a little boy were gathered with something of the same wistfulness. The little boy indeed happened to look round for a moment, upon which, with the keenness of the predatory age, he recognised in our young man a source of pleasures from which he lately had been weaned. He bounded forward with irrepressible cries of "Geegee!" and Peter lifted him aloft for an embrace. On putting him down the pilgrim from Jersey Villas stood confronted with a sensibly severe Miss Teagle, who had followed her little charge. "What's the matter with the old woman?" he asked himself as he offered her a hand which she treated as the merest detail. Whatever it was, it was (and very properly, on the part of a loyal *suivante*) the same complaint as that of her employer, to whom, from a distance, for Mrs. Ryves had not advanced an inch, he flourished his hat as she stood looking at him with a face that he imagined rather white. Mrs. Ryves's response to this salutation was to shift her position in such a manner as to appear again absorbed in the Calais boat. Peter Baron, however, kept hold of the child, whom Miss Teagle artfully endeavoured to wrest from him—a policy in which he was aided by Sidney's own rough but instinctive loyalty; and he was thankful for the happy effect of being dragged by his jubilant friend in the very direction in which he had tended for so many hours. Mrs. Ryves turned once more as he came near, and then, for the sweet, strained smile with which she asked him if he were on his way to France, he saw that if she had been angry at his having followed her she had quickly got over it.

"No, I'm not crossing; but it came over me that you might be, and that's why I hurried down—to catch you before you went off."

"Oh, we can't go—more's the pity; but why, if we could," Mrs. Ryves inquired, "should you wish to prevent it?"

"Because I've something to ask you first, something that may take some time." He saw now that her embarrassment had really not been resentful; it had been nervous, tremulous, as the emotion of an unexpected pleasure might have been. "That's really why I determined last night, without asking

your leave first to pay you this little visit—that and the intense
desire for another bout of horse-play with Sidney. Oh, I've
come to see you," Peter Baron went on, "and I won't make
any secret of the fact that I expect you to resign yourself
gracefully to the trial and give me all your time. The day's
lovely, and I'm ready to declare that the place is as good as
the day. Let me drink deep of these things, drain the cup like
a man who hasn't been out of London for months and months.
Let me walk with you and talk with you and lunch with you—
I go back this afternoon. Give me all your hours in short, so
that they may live in my memory as one of the sweetest
occasions of life."

The emission of steam from the French packet made such
an uproar that Baron could breathe his passion into the young
woman's ear without scandalising the spectators; and the
charm which little by little it scattered over his fleeting visit
proved indeed to be the collective influence of the conditions
he had put into words. "What is it you wish to ask me?" Mrs.
Ryves demanded, as they stood there together; to which he
replied that he would tell her all about it if she would send
Miss Teagle off with Sidney. Miss Teagle, who was always
anticipating her cue, had already begun ostentatiously to gaze
at the distant shores of France and was easily enough induced
to take an earlier start home and rise to the responsibility of
stopping on her way to contend with the butcher. She had
however to retire without Sidney, who clung to his recovered
prey, so that the rest of the episode was seasoned, to Baron's
sense, by the importunate twitch of the child's little, plump,
cool hand. The friends wandered together with a conjugal
air and Sidney not between them, hanging wistfully, first,
over the lengthened picture of the Calais boat, till they could
look after it, as it moved rumbling away, in a spell of silence
which seemed to confess—especially when, a moment later,

their eyes met—that it produced the same fond fancy in each. The presence of the boy moreover was no hindrance to their talking in a manner that they made believe was very frank. Peter Baron presently told his companion what it was he had taken a journey to ask, and he had time afterwards to get over his discomfiture at her appearance of having fancied it might be something greater. She seemed disappointed (but she was forgiving) on learning from him that he had only wished to know if she judged ferociously his not having complied with her request to respect certain seals.

"How ferociously do you suspect me of having judged it?" she inquired.

"Why, to the extent of leaving the house the next moment."

They were still lingering on the great granite pier when he touched on this matter, and she sat down at the end while the breeze, warmed by the sunshine, ruffled the purple sea. She coloured a little and looked troubled, and after an instant she repeated interrogatively: "The next moment?"

"As soon as I told you what I had done. I was scrupulous about this, you will remember; I went straight downstairs to confess to you. You turned away from me, saying nothing; I couldn't imagine—as I vow I can't imagine now—why such a matter should appear so closely to touch you. I went out on some business and when I returned you had quitted the house. It had all the look of my having offended you, of your wishing to get away from me. You didn't give me time to tell you how it was that, in spite of your advice, I determined to see for myself what my discovery represented. You must do me justice and hear what determined me."

Mrs. Ryves got up from her seat and asked him, as a particular favour, not to allude again to his discovery. It was no concern of hers at all, and she had no warrant for prying into his secrets. She was very sorry to have been for a moment so absurd as to appear to do so, and she humbly begged his pardon for her meddling. Saying this she walked on with a charming colour in her cheek, while he laughed out, though he was really bewildered, at the endless capriciousness of women. Fortunately the incident didn't spoil the hour, in which there were other sources of satisfaction, and they took their course in her lodgings with such pleasant little pauses and excursions by the way as permitted her to show him the objects of interest at Dover. She let him stop at a wine-merchant's and buy a bottle for luncheon, of which, in its order, they partook, together with a pudding invented by Miss Teagle, which, as they hypocritically swallowed it, made them look at each other in an intimacy of indulgence. They came out again and, while Sidney grubbed in the gravel of the shore, sat selfishly on the Parade, to the disappointment of Miss Teagle, who had fixed her hopes on a fly and a ladylike visit to the castle. Baron had his eye on his watch—he had to think of his train and the dismal return and many other melancholy things; but the sea in the afternoon light was a more appealing picture; the wind had gone down, the Channel was crowded, the sails of the ships were white in the purple distance. The young man asked his companion (he had asked her before) when she was to come back to Jersey Villas, and she had said that she should probably stay at Dover another week. It was dreadfully expensive, but it was doing the child all the good in the world, and if Miss Teagle could go up for some things she should probably be able to manage an extension. Earlier in the day she had said that she perhaps wouldn't return to Jersey Villas at all, or only return to wind up her connection with Mrs. Bundy. At another moment she had spoken of an early date, an immediate reoccupation of the wonderful parlours. Baron saw that she had no plan, no real reasons, that she was vague and, in secret, worried and nervous, waiting for something that didn't depend on herself. A silence of several minutes had fallen upon them while they watched the shining sails; to which Mrs. Ryves put an end by exclaiming abruptly, but without completing her sentence: "Oh, if you had come to tell me you had destroyed them—"

"Those terrible papers? I like the way you talk about 'destroying!' You don't even know what they are."

"I don't want to know; they put me into a state."

"What sort of state?"

"I don't know; they haunt me."

"They haunted me; that was why, early one morning, suddenly, I couldn't keep my hands off them. I had told you I wouldn't touch them. I had deferred to your whim, your superstition (what is it?) but at last they got the better of me. I had lain awake all night threshing about, itching with curiosity. It made me ill; my own nerves (as I may say) were irritated, my capacity to work was gone. It had come over me in the small hours in the shape of an obsession, a fixed idea, that there was nothing in the ridiculous relics and that my exaggerated scruples were making a fool of me. It was ten to one they were rubbish, they were vain, they were empty; that they had been even a practical joke on the part of some weak-minded gentleman of leisure, the former professor of the confounded davenport. The longer I hovered about them with such precautions the longer I was taken in, and the sooner I exposed their insignificance the sooner I should get back to my usual occupations. This conviction made my hands so uncontrollable that that morning before breakfast I broke one of the seals. It took me but a few minutes to perceive that the contents were not rubbish; the little bundle contained old letters—very curious old letters."

"I know—I know; 'private and confidential.' So you broke

the other seals?" Mrs. Ryves looked at him with the strange apprehension he had seen in her eyes when she appeared at his door the moment after his discovery.

"You know, of course, because I told you an hour later, though you would let me tell you very little."

Baron, as he met his queer gaze, smiled hard at her to prevent her guessing that he smarted with the fine reproach conveyed in the tone of her last words; but she appeared able to guess everything, for she reminded him that she had not had to wait that morning till he came downstairs to know what had happened above, but had shown him at the moment how she had been conscious of it an hour before, had passed on her side the same tormented night as he, and had had to exert extraordinary self-command not to rush up to his rooms while the study of the open packets was going on. "You're so sensitively organised and you've such mysterious powers that you're uncanny," Baron declared.

"I feel what takes place at a distance; that's all."

"One would think somebody you liked was in danger."

"I told you that that was what was present to me the day I came up to see you."

"Oh, but you don't like me so much as that," Baron argued, laughing.

She hesitated. "No, I don't know that I do."

"It must be for someone else—the other person connected. The other day, however, you wouldn't let me tell you that person's name."

Mrs. Ryves, at this, rose quickly. "I don't want to know it; it's none of my business."

"No, fortunately, I don't think it is," Baron rejoined, walking with her along the Parade. She had Sidney by the hand now, and the young man was on the other side of her. They moved toward the station—she had offered to go part of the way. "But with your miraculous gift it's a wonder you haven't divined."

"I only divine what I want," said Mrs. Ryves.

"That's very convenient!" exclaimed Peter, to whom Sidney had presently come round again. "Only, being thus in the dark, it's difficult to see your motive for wishing the papers destroyed."

Mrs. Ryves meditated, looking fixedly at the ground. "I thought you might do it to oblige me."

"Does it strike you that such an expectation, formed in such conditions, is reasonable?"

Mrs. Ryves stopped short, and this time she turned on him the clouded clearness of her eyes. "What do you mean to do with them?"

It was Peter Baron's turn to meditate, which he did, on the empty asphalt of the Parade (the "season," at Dover, was not yet), where their shadows were long in the afternoon light. He was under such a charm as he had never known, and he wanted immensely to be able to reply: "I'll do anything you like if you'll love me." These words, however, would have represented a responsibility and have constituted what was vulgarly termed an offer. An offer of what? he quickly asked himself here, as he had already asked himself after making in spirit other awkward dashes in the same direction—of what but his poverty, his obscurity, his attempts that had come to nothing, his abilities for which there was nothing to show? Mrs. Ryves was not exactly a success, but she was a greater success than Peter Baron. Poor as he was he hated the sordid (he knew she didn't love it), and he felt small for talking of marriage. Therefore he didn't put the question in the words it would have pleased him most to hear himself utter, but he compromised, with an angry young pang, and said to her: "What will you do for me if I put an end to them?"

She shook her head sadly—it was always her prettiest movement. "I can promise nothing—oh no, I can't promise! We must part now," she added. "You'll miss your train."

He looked at his watch, taking the hand she held out to him. She drew it away quickly, and nothing then was left him, before hurrying to the station, but to catch up Sidney and squeeze him till he uttered a little shriek. On the way back to town the situation struck him as grotesque.

V

It tormented him so the next morning that after threshing it out a little further he felt he had something of a grievance. Mrs. Ryves's intervention had made him acutely uncomfortable, for she had taken the attitude of exerting pressure without, it appeared, recognising on his part an equal right. She had imposed herself as an influence, yet she held herself aloof as a participant; there were things she looked to him to do for her, yet she could tell him of no good that would come to him from the doing. She could either have had less to say or have been willing to say more, and he asked himself why he should be the sport of her moods and her mysteries. He perceived her knack of punctual interference to be striking, but it was just this apparent infallibility that he resented. Why didn't she set up at once as a professional clairvoyant and eke out her little income more successfully? In purely private life such a gift was disconcerting; her divinations, her evasions disturbed at any rate his own tranquillity.

What disturbed it still further was that he received early in the day a visit from Mr. Locket, who, leaving him under no illusion as to the grounds of such an honour, remarked as soon as he had got into the room or rather while he still panted on the second flight and the smudged little slavey held open Baron's door, that he had taken up his young friend's invitation to look at Sir Dominick Ferrand's letters for himself. Peter drew them forth with a promptitude intended to show that he recognised the commercial character of the call and without attenuating the inconsequence of this departure from the last determination he had expressed to Mr. Locket. He showed his visitor the davenport and the hidden recess, and he smoked a cigarette, humming softly, with a sense of unwonted advantage and triumph, while the cautious editor sat silent and handed the papers. For all his caution Mr. Locket was unable to keep a warmer light out of his judicial eye as he said to Baron at last with sociable brevity—a tone that took many things for granted: "I'll take them home with me—they require much attention."

The young man looked at him a moment. "Do you think they're genuine?" He didn't mean to be mocking, he meant not to be; but the words sounded so to his own ear, and he could see that they produced that effect on Mr. Locket.

"I can't in the least determine. I shall have to go into them at my leisure, and that's why I ask you to lend them to me."

He had shuffled the papers together with a movement charged, while he spoke, with the air of being preliminary to that of thrusting them into a little black bag which he had brought with him and which, resting on the shelf of the davenport, struck Peter, who viewed it askance, as an object darkly editorial. It made our young man, somehow, suddenly apprehensive; the advantage of which he had just been conscious was about to be transferred by a quiet process of legerdemain to a person who already had advantages enough. Baron, in short, felt a deep pang of anxiety; he couldn't have said why. Mr. Locket took decidedly too many things for granted, and the explorer of Sir Dominick Ferrand's irregularities remembered afresh how clear he had been after all about his indisposition to traffic in them. He asked his visitor to what end he wished to remove the letters, since on the one hand there was no question now of the article in the Promiscuous which was to reveal their existence, and on the other he himself, as their owner, had a thousand insurmountable scruples about putting them into circulation.

Mr. Locket looked over his spectacles as over the battlements of a fortress. "I'm not thinking of the end—I'm thinking of the beginning. A few glances have assured me that such documents ought to be submitted to some competent eye."

"Oh, you mustn't show them to anyone!" Baron exclaimed.

"You may think me presumptuous, but the eye that I venture to allude to in those terms—"

"Is the eye now fixed so terribly on *me?*" Peter laughingly interrupted. "Oh, it would be interesting, I confess, to know how they strike a man of your acuteness!" It had occurred to him that by such a concession he might endear himself to a literary umpire hitherto implacable. There would be no question of his publishing Sir Dominick Ferrand, but he might, in due acknowledgment of services rendered, form the habit of publishing Peter Baron. "How long would it be your idea to retain them?" he inquired, in a manner which, he immediately became aware, was what incited Mr. Locket to begin stuffing the papers into his bag. With this perception he came quickly closer and, laying his hand on the gaping receptacle, lightly drew its two lips together. In this way the two men stood for a few seconds, touching, almost in the attitude of combat, looking hard into each other's eyes.

The tension was quickly relieved however by the surpised flush which mantled on Mr. Locket's brow. He fell back a few steps with an injured dignity that might have been a protest against physical violence. "Really, my dear young sir, your attitude is tantamount to an accusation of intended bad faith. Do you think I want to steal the confounded things?" In reply to such a challenge Peter could only hastily declare that he was guilty of no discourteous suspicion—he only wanted a limit named, a pledge of every precaution against accident. Mr. Locket admitted the justice of the demand, assured him he would restore the property within three days, and completed, with Peter's assistance, his little arrangements for removing it discreetly. When he was ready, his treacherous reticule distended with its treasures, he gave a lingering look at the inscrutable davenport. "It's how they ever got into that thing that puzzles one's brain!"

"There was some concatenation of circumstances that would doubtless seem natural enough if it were explained, but that one would have to remount the stream of time to ascertain. To one course I have definitely made up my mind: not to make any statement or any inquiry at the shop. I simply accept the mystery," said Peter, rather grandly.

"That would be thought a cheap escape if you were to put it into a story," Mr. Locket smiled.

"Yes, I shouldn't offer the story to *you*. I shall be impatient till I see my papers again," the young man called out, as his visitor hurried downstairs.

That evening, by the last delivery, he received, under the Dover postmark, a letter that was not from Miss Teagle. It was a slightly confused but altogether friendly note, written that morning after breakfast, the ostensible purpose of which was to thank him for the amiability of his visit, to express regret at any appearance the writer might have had of meddling with what didn't concern her, and to let him know that the evening before, after he had left her, she had in a moment of inspiration got hold of the tail of a really musical idea—a perfect accompaniment for the song he had so kindly given her. She had scrawled, as a specimen, a few bars at the end of her note, mystic, mocking musical signs which had no sense for her correspondent. The whole letter testified to a restless but rather pointless desire to remain in communication with him. In answering her, however, which he did that night before going to bed, it was on this bright possibility of their collaboration, its advantages for the future of each of them, that Baron principally expatiated. He spoke of this future with an eloquence of which he would have defended the sincerity, and drew of it a picture extravagantly rich. The next morning, as he was about to settle himself to tasks for some time terribly neglected, with a sense that after all it was rather a relief not to be sitting so close to Sir Dominick Ferrand, who had become dreadfully distracting; at the very moment at which he habitually addressed his preliminary invocation to the muse, he was agitated by the arrival of a telegram which proved to be an urgent request from Mr. Locket that he would immediately come down and see him. This represented, for poor Baron, whose funds were very low, another morning sacrificed, but somehow it didn't even occur to him that he might impose his own time upon the editor of Promiscuous, the keeper of the keys of renown. He had some of the plasticity of the raw contributor. He gave the muse another holiday, feeling she was really ashamed to take it, and in course of time found himself in Mr. Locket's own chair at Mr. Locket's own table—so much nobler an expanse than that slippery slope of the davenport—considering with quick intensity, in the white flash of certain words just brought out by his host, the quantity of happiness, of emancipation that might reside in a hundred pounds.

Yes, that was what it meant: Mr. Locket, in the twenty-four hours, had discovered so much in Sir Dominick's literary remains that his visitor found him primed with an offer. A hundred pounds would be paid to him that day, that minute, and no questions would be either asked or answered. "I take all the risks, I take all the risks," the editor of the Promiscuous repeated. The letters were out on the table, Mr. Locket was on the hearthrug, like an orator on a platform, and Peter, under the infleunce of his sudden ultimatum, had dropped, rather weakly, into the seat which happened to be nearest and which, as he became conscious it moved on a pivot, he whirled round so as to enable himself to look at his tempter with an eye intended to be cold. What surprised him most was to find Mr. Locket taking exactly the line about the expediency of publication which he would have expected Mr. Locket not to take. "Hush it all up; a barren scandal, an offence that can't be remedied, is the thing in the world that least justifies an airing—" some such line as that was the line he would have thought natural to a man whose life was spent in weighing questions of propriety and who had only the other day objected, in the light of his virtue, to a work of the most disinterested art. But the author of that incorruptible masterpiece had put his finger on the place in saying to his interlocutor on the occasion of his last visit that, if given to the world in the pages of the Promiscuous, Sir Dominick's aberrations would sell the edition. It was not necessary for Mr. Locket to reiterate to his young friend his phrase about their making a sensation. If he wished to purchase the "rights," as theatrical people said, it was not to protect a celebrated name or to lock them up in a cupboard. That formula of Baron's covered all the ground, and one edition was a low estimate of the probable performance of the magazine.

Peter left the letters behind him and, on withdrawing

from the editorial presence, took a long walk on the Em-
bankment. His impressions were at war with each other—
he was flurried by possibilities of which he yet denied the
existence. He had consented to trust Mr. Locket with the
papers a day or two longer, till he should have thought out
the terms on which he might—in the event of certain occurrences—be induced to dispose of them. A hundred
pounds were not this gentleman's last word, nor perhaps was
mere unreasoning intractability Peter's own. He sighed as he
took no note of the pictures made by barges—sighed because
it all might mean money. He needed money bitterly; he
owned it in disquieting quarters. Mr. Locket had put it before
him that he had a high responsibility—that he might vindicate
the disfigured truth, contribute a chapter to the history of
England. "You haven't a right to suppress such momentous
facts," the hungry little editor had declared, thinking how the
series (he would spread it into three numbers) would be the
talk of the town. If Peter had money he might treat himself
to ardour, to bliss. Mr. Locket had said, no doubt justly
enough, that there were ever so many questions one would
have to meet should one venture to play so daring a game.
These questions, embarrassments, dangers—the danger, for
instance, of the cropping-up of some lurking litigious relative—he would take over unreservedly and bear the brunt
of dealing with. It was to be remembered that the papers
were discredited, vitiated by their childish pedigree; such a
preposterous origin, suggesting, as he had hinted before, the
feeble ingenuity of a third-rate novelist, was a thing he should
have to place himself at the positive disadvantage of being
silent about. He would rather give no account of the matter
at all than expose himself to the ridicule that such a story
would infallibly excite. Couldn't one see them in advance,
the clever, taunting things the daily and weekly papers would

say? Peter Baron and his guileless side, but he felt, as he worried with a stick that betrayed him the granite parapets of the Thames, that he was not such a fool as not to know how Mr. Locket would "work" the mystery of his marvellous find. Nothing could help it on better with the public than the impenetrability of the secret attached to it. If Mr. Locket should only be able to kick up dust enough over the circumstances that had guided his hand his fortune would literally be made. Peter thought a hundred pounds a low bid, yet he wondered how the Promiscuous could bring itself to offer such a sum—so large it loomed in the light of literary remuneration as hitherto revealed to our young man. The explanation of this anomaly was of course that the editor shrewdly saw a dozen ways of getting his money back. There would be in the "sensation," at a later stage, the making of a book in large type—the book of the hour; and the profits of this scandalous volume or, if one preferred the name, this reconstruction, before an impartial posterity, of a great historical hambug, the sum "down," in other words, that any lively publisher would give for it, figured vividly in Mr. Locket's calculations. It was therefore altogether an opportunity of dealing at first hand with the lively publisher that Peter was invited to forego. Peter gave a masterful laugh, rejoicing in his heart that, on the spot, in the *repaire* he had lately quitted, he had not been tempted by a figure that would have approximately represented the value of his property. It was a good job, he mentally added as he turned his face homeward, that there was so little likelihood of his having to struggle with that particular pressure.

VI

When, half an hour later, he approached Jersey Villas, he noticed that the house-door was open; then, as he reached the gate, saw it make a frame for an unexpected presence. Mrs. Ryves, in her bonnet and jacket, looked out from it as if she were expecting something—as if she had been passing to and fro to watch. Yet when he had expressed to her that it was a delightful welcome she replied that she had only thought there might possibly be a cab in sight. He offered to go and look for one, upon which it appeared that after all she was not, as yet at least, in need. He went back with her into her sitting-room, where she let him know that within a couple of days she had seen clearer what was best; she had determined to quit Jersey Villas and had come up to take away her things, which she had just been packing and getting together.

"I wrote you last night a charming letter in answer to yours," Baron said. "You didn't mention in yours that you were coming up."

"It wasn't your answer that brought me. It hadn't arrived when I came away."

"You'll see when you get back that my letter is charming."

"I daresay." Baron had observed that the room was not, as she had intimidated, in confusion—Mrs. Ryves's preparations for departure were not striking. She saw him look round and, standing in front of the fireless grate with her hands behind her, she suddenly asked: "Where have you come from now?"

"From an interview with a literary friend."

"What are you concocting between you?"

"Nothing at all. We've fallen out—we don't agree."

"Is he a publisher?"

"He's an editor."

"Well, I'm glad you don't agree. I don't know what he wants, but, whatever it is, don't do it."

"He must do what *I* want!" said Baron.

"And what's that?"

"Oh, I'll tell you when he has done it!" Baron begged her to let him hear the "musical idea" she had mentioned in her letter; on which she took off her hat and jacket and, seating herself at her piano, gave him, with a sentiment of which the very first notes thrilled him, the accompaniment of his song. She phrased the words with her sketchy sweetness, and he sat there as if he had been held in a velvet vise, throbbing with the emotion, irrecoverable ever after in its freshness, of the young artist in the presence for the first time of "production"—the proofs of his book, the hanging of his picture, the rehearsal of his play. When she had finished he asked again for the same delight, and then for more music and for more; it did him such a world of good, kept him quiet and safe, smoothed out the creases of his spirit. She dropped her own experiments and gave him immortal things, and he lounged there, pacified and charmed, feeling the mean little room grow large and vague and happy possibilities come back. Abruptly, at the piano, she called out to him: "Those papers of yours—the letters you found—are not in the house?"

"No, they're not in the house."

"I was sure of it! No matter—it's all right!" she added. She herself was pacified—trouble was a false note. Later he was on the point of asking her how she knew the objects she had mentioned were not in the house; but he let it pass. The

subject was a profitless riddle—a puzzle that grew grotesquely bigger, like some monstrosity seen in the darkness,
as one opened one's eyes to it. He closed his eyes—he wanted
another vision. Besides, she had shown him that she had
extraordinary senses—her explanation would have been
stranger than the fact. Moreover they had other things to talk
about, in particular the question of her putting off her return
to Dover till the morrow and dispensing meanwhile with the
valuable protection of Sidney. This was indeed but another
face of the question of her dining with him somewhere that
evening (where else should she dine?)—accompanying him,
for instance, just for an hour of Bohemia, in their deadly
respectable lives, to a jolly little place in Soho. Mrs. Ryves
declined to have her life abused, but in fact, at the proper
moment, at the jolly little place, to which she did accompany
him—it dealt in macaroni and Chianti—the pair put their
elbows on the crumpled cloth and, face to face, with their
little emptied coffee-cups pushed away and the young man's
cigarette lighted by her command, became increasingly confidential. They went afterwards to the theatre, in cheap places,
and came home in "busses" and under umbrellas.

On the way back Peter Baron turned something over in
his mind as he had never turned anything before; it was the
question of whether, at the end, she would let him come into
her sitting-room for five minutes. He felt on this point a
passion of suspense and impatience, and yet for what would
it be but to tell her how poor he was? This was literally the
moment to say it, so supremely depleted had the hour of
Bohemia left him. Even Bohemia was too expensive, and yet
in the course of the day his whole temper on the subject of
certain fitnesses had changed. At Jersey Villas (it was near
midnight, and Mrs. Ryves, scratching a light for her glimmering taper, had said: "Oh, yes, come in for a minute if you

like!"), in her precarious parlour, which was indeed, after the
brilliances of the evening, a return to ugliness and truth, she
let him stand while he explained that he had certainly everything in the way of fame and fortune still to gain, but that
youth and love and faith and energy—to say nothing of her
supreme dearness—were all on his side. Why, if one's beginnings were rough, should one add to the hardness of the
conditions by giving up the dream which, if she would only
hear him out, would make just the blessed difference?
Whether Mrs. Ryves heard him out or not is a circumstance
as to which this chronicle happens to be silent; but after he
had got possession of both her hands and breathed into her
face for a moment all the intensity of his tenderness—in the
relief and joy of utterance he felt it carry him like a rising
flood—she checked him with better reasons, with a cold,
sweet afterthought in which he felt there was something deep.
Her procrastinating head-shake was prettier than ever, yet it
had never meant so many fears and pains—impossibilities
and memories, independences and pieties, and a sort of un-
complaining ache for the ruin of a friendship that had been
happy. She had liked him—if she hadn't she wouldn't have
let him think so!—but she protested that she had not, in the
odious vulgar sense, "encouraged" him. Moreover she
couldn't talk of such things in that place, at that hour, and
she begged him not to make her regret her good-nature in
staying over. There were peculiarities in her position, considerations insurmountable. She got rid of him with kind and
confused words, and afterwards, in the dull, humiliated night,
he felt that he had been put in his place. Women in her
situation, women who after having really loved and lost, usually lived on into the new dawns in which old ghosts steal
away. But there was something in his whimsical neighbour
that struck him as terribly invulnerable.

VII

"I've had time to look a little further into what we're prepared to do, and I find the case is one in which I should consider the advisability of going to an extreme length," said Mr. Locket. Jersey Villas the next morning had had the privilege of again receiving the editor of the Promiscuous, and he sat once more at the davenport, where the bone of contention, in the shape of a large, loose heap of papers that showed how much they had been handled, was placed well in view. "We shall see our way to offering you three hundred, but we shouldn't, I must positively assure you, see it a single step further."

Peter Baron, in his dressing-gown and slippers, with his hands in his pockets, crept softly about the room, repeating, below his breath and with inflections that for his own sake he endeavoured to make humorous: "Three hundred—three hundred." His state of mind was far from hilarious, for he felt poor and sore and disappointed; but he wanted to prove to himself that he was gallant—was made, in general and in particular, of undiscourageable stuff. The first thing he had been aware of on stepping into his front room was that a four-wheeled cab, with Mrs. Ryves's luggage upon it, stood at the door of No.3. Permitting himself, behind his curtain, a pardonable peep, he saw the mistress of his thoughts come out of the house, attended by Mrs. Bundy, and take her place in the modest vehicle. After this his eyes rested for a long time on the sprigged cotton back of the landlady, who kept bobbing at the window of the cab an endlessly moralising old head. Mrs. Ryves had really taken flight—he had made Jersey Villas impossible for her—but Mrs. Bundy, with a magnanimity unprecedented in the profession, seemed to express a belief in the purity of her motives. Baron felt that his own separation had been, for the present at least, effected; every instinct of delicacy prompted him to stand back.

Mr. Locket talked a long time, and Peter Baron listened and waited. He reflected that his willingness to listen would probably excite hopes in his visitor—hopes which he himself was ready to contemplate without a scruple. He felt no pity for Mr. Locket and had no consideration for his suspense or for his possible illusions; he only felt sick and forsaken and in want of comfort and money. Yet it was a kind of outrage to his dignity to have the knife held to his throat, and he was irritated above all by the ground on which Mr. Locket put the question—the ground of a service rendered to historical truth. It might be—he wasn't clear; it might be—the question was deep, too deep, probably, for his wisdom; at any rate he had to control himself not to interrupt angrily such dry, in-terested palaver, the false voice of commerce and of cant. He stared tragically out of the window and saw the stupid rain begin to fall; the day was duller even than his own soul, and Jersey Villas looked so sordidly hideous that it was no wonder Mrs. Ryves couldn't endure them. Hideous as they were he should have to tell Mrs. Bundy in the course of the day that he was obliged to seek humbler quarters. Suddenly he interrupted Mr. Locket; he observed to him: "I take it that if I should make you this concession the hospitality of the Promiscuous would be by that very fact unrestrictedly secured to me."

Mr. Locket stared. "Hospitality—secured?" He thumbed the proposition as if it were a hard peach.

"I mean that of course you wouldn't—in courtesy, in gratitude—keep on declining my things."

"I should give them my best attention—as I've always done in the past."

Peter Baron hesitated. It was a case in which there would have seemed to be some chance for the ideally shrewd aspirant in such an advantage as he possessed; but after a moment the blood rushed into his face with the shame of the idea of pleading for his productions in the name of anything but their merit. It was as if he had stupidly uttered evil of them. Nevertheless he added the interrogation: "Would you for instance publish my little story?"

"The one I read (and objected to some features of) the other day? Do you mean—a—with the alteration?" Mr. Locket continued.

"Oh, no, I mean utterly without it. The pages you want altered contain, as I explained to you very lucidly, I think, the very *raison d'être* of the work, and it would therefore, it seems to me, be an imbecility of the first magnitude to cancel them." Peter had really renounced all hope that his critic would understand what he meant, but, under favour of circumstances, he couldn't forbear to taste the luxury, which probably never again would come within his reach, of being really plain, for one wild moment, with an editor.

Mr. Locket gave a constrained smile. "Think of the scandal, Mr. Baron."

"But isn't this other scandal just what you're going in for?"

"It will be a great public service."

"You mean it will be a big scandal, whereas my poor story would be a very small one, and that it's only out of a big one that money's to be made."

Mr. Locket got up—he too had his dignity to vindicate. "Such a sum as I offer you ought really to be an offset against all claims."

"Very good—I don't mean to make any, since you don't really care for what I write. I take note of your offer," Peter pursued, "and I engage to give you to-night (in a few words left by my own hand at your house) my absolutely definite and final reply."

Mr. Locket's movements, as he hovered near the relics of the eminent statesman, were those of some feathered parent fluttering over a threatened nest. If he had brought his huddled brood back with him this morning it was because he had felt sure enough of closing the bargain to be able to be graceful. He kept a glittering eye on the papers and remarked that he was afraid that before leaving them he must elicit some assurance that in the meanwhile Peter would not place them in any other hands. Peter, at his, gave a laugh of harsher cadence than he intended, asking, justly enough, on what privilege his visitor rested such a demand and why he himself was disqualified from offering his wares to the highest bidder. "Surely you wouldn't hawk such things about?" cried Mr. Locket; but before Baron had time to retort cynically he added: "I'll publish your little story."

"Oh, thank you!"

"I'll publish anything you'll send me," Mr. Locket continued, as he went out. Peter had before this virtually given his word that for the letters he would treat only with the Promiscuous.

The young man passed, during a portion of the rest of the day, the strangest hours of his life. Yet he thought of them afterwards not as a phase of temptation, though they had been full of the emotion that accompanies an intense vision of alternatives. The struggle was already over; it seemed to him that, poor as he was, he was not poor enough to take Mr. Locket's money. He looked at the opposed courses with the self-possession of a man who has chosen, but this self-possession was in itself the most exquisite of excitements. It was really a high revulsion and a sort of noble pity. He seemed indeed to have his finger upon the pulse of

history and to be in the secret of the gods. He had them all
in his hand, the tablets and the scales and the torch. He
couldn't keep a character together, but he might easily pull
one to pieces. That would be "creative work" of a kind—he
could reconstruct the character less pleasingly, could show
an unknown side of it. Mr. Locket had had a good deal to
say about responsibility; and responsibility in truth sat there
with him all the morning, while he revolved in his narrow
cage and, watching the crude spring rain on the windows,
thought of the dismalness to which, at Dover, Mrs. Ryves
was going back. This influence took in fact the form, put on
the physiognomy of poor Sir Dominick Ferrand; he was at
present as perceptible in it, as coldly and strangely personal,
as if he had been a haunting ghost and had risen beside his
own old hearthstone. Our friend was accustomed to his company and indeed had spent so many hours in it of late, following him up at the museum and comparing his different
portraits, engravings and lithographs, in which there seemed
to be conscious, pleading eyes for the betrayer, that their
queer intimacy had grown as close as an embrace. Sir Dominick was very dumb, but he was terrible in his dependence,
and Peter would not have encouraged him by so much curiosity nor reassured him by so much deference had it not
been for the young man's complete acceptance of the im-
possibility of getting out of a tight place by exposing an individual. It didn't matter that the individual was dead; it didn't
matter that he was dishonest. Peter felt him sufficiently alive
to suffer; he perceived the rectification of history so conscientiously desired by Mr. Locket to be somehow for himself
not an imperative task. It had come over him too definitely
that in a case where one's success was to hinge upon an act
of extradition it would minister most to an easy conscience
to let the success go. No, no—even should he be starving

he couldn't make money out of Sir Dominick's disgrace. He was almost surprised at the violence of the horror with which, as he shuffled mournfully about, the idea of any such profit inspired him. What was Sir Dominick to him after all? He wished he had never come across him.

In one of his brooding pauses at the window—the window out of which never again apparently should he see Mrs. Ryves glide across the little garden with the step for which he had liked her from the first—he became aware that the rain was about to intermit and the sun to make some grudging amends. This was a sign that he might go out; he had a vague perception that there were things to be done. He had work to look for, and a cheaper lodging, and a new idea (every idea he had ever cherished had left him), in addition to which the promised little word was to be dropped at Mr. Locket's door. He looked at his watch and was surprised at the hour, for he had nothing but a heartache to show for so much time. He would have to dress quickly, but as he passed to his bedroom his eye was caught by the little pyramid of letters which Mr. Locket had constructed on his davenport. They startled him and, staring at them, he stopped for an instant, half-amused, half-annoyed at their being still in existence. He had so completely destroyed them in spirit that he had taken the act for granted, and he was now reminded of the orderly stages of which an intention must consist to be sincere. Baron went at the papers with all his sincerity, and at his empty grate (where there lately had been no fire and he had only to remove a horrible ornament of tissue-paper dear to Mrs. Bundy) he burned the collection with infinite method. It made him feel happier to watch the worst pages turn to illegible ashes—if happiness be the right word to apply to his sense, in the process, of something so crisp and crackling that it suggested the death-rustle of banknotes.

When ten minutes later he came back into his sitting-room, he seemed to himself oddly, unexpectedly in the presence of a bigger view. It was as if some interfering mass had been so displaced that he could see more sky and more country. Yet the opposite houses were naturally still there, and if the grimy little place looked lighter it was doubtless only because the rain had indeed stopped and the sun was pouring in. Peter went to the window to open it to the altered air, and in doing so beheld at the garden gate the humble "growler" in which a few hours before he had seen Mrs. Ryves take her departure. It was unmistakable—he remembered the knock-kneed white horse; but this made the fact that his friend's luggage no longer surmounted it only the more mystifying. Perhaps the cabman had already removed the luggage—he was now on his box smoking the short pipe that derived relish from inaction paid for. As Peter turned into the room again his ears caught a knock at his own door, a knock explained, as soon as he had responded, by the hard breathing of Mrs. Bundy.

"Please, sir, it's to say she've come back."

"What has she come back for?" Baron's question sounded ungracious, but his heartache had given another throb, and he felt a dread of another wound. It was like a practical joke.

"I think it's for you, sir," said Mrs. Bundy. "She'll see you for a moment, if you'll be so good, in the old place."

Peter followed his hostess downstairs, and Mrs. Bundy ushered him, with her company flourish, into the apartment she had fondly designated.

"I went away this morning, and I've only returned for an instant," said Mrs. Ryves, as soon as Mrs. Bundy had closed the door. He saw that she was different now; something had happened that had made her indulgent.

"Have you been all the way to Dover and back?"

"No, but I've been to Victoria. I've left my luggage there—I've been driving about."

"I hope you've enjoyed it."

"Very much. I've been to see Mr. Morrish."

"Mr. Morrish?"

"The musical publisher. I showed him our song. I played it for him, and he's delighted with it. He declares it's just the thing. He has given me fifty pounds. I think he believes in us," Mrs. Ryves went on, while Baron stared at the wonder—too sweet to be safe, it seemed to him as yet—of her standing there again before him and speaking of what they had in common. "Fifty pounds! fifty pounds!" she exclaimed, fluttering at him her happy cheque. She had come back, the first thing, to tell him, and of course his share of the money would be the half. She was rosy, jubilant, natural, she chattered like a happy woman. She said they must do more, ever so much more. Mr. Morrish had practically promised that he would take anything that was as good as that. She had kept her cab because she was going to Dover; she couldn't leave the others alone. It was a vehicle infirm and inert, but Baron, after a little, appreciated its pace, for she had consented to his getting in with her and driving, this time in earnest, to Victoria. She had only come to tell him the good news—she repeated this assurance more than once. They talked of it so profoundly that it drove everything else for the time out of his head—his duty to Mr. Locket, the remarkable sacrifice he had just achieved, and even the odd coincidence, matching with the oddity of all the others, of her having reverted to the house again, as if with one of her famous divinations, at the very moment the trumpery papers, the origin really of their intimacy, had ceased to exist. But she, on her side, also had evidently forgotten the trumpery papers: she never mentioned them again, and Peter Baron never boasted of what he had done with them. He was silent for a while, from curiosity to see if her fine nerves had really given her a hint; and then later, when it came to be a question of his permanent attitude, he was silent, prodigiously, religiously, tremulously silent, in consequence of an extraordinary conversation that he had with her.

This conversation took place at Dover, when he went down to give her the money for which, at Mr. Morrish's bank, he had exchanged the cheque she had left with him. That cheque, or rather certain things it represented, had made somehow all the difference in their relations. The difference was huge, and Baron could think of nothing but this confirmed vision of their being able to work fruitfully together that would account for so rapid a change. She didn't talk of impossibilities now—she didn't seem to want to stop him off; only when, the day following his arrival at Dover with the fifty pounds (he had after all to agree to share them with her—he couldn't expect her to take a present of money from him), he returned to the question over which they had had their little scene the night they dined together—on this occasion (he had brought a protmanteau and he was staying) she mentioned that there was something very particular she had it on her conscience to tell him before letting him commit himself. There dawned in her face as she approached the subject a light of warning that frightened him; it was charged with something so strange that for an instant he held his breath. This flash of ugly possibilities passed however, and it was with the gesture of taking still tenderer possession of her, checked indeed by the grave, important way she held up a finger, that he answered: "Tell me everything—tell me!"

"You must know what I am—who I am; you must know especially what I'm not! There's a name for it, a hideous, cruel name. It's not my fault! Others have known, I've had to speak of it—it has made a great difference in my life. Surely you must have guessed!" she went on, with the thinnest quaver of irony, letting him now take her hand, which felt as cold as her hard duty. "Don't you see I've no belongings, no relations, no friends, nothing at all, in all the world, of my own? I was only a poor girl."

"A poor girl?" Baron was mystified, touched, distressed, piecing dimly together what she meant, but feeling, in a great surge of pity, that it was only something more to love her for.

"My mother—my poor mother," said Mrs. Ryves. She paused with this, and through gathering tears her eyes met his as if to plead with him to understand. He understood, and drew her closer, but she kept herself free still, to continue: "She was a poor girl—she was only a governess; she was alone, she thought he loved her. He did—I think it was the only happiness she ever knew. But she died of it."

"Oh, I'm so glad you tell me—it's so grand of you!" Baron murmured. "Then—your father?" He hesitated, as if with his hands on old wounds.

"He had his own troubles, but he was kind to her. It was all misery and folly—he was married. He wasn't happy—there were good reasons, I believe, for that. I know it from letters, I know it from a person who's dead. Everyone is dead now—it's too far off. That's the only good thing. He was very kind to me; I remember him, though I didn't know then, as a little girl, who he was. He put me with some very good people—he did what he could for me. I think, later, his wife knew—a lady who came to see me once after his death. I was a very little girl, but I remember many things. What he could he did—something that helped me afterwards, something that helps me now. I think of him with a strange pity—I *see* him!" said Mrs. Ryves, with the faint past in her eyes.

"You mustn't say anything against him," she added, gently and gravely.

"Never—never; for he has only made it more of a rapture to care for you."

"You must wait, you must think; we must wait together," she went on. "You can't tell, and you must give me time. Now that you know, it's all right; but you had to know. Doesn't it make us better friends?" asked Mrs. Ryves, with a tired smile which had the effect of putting the whole story further and further away. The next moment, however, she added quickly, as if with the sense that it couldn't be far enough: "You don't know, you can't judge, you must let it settle. Think of it, think of it; oh you will, and leave it so. I must have time myself, oh I must! Yes, you must believe me."

She turned away from him, and he remained looking at her a moment. "Ah, how I shall work for you!" he exclaimed.

"You must work for yourself; I'll help you." Her eyes had met his eyes again, and she added, hesitating, thinking: "You had better know, perhaps, who he was."

Baron shook his head, smiling confidently. "I don't care a straw."

"I do—a little. He was a great man."

"There must indeed have been some good in him."

"He was a high celebrity. You've often heard of him."

Baron wondered an instant. "I've no doubt you're a princess!" he said with a laugh. She made him nervous.

"I'm not ashamed of him. He was Sir Dominick Ferrand."

Baron saw in her face, in a few seconds, that she had seen something in his. He knew that he stared, then turned pale; it had the effect of a powerful shock. He was cold for an instant, as he had just found her, with the sense of danger, the confused horror of having dealt with a blow. But the blood rushed back to its courses with his still quicker consciousness of safety, and he could make out, as he recovered his balance, that his emotion struck her simply as a violent surprise. He gave a muffled murmur: "Ah, it's you, my beloved!" which lost itself as he drew her close and held her long, in the intensity of his embrace and the wonder of his escape. It took more than a minute for him to say over to himself often enough, with his hidden face: "Ah, she must never, never know!"

She never knew; she only learned, when she asked him casually, that he had in fact destroyed the old documents she had had such a comic caprice about. The sensibility, the curiosity they had had the queer privilege of exciting in her had lapsed with the event as irresponsibly as they had arisen, and she appeared to have forgotten, or rather to attribute now to other causes, the agitation and several of the odd incidents that accompanied them. They naturally gave Peter Baron rather more to think about, much food, indeed, for clandestine meditation, some of which, in spite of the pains he took not to be caught, was noted by his friend and interpreted, to his knowledge, as depression produced by the long probation she succeeded in imposing on him. He was more patient than she could guess, with all her guessing, for if he was put to the proof she herself was not left undissected. It came back to him again and again that if the documents he had burned proved anything they proved that Sir Dominick Ferrand's human errors were not all of one order. The woman he loved was the daughter of her father, he couldn't get over that. What was more to the point was that as he came to know her better and better—for they did work together under Mr. Morrish's protection—his affection was a quantity still less to be neglected. He sometimes wondered, in the light of her general straightness (their marriage had brought out even more than he believed there was of it) whether the relics in the davenport were genuine. That piece of furniture is still almost as useful to him as Mr. Morrish's patronage. There is a tremendous run, as this gentleman calls it, on several of their songs. Baron nevertheless still tries his hand also at prose, and his offerings are now not always declined by the magazines. But he has never approached the Promiscuous again. This periodical published in due course a highly eulogistic study of the remarkable career of Sir Dominick Ferrand.

THE LAST OF
THE VALERII

I had had occasion to declare more than once that if my goddaughter married a foreigner I should refuse to give her away. And yet when the young Conte Valerio was presented to me, in Rome, as her accepted and plighted lover, I found myself looking at the happy fellow, after a momentary stare of amazement, with a certain paternal benevolence; thinking, indeed, that from the picturesque point of view (she with her yellow locks and he with his dusky ones), they were a strikingly well-assorted pair. She brought him up to me half proudly, half timidly, pushing him before her, and begging me with one of her dovelike glances to be very polite. I don't know that I am particularly addicted to rudeness; but she was so deeply impressed with his grandeur that she thought it impossible to do him honor enough. The Conte Valerios' grandeur was doubtless nothing for a young American girl, who had the air and almost the habits of a princess, to sound her trumpet about; but she was desperately in love with him, and not only her heart, but her imagination, was touched. He was extremely handsome, and with a more significant sort of beauty than is common in the handsome Roman race. He had a sort of sunken depth of expression, and a grave, slow smile, suggesting no great quickness of wit, but an unimpassioned intensity of feeling which promised well for Martha's happiness. He had little of the light, inexpensive urbanity of his countrymen, and more of a sort of heavy sincerity in his gaze which seemed to suspend response until he was sure he understood you. He was perhaps a little stupid, and I fancied that to a political or aesthetic question the response would be particularly slow. "He is good, and strong, and brave," the young girl however assured me; and I easily believed her. Strong the Conte Valerio certainly was; he had a head and throat like some of the busts in the Vatican. To my eye, which has looked at things now so long with the painter's purpose, it was a real perplexity to see such a throat rising out of the white cravat of the period. It sustained a head as massively round as that of the familiar bust of the Emperor Caracalla, and covered with the same dense sculptural crop of curls. The young man's hair grew superbly; it was such hair as the old Romans must have had when they walked bareheaded and bronzed about the world. It made a perfect arch over his low, clear forehead, and prolonged itself on cheek and chin in a close, crisp beard, strong with its own strength and unstiffened by the razor. Neither his nose nor his mouth was delicate; but they were powerful, shapely, and manly. His complexion was of a deep glowing brown which no emotion would alter, and his large, lucid eyes seemed to stare at you like a pair of polished agates. He was of middle stature, and his chest was of so generous a girth that you half expected to hear his linen crack with its even respirations. And yet, with his simple human smile, he looked neither like a young bullock nor a gladiator. His powerful voice was the least bit harsh, and his large, ceremonious reply to my compliment had the massive sonority with which civil speeches must have been uttered in the age of Augustus. I had always considered my goddaughter a very American little person, in all delightful meanings of the word, and I doubted if this sturdy young Latin would understand the transatlantic element in her nature; but, evidently, he would make her a loyal and ardent lover. She seemed to me, in her blond prettiness, so tender, so appealing, so bewitching, that it was impossible to believe he had not more thoughts for all this than for the pretty fortune which it yet bothered me to believe that he must, like a good Italian, have taken the exact measure of. His own worldly goods consisted of the paternal estate, a villa within the walls of Rome, which his scanty funds had suffered to fall into sombre disrepair. "It's the Villa she's in love with, quite as much as the Count," said her mother. "She dreams of converting the Count; that's all very well. But she dreams of refurnishing the Villa!"

The upholsterers were turned into it, I believe, before the wedding, and there was a great scrubbing and sweeping of salons and raking and weeding of alleys and avenues. Martha made frequent visits of inspection while these ceremonies were taking place; but one day, on her return, she came into my little studio with an air of amusing horror. She had found them *scraping* the sarcophagus in the great ilex-walk; divesting it of its mossy coat, disincrusting it of the sacred green mould of the ages! This was their idea of making the Villa comfortable. She had made them transport it to the dampest place they could find; for, next after that slow-coming, slow-going smile of her lover, it was the rusty complexion of his patrimonial marbles that she most prized. The young Count's conversion proceeded less rapidly, and indeed I believe that his betrothed brought little zeal to the affair. She loved him so devoutly that she believed no change of faith could better him, and she would have been willing for his sake to say her prayers to the sacred Bambino at Epiphany. But he had the good taste to demand no such sacrifice, and I was struck with the happy promise of a scene of which I was an accidental observer. It was at St. Peter's, one Friday afternoon, during the vesper service which takes place in the chapel of the Choir. I met my goddaughter wandering happily on her lover's arm, her mother being established on her campstool near the chapel door. The crowd was collected thereabouts, and the body of the church was empty. Now and then the high voices of the singers escaped into the outer vastness and melted slowly away in the incense-thickened air. Something in the young girl's step and that clasp of her arm in her lover's told me that her contentment was perfect. As she threw back her head and gazed into the magnificent immensity of vault and dome, I felt that she was in the enviable mood in which all consciousness revolves on a single centre, and that her sense of the splendors around her was one with the ecstasy of her trust. They stopped before that sombre group of confessionals which proclaims so portentously the world's sinfulness, and Martha seemed to make some almost passionate protestation. A few minutes later I overtook them.

"Don't you agree with me, dear friend," said the Count, who always addressed me with the most affectionate deference, "that before I marry so pure and sweet a creature as this, I ought to go into one of those places and confess every sin I ever was guilty of—every evil thought and impulse and desire of my grossly evil nature?"

Martha looked at him, half in deprecation, half in homage, with a look which seemed at once to insist that her lover could have no vices, and to plead that, if he had, there would be something magnificent in them. "Listen to him!" she said, smiling. "The list would be long, and if you waited to finish it, you would be late for the wedding! But if you confess your sins for me, it's only fair I should confess mine for you. Do you know what I have been saying to Camillo?" she added, turning to me with the half-filial confidence she had always shown me and with a rosy glow in her cheeks; "that I want to do something more for him than girls commonly do for their lovers—to take some step, to run some risk, to break some law, even! I'm willing to change my religion, if he bids me. There are moments when I'm terribly tired of simply staring at Catholicism; it will be a relief to come into a church to kneel. That's after all, what they are meant for! Therefore, Camillo *mio,* if it casts a shade across your heart to think that I'm a heretic, I'll go and kneel down to that good old priest who has just entered the confessional yonder and say to him, 'My father, I repent, I abjure, I believe. Baptize me in the only faith.'"

"If it's as a compliment to the Count," I said, "it seems to me he ought to anticipate it by turning Protestant."

She had spoken lightly and with a smile, and yet with an undertone of girlish ardor. The young man looked at her with a solemn, puzzled face and shook his head. "Keep your religion," he said. "Everyone his own. If you should attempt to embrace mine, I'm afraid you would close your arms about a shadow. I'm a poor Catholic! I don't understand all these chants and ceremonies and splendors. When I was a child I never could learn my catechism. My poor old confessor long ago gave me up; he told me I was a good boy but a *pagan!* You must not be a better Catholic than your husband. I don't understand your religion any better, but I beg you not to change it for mine. If it has helped to make you what you are, it must be good." And taking the young girl's hand, he was about to raise it affectionately to his lips; but suddenly remembering that they were in a place unaccordant with profane passions, he lowered it with a comical smile. "Let us go!" he murmured, passing his hand over his forehead. "This heavy atmosphere of St. Peter's always stupifies me."

They were married in the month of May, and we separated for the summer, the Contessa's mamma going to illuminate the domestic circle in New York with her reflected dignity. When I returned to Rome in the autumn, I found the young couple established at the Villa Valerio, which was being gradually reclaimed from its antique decay. I begged that the hand of improvement might be lightly laid on it, for as an unscrupulous old genre painter, with an eye to "subjects," I preferred that ruin should accumulate. My goddaughter was quite of my way of thinking, and she had a capital sense of the picturesque. Advising with me often as to projected changes, she was sometimes more conservative than myself; and I more than once smiled at her archaeological zeal, and declared that I believed she had married the Count because he was like a statue of the Decadence. I had a constant invitation to spend my days at the Villa, and my easel was always planted in one of the garden walks. I grew to have a painter's passion for the place, and to be intimate with every tangled shrub and twisted tree, every moss-coated vase and mouldy sarcophagus and sad, disfeatured bust of those grim old Romans who could so ill afford to become more meagre-visaged. The place was of small extent; but though there were many other villas more pretentious and splendid, none seemed to me more deeply picturesque, more romantically idle and untrimmed, more encumbered with precious antique rubbish, and haunted with half-historic echoes. It contained an old ilex-walk in which I used religiously to spend half an hour every day—half an hour being, I confess, just as long as I could stay without beginning to sneeze. The trees arched and intertwisted here along their dusky vista in the quaintest symmetry; and as it was exposed uninterruptedly to the west, the low evening sun used to transfuse it with a sort of golden mist and play through it—over leaves and knotty boughs and mossy marbles—with a thousand crimson fingers. It was filled with disinterred fragments of sculpture—nameless statues and noseless heads and rough-hewn sarcophagi, which made it deliciously solemn. The statues used to stand there in the perpetual twilight like conscious things, brooding on their gathered memories. I used to linger about them, half expecting they would speak and tell me their stony secrets—whisper heavily the whereabouts of their mouldering fellows, still unrecovered from the soil.

My goddaughter was idyllically happy and absolutely in love. I was obliged to confess that even rigid rules have their exceptions, and that now and then an Italian count is an honest fellow. Camillo was one to the core, and seemed quite content to be adored. Their life was a childlike interchange of caresses, as candid and unmeasured as those of a shepherd and the shepherdess in a bucolic poem. To stroll in the ilex walk and feel her husband's arm about her waist and his shoulder against her cheek; to roll cigarettes for him while he puffed them in the great marble-paved rotunda in the centre of the house; to fill his glass from an old rusty red amphora—these graceful occupations satisfied the young Countess.

She rode with him sometimes in the grassy shadow of aqueducts and tombs, and sometimes suffered him to show his beautiful wife at Roman dinners and balls. She played dominos with him after dinner, and carried out in a desultory way a daily scheme of reading him the newspapers. This observance was subject to fluctuations caused by the Count's invincible tendency to go to sleep—a failing his wife never attempted to disguise or palliate. She would sit and brush the flies from him while he lay picturesquely snoozing, and, if I ventured near him, would place her finger on her lips and whisper that she thought her husband was as handsome asleep as awake. I confess I often felt tempted to reply to her that he was at least as entertaining, for the young man's happiness had not multiplied the topics on which he readily conversed. He had plenty of good sense, and his opinions on practical matters were always worth having. He would often come and sit near me while I worked at my easel and offer a friendly criticism. His taste was a little crude, but his eye was excellent, and his measurement of the resemblance between some point of my copy and the original as trust-worthy as that of a mathematical instrument. But he seemed to me to have either a strange reserve or a strange simplicity; to be fundamentally unfurnished with "ideas." He had no beliefs nor hopes nor fears—nothing but sense, appetites, and serenely luxurious tastes. As I watched him strolling about looking at his fingernails, I often wondered whether he had anything that could properly be termed a soul, and whether good health and good nature were not the sum of his advantages. "It's lucky he's good-natured," I used to say to myself; "for if he were not, there is nothing in his con-science to keep him in order. If he had irritable nerves instead of quiet ones, he would strangle us as the infant Hercules strangled the poor little snakes. He's the natural man! Hap-pily, his nature is gentle; I can mix my colors at my ease." I wondered what he thought about and what passed through his mind in the sunny leisure which seemed to shut him in from that modern workaday world of which, in spite of my passion for bedaubing old panels with ineffective portraiture of mouldy statues against screens of box, I still flattered myself I was a member. I went so far as to believe that he sometimes withdrew from the world altogether. He had moods in which his consciousness seemed so remote and his mind so irresponsive and dumb, that nothing but a powerful caress or a sudden violence was likely to arouse him. Even his lavish tenderness for his wife had a quality which I but half relished. Whether or not he had a soul himself, he seemed not to suspect that she had one. I took a godfatherly interest in what it had not always seemed to me crabbed and pedantic talk of as her moral development. I fondly believed her to be a creature susceptible of the finer spiritual emotions. But what was becoming of her spiritual life in this interminable heathenish honeymoon? Some fine day she would find herself tired of the Count's *beaux yeux* and make an appeal to his mind. She had, to my knowledge, plans of study, of charity, of worthily playing her part as a Contessa Valerio—a position as to which the family records furnished the most inspiring examples. But if the Count found the newspapers soporific, I doubted if he would turn Dante's pages very fast for his wife, or smile with much zest at the anecdotes of Vasari. How could he advise her, instruct her, sustain her? And if she became a mother, how could he share her responsibilities? He doubtless would assure his little son and heir a stout pair of arms and legs and a magnificent crop of curls, and sometimes remove his cigarette to kiss a dimpled spot; but I found it hard to picture him lending his voice to teach the lusty urchin his alphabet or his prayers, or the rudiments of infant virtue. One accomplishment indeed the Count possessed which would make him an agreeable playfellow: he carried in his pocket a collection of precious fragments of antique pavement—bits of porphyry and malachite and lapis and basalt—disinterred on his own soil and brilliantly polished by use. With these you might see him occupied by the half-hour, playing the simple game of catch-and-toss, ranging them in a circle, tossing them in rotation, and catching them on the back of his hand. His skill was remarkable; he would send a stone five feet into the air, and pitch and catch and transpose the rest before he received it again. I watched with affectionate jealousy for the signs of a dawning sense, on Martha's part, that she was the least bit strangely mated. Once or twice, as the weeks went by, I fancied I read them, and that she looked at me with eyes which seemed to remember certain old talks of mine in which I had declared—with such verity as you please—that a Frenchman, an Italian, a Spaniard, might be a very good fellow, but that he never really respected the woman he pretended to love. For the most part, however, these dusky broodings of mine spent themselves easily in the charmed atmosphere of our romantic home. We were out of the modern world and had no business with modern scruples. The place was so bright, so still, so sacred to the silent, imperturbable past, that drowsy contentment seemed a natural law; and sometimes when, as I sat at my work, I saw my companions passing arm-in-arms across the end of one of the long-drawn vistas, and, turning back to my palette, found my colors dimmer for the radiant vision, I could easily believe that I was some loyal old chronicler of a perfectly poetical legend.

It was a help to ungrudging feelings that the Count, yielding to his wife's urgency, had undertaken a series of systematic excavations. To excavate is an expensive luxury, and neither Camillo nor his latter forefathers had possessed the means for a disinterested pursuit of archaeology. But his young wife had persuaded herself that the much-trodden soil of the Villa was as full of buried treasures as a bridecake of plums, and that it would be a pretty compliment to the ancient house which had accepted her as a mistress, to devote a portion of her dowry to bringing its mouldy honors to the light. I think she was not without a fancy that this liberal process would help to disinfect her Yankee dollars of the impertinent odor of trade. She took learned advice on the subject, and was soon ready to swear to you, proceeding from irrefutable premises, that a colossal gilt-bronze Minerva mentioned by Strabo was placidly awaiting resurrection at a point twenty rods from the northwest angle of the house. She had a couple of grotesque old antiquaries to lunch, whom having plied with unwonted potations, she walked off their legs in the grounds; and though they agreed on nothing else in the world, they individually assured her that properly conducted researches would probably yield an unequalled harvest of discoveries. The Count had been not only indifferent, but even averse, to the scheme, and had more than once arrested his wife's complacent allusions to it by an unaccustomed acerbity of tone. "Let them lie, the poor disinherited gods, the Minerva, the Apollo, the Ceres you are so sure of finding," he said, "and don't break their rest. What do you want of them? We can't worship them. Would you put them on pedestals to stare and mock at them? If you can't believe in them, don't disturb them. Peace be with them!" I remember being a good deal impressed by a vigorous confession drawn from him by his wife's playfully declaring in answer to some remonstrances in this strain that he was absolutely superstitious. "Yes, by Bacchus, I am superstitious!" he cried. "Too much so, perhaps! But I'm an old Italian, and you must take me as you find me. There have been things seen and done here which leave strange influences behind! They don't touch you, doubtless, who come of another race. But they touch me, often, in the whisper of the leaves and the odor of the mouldy soil and the blank eyes of the old statues. I can't bear to look the statues in the face. I seem to see other strange eyes in

the empty sockets, and I hardly know what they say to me.
I call the poor old statues ghosts. In conscience, we've enough
on the place already, lurking and peering in every shady nook.
Don't dig up any more, or I won't answer for my wits!"

This account of Camillo's sensibilities was too fantastic
not to seem to his wife almost a joke; and though I imagined
there was more in it, he made a joke so seldom that I should
have been sorry to cut short the poor girl's smile. With her
smile she carried her point, and in a few days arrived a kind
of archaeological detective, with a dozen workmen armed
with pickaxes and spades. For myself, I was secretly vexed
at these energetic measures; for, though fond of disinterred
statues, I disliked the disinterment, and deplored the profane
sounds which were henceforth to jar upon the sleepy stillness
of the gardens. I especially objected to the personage who
conducted the operations; an ugly little dwarfish man who
seemed altogether a subterranean genius, an earthy gnome
of the underworld, and went prying about the grounds with
a malicious smile which suggested more delight in the money
the Signor Conte was going to bury than in the expected
marbles and bronzes. When the first sod had been turned,
the count's mood seemed to alter, and his curiosity got the
better of his scruples. He sniffed delightedly the odor of the
humid earth, and stood watching the workmen, as they struck
constantly deeper, with a kindling wonder in his eyes. Whenever a pickaxe rang against a stone he would utter a sharp
cry, and be deterred from jumping into the trench only by
the little explorer's assurance that it was a false alarm. The
near prospect of discoveries seemed to act upon his nerves,
and I met him more than once strolling restlessly among his
cedarn alleys, as if at last he had fallen a thinking. He took
me by the arm and made me walk with him, and discoursed
ardently of the chance of a "find." I rather marvelled at his

sudden zeal, and wondered whether he had an eye to the past or to the future—to the beauty of possible Minervas and Apollos or to their market value. Whenever the Count would come and denounce his little army of spadesmen for a set of loitering vagabonds, the little explorer would glance at me with a sarcastic twinkle which seemed to hint that excavations were a snare. We were kept some time in suspense, for several false beginnings were made. The earth was probed in the wrong places. The Count began to be discouraged and to prolong his abbreviated siesta. But the little expert, who had his own ideas, shrewdly continued his labors; and as I sat at my easel I heard the spades ringing against the dislodged stones. Now and then I would pause, with an uncontrollable acceleration of my heartbeats. "It *may* be," I would say, "that some marble masterpiece if stirring there beneath its lightening weight of earth! There are as good fish in the sea . . . ! I *may* be summoned to welcome another Antinous back to fame—a Venus, a Faun, an Augustus!"

One morning it seemed to me that I had been hearing for half an hour a livelier movement of voices than usual; but as I was preoccupied with a puzzling bit of work, I made no inquiries. Suddenly a shadow fell across my canvas, and I turned round. The little explorer stood beside me, with a glittering eye, cap in hand, his forehead bathed in perspiration. Resting in the hollow of his arm was an earth-stained fragment of marble. In answer to my questioning glance he held it up to me, and I saw it was a woman's shapely hand. "Come!" he simply said, and led the way to the excavation. The workmen were so closely gathered round the open trench that I saw nothing till he made them divide. Then, full in the sun and flashing it back, almost, in spite of her dusky incrustations, I beheld, propped up with stones against a heap of earth, a majestic marble image. She seemed to me almost colossal, though I afterwards perceived that she was of perfect human proportions. My pulses began to throb, for I felt she was something great, and that it was great to be among the first to know her. Her marvellous beauty gave her an almost human look, and her absent eyes seemed to wonder back at us. She was amply draped, so that I saw that she was not a Venus. "She's a Juno," said the excavator, decisively; and she seemed indeed an embodiment of celestial supremacy and repose. Her beautiful head, bound with a single band, could have bent only to give the nod of command; her eyes looked straight before her; her mouth was implacably grave; one hand, outstretched, appeared to have held a kind of imperial wand, the arm from which the other had been broken hung at her side with the most classical majesty. The workmanship was of the rarest finish; and though perhaps there was a sort of vaguely modern attempt at character in her expression, she was wrought, as a whole, in the large and simple manner of the great Greek period. She was a masterpiece of skill and a marvel of preservation. "Does the Count know?" I soon asked, for I had a guilty sense that our eyes were taking something from her.

"The Signor Conte is at his siesta," said the explorer, with his sceptical grin. "We don't like to disturb him."

"Here he comes!" cried one of the workmen, and we made way for him. His siesta had evidently been suddenly broken, for his face was flushed and his hair disordered.

"Ah, my dream—my dream was right, then!" he cried, and stood staring at the image.

"What was your dream?" I asked, as his face seemed to betray more dismay than delight.

"That they'd found a Juno; and that she rose and came and laid her marble hand on mine. Eh?" said the Count, excitedly.

A kind of awestruck, guttural *a-ah!* burst from the listening workmen.

"This is the hand!" said the little explorer, holding up his perfect fragment. "I've had it this half-hour, so it can't have touched you."

"But you're apparently right as to her being a Juno," I said. "Admire her at your leisure." And I turned away; for if the Count was superstitious, I wished to leave him free to relieve himself. I repaired to the house to carry the news to my goddaughter, whom I found slumbering—dreamlessly, it appeared—over a great archaeological octavo. "They've touched bottom," I said. "They've found a Juno of Praxiteles at the very least!" She dropped her octavo, and rang for a parasol. I described the statue, but not graphically, I presume, for Martha gave a little sarcastic grimace.

"A long, fluted *peplum?*" she said. "How very odd! I don't believe she's beautiful."

"She's beautiful enough, *figlioccia mia,*" I answered, "to make you jealous."

We found the Count standing before the resurgent goddess in fixed contemplation, with folded arms. He seemed to have recovered from the irritation of his dream, but I thought his face betrayed a still deeper emotion. He was pale, and gave no response as his wife caressingly clasped his arm. I'm not sure, however, that his wife's attitude was not a livelier tribute to the perfection of the image. She had been laughing at my rhapsody as we walked from the house, and I had bethought myself of a statement I had somewhere seen, that women lacked the perception of the purest beauty. Martha, however, seemed slowly to measure our Juno's infinite stateliness. She gazed a long time silently, leaning against her husband, and then stepped half timidly down on the stones which formed a rough base for the figure. She laid her two

HENRY JAMES

rosy, ungloved hands upon the stony fingers of the goddess, and remained for some moments pressing them in her warm grasp, and fixing her living eyes upon the inexpressive brow. When she turned round her eyes were bright with an admiring tear—a tear which her husband was too deeply absorbed to notice. He had apparently given orders that the workmen should be treated to a cask of wine, in honor of their discovery. It was now brought and opened on the spot, and the little explorer, having drawn the first glass, stepped forward, hat in hand, and obsequiously presented it to the Countess. She only moistened her lips with it and passed it to her husband. He raised it mechanically to his own; then suddenly he stopped, held it a moment aloft, and poured it out slowly and solemnly at the feet of Juno.

"Why, it's a libation!" I cried. He made no answer, and walked slowly away.

There was no more work done that day. The laborers lay on the grass, grazing with the native Roman relish of a fine piece of sculpture, but wasting no wine in pagan ceremonies. In the evening the Count paid the Juno another visit, and gave orders that on the morrow she should be transferred to the Casino. The Casino was a deserted garden-house, built in not ungraceful imitation of an Ionic temple, in which Camillo's ancestors must often have assembled to drink cool syrups from Venetian glasses, and listen to learned madrigals. It contained several dusty fragments of antique sculpture, and it was spacious enough to enclose that richer collection of which I began fondly to regard the Juno as but the nucleus. Here, with short delay, this fine creature was placed, serenely upright, a reversed funereal *cippus* forming a sufficiently solid pedestal. The little explorer, who seemed an expert in all the offices of restoration, rubbed her and scraped her with mysterious art, removed her earthly stains, and doubled the lustre

268

of her beauty. Her mellow substance seemed to glow with a kind of renascent purity and bloom, and, but for her broken hand, you might have fancied she had just received the last stroke of the chisel. Her fame remained no secret. Within two or three days half a dozen inquisitive *conoscenti* posted out to obtain sight of her. I happened to be present when the first of these gentlemen (a German in blue spectacles, with a portfolio under his arm) presented himself at the Villa. The Count, hearing his voice at the door, came forward and eyed him coldly from head to foot.

"Your new Juno, Signor Conte," began the German, "is, in my opinion, much more likely to be a certain Proserpine—"

"I've neither a Juno nor a Proserpine to discuss with you," said the Count, curtly. "You're misinformed."

"You've dug up no statue?" cried the German. "What a scandalous hoax!"

"None worthy of your learned attention. I'm sorry you should have the trouble of carrying your little notebook so far." The Count had suddenly become witty!

"But you've something, surely. The rumor is running through Rome."

"The rumor be damned!" cried the Count, savagely. "I've *nothing*—do you understand? Be so good as to say so to your friends."

The answer was explicit, and the poor archaeologist departed, tossing his flaxen mane. But I pitied him, and ventured to remonstrate with the Count. "She might as well be still in the earth, if no one is to see her," I said.

"*I'm* to see her: that's enough!" he answered with the same unnatural harshness. Then, in a moment, as he caught me eyeing him askance in troubled surprise, "I hated his great portfolio. He was going to make some hideous drawing of her."

"Ah, that touches me," I said. "I too have been planning to make a little sketch."

He was silent for some moments, after which he turned and grasped my arm, with less irritation, but with extraordinary gravity. "Go in there towards twilight," he said, "and sit for an hour and look at her. I think you'll give up your sketch. If you don't my good old friend—you're welcome!"

I followed his advice, and, as a friend, I gave up my sketch. But an artist is an artist, and I secretly longed to attempt one. Orders strictly in accordance with the Count's reply to our German friend were given to the servants, who, with an easy Italian conscience and a gracious Italian persuasiveness, assured all subsequent inquirers that they had been regrettably misinformed. I have no doubt, indeed, that, in default of larger opportunity, they made condolence remunerative. Further excavation was, for the present, suspended, as implying an affront to the comparable Juno. The workmen departed, but the little explorer still haunted the premises and sounded the soil for his own entertainment. One day he came to me with his usual ambiguous grimace. "The beautiful hand of the Juno," he murmured; "what has become of it?"

"I've not seen it since you called me to look at her. I remember when I went away it was lying on the grass near the excavation."

"Where I placed it myself! After that it disappeared. *Ecco!*"

"Do you suspect one of your workmen? Such a fragment as that would bring more scudi than most of them ever looked at."

"Some, perhaps, are greater thieves than others. But if I were to call up the worst of them and accuse him, the Count would interfere."

"He must value that beautiful hand, nevertheless."

The little expert in disinterment looked about him and winked. "He values it so much that he himself purloined it. That's my belief, and I think that the less we say about it the better."

"Purloined it, my dear sir? After all, it's his own property."

"Not so much as that comes to! So beautiful a creature is more or less the property of everyone; we've all a right to look at her. But the Count treats her as if she were a sacrosanct image of the Madonna. He keeps her under lock and key, and pays her solitary visits. What does he do, after all? When a beautiful woman is in stone, all he can do is to look at her. And what does he do with that precious hand? He keeps it in a silver box; he has made a relic of it!" And this cynical personage began to chuckle grotesquely and walked away.

He left me musing uncomfortably, and wondering what the deuce he meant. The Count certainly chose to make a mystery of the Juno, but his seemed a natural incident of the first rapture of possession. I was willing to wait for a free access to her, and in the meantime I was glad to find that there was a limit to his constitutional apathy. But as the days elapsed I began to be conscious that his enjoyment was not communicative, but strangely cold and shy and sombre. That he should admire a marble goddess was no reason for his despising mankind; yet he really seemed to be making invidious comparisons between us. From this untender proscription his charming wife was not excepted. At moments when I tried to persuade myself that he was neither worse nor better company than usual, her face condemned my optimism. She said nothing, but she wore a constant look of pathetic perplexity. She sat at times with her eyes fixed on him with a kind of imploring curiosity, as if pitying surprise held resentment yet awhile in check. What passed between them in private, I had, of course, no warrant to inquire. Nothing, I imagined—and that was the misery! It was part of the misery, too, that he seemed impenetrable to these mute glances, and looked over her head with an air of superb abstraction. Occasionally he noticed me looking at him in urgent deprecation, and then for a moment his heavy eye would sparkle, half, as it seemed, in defiant irony and half with a strangely stifled impulse to justify himself. But from his wife he kept his face inexorably averted; and when she approached him with some persuasive caress, he received it with an ill-concealed shudder. I inwardly protested and raged. I grew to hate the Count and everything that belonged to him. "I was a thousand times right," I cried; "an Italian count may be mighty fine, but he won't *wear!* Give us some wholesome young fellow of our own blood, who'll pay us none of these dusky old-world tricks. Painter as I am, I'll never recommend a picturesque husband!" I lost my pleasure in the Villa, in the purple shadows and glowing lights, the mossy marbles and the long-trailing profile of the Alban Hills. My painting stood still; everything looked ugly. I sat and fumbled with my palette, and seemed to be mixing mud with my colors. My head was stuffed with dismal thoughts; an intolerable weight seemed to lie upon my heart. The Count became, to my imagination, a dark efflorescence of the evil germs which history had implanted in his line. No wonder he was foredoomed to be cruel. Was not cruelty a tradition in his race, and crime an example? The unholy passions of his forefathers stirred blindly in his untaught nature and clamored dumbly for an issue. What a heavy heritage it seemed to me, as I reckoned it up in my melancholy musings, the Count's interminable ancestry! Back to the profligate revival of arts and vices—back to the bloody medley of mediaeval wars—back through the long, fitfully glaring dusk of the early ages to its ponderous origin in the solid Roman state—back through all the darkness of history it seemed to stretch, losing every feeblest claim on my sympathies as it went. Such a record was in itself a curse; and my poor girl had expected it to sit as lightly and gratefully on her consciousness as her feather on her hat! I have little idea how long this painful situation lasted. It seemed the longer from my goddaughter's continued reserve, and my inability to offer her a word of consolation. A sensitive woman, disappointed in marriage, exhausts her own ingenuity before she takes counsel. The Count's preoccupations, whatever they were, made him increasingly restless; he came and went at random, with nervous abruptness; he took long rides alone, and, as I inferred, rarely went through the form of excusing himself to his wife; and still, as time went on, he came no nearer explaining his mystery. With the lapse of time, however, I confess that my apprehensions began to be tempered with pity. If I had expected to see him propitiate his urgent ancestry by a crime, now that his native rectitude seemed resolute to deny them this satisfaction, I felt a sort of grudging gratitude. A man couldn't be so gratuitously sombre without being unhappy. He had always treated me with that antique deference to a grizzled beard for which elderly men reserve the flower of their general tenderness for waning fashions, and I thought it possible he might suffer me to lay a healing hand upon his trouble. One evening, when I had taken leave of my goddaughter and given her my useless blessing in a silent kiss, I came out and found the Count sitting in the garden in the mild starlight, and staring at a mouldy Hermes, nestling in a clump of oleander. I sat down by him and informed him roundly that his conduct needed explanation. He half turned his head, and his dark pupil gleamed an instant.

"I understand," he said, "you think me crazy!" And he tapped his forehead.

"No, not crazy, but unhappy. And if unhappiness runs its course too freely, of course, our poor wits are sorely tried."

He was silent awhile, and then, "I'm not unhappy!" he cried abruptly. "I'm prodigiously happy. You wouldn't believe the satisfaction I take in sitting here and staring at that old weatherworn Hermes. Formerly I used to be afraid of him: his frown used to remind me of a little bushy-browed old priest who taught me Latin and looked at me terribly over the book when I stumbled in my Virgil. But now it seems to me the friendliest, jolliest thing in the world, and suggests the most delightful images. He stood pouting his great lips in some old Roman's garden two thousand years ago. He saw the sandalled feet treading the alleys and the rose-crowned heads bending over the wine; he knew the old feasts and the old worship, the old Romans and the old gods. As I sit here he speaks to me, in his own dumb way, and describes it all! No, no, my friend, I'm the happiest of men!"

I had denied that I thought he was crazy, but I suddenly began to suspect it, for I found nothing reassuring in this singular rhapsody. The Hermes, for a wonder, had kept his nose; and when I reflected that my dear Countess was being neglected for this senseless pagan block, I secretly promised myself to come the next day with a hammer and deal him such a lusty blow as would make him too ridiculous for a sentimental tête-à-tête. Meanwhile, however, the Count's infatuation was no laughing matter, and I expressed my sincerest conviction when I said, after a pause, that I should recommend him to see either a priest or a physician.

He burst into uproarious laughter. "A priest! What should I do with a priest, or he with me? I never loved them, and I feel less like beginning than ever. A priest, my dear friend," he repeated, laying his hand on my arm, "don't set a priest at me, if you value *his* sanity! My confession would frighten the poor man out of his wits. As for a doctor, I never was better in my life; and unless," he added abruptly, rising, and eyeing me askance, "you want to poison me, in Christian charity I advise you to leave me alone."

Decidedly, the Count *was* unsound, and I had no heart, for some days, to go back to the Villa. How should I treat him, what stand should I take, what course did Martha's happiness and dignity demand? I wandered about Rome, revolving these questions, and one afternoon found myself in the Pantheon. A light spring shower had begun to fall, and I hurried for refuge into the great temple which its Christian altars have but half converted into a church. No Roman monument retains a deeper impress of ancient life, or verifies more forcibly those prodigious beliefs which we are apt to regard as dim fables. The huge dusky dome seems to the spiritual ear to hold a vague reverberation of pagan worship, as a gathered shell holds the rumor of the sea. Three or four persons were scattered before the various altars; another stood near the centre, beneath the aperture in the dome. As I drew near I perceived this was the Count. He was planted with his hands behind him, looking up first at the heavy rainclouds, as they crossed the great bull's-eye, and then down at the besprinkled circle on the pavement. In those days the pavement was rugged and cracked and magnificently old, and this ample space, in free communion with the weather, had become as mouldy and mossy and verdant as a strip of garden soil. A tender herbage had sprung up in the crevices of the slabs, and the little microscopic shoots were twinkling in the rain. This great weather-current, through the uncapped vault, deadens most effectively the customary odors of incense and tallow, and transports one to a faith that was on friendly terms with nature. It seemed to have performed this office for the Count; his face wore an indefinable expression of ecstasy, and he was so rapt in comtemplation that it was some time before he noticed me. The sun was struggling through the clouds without, and yet a thin rain continued to fall and came drifting down into our gloomy enclosure in a sort of illuminated drizzle. The Count watched it with the fascinated stare of a child watching a fountain, and then turned away, pressing his hand to his brow, and walked over to one of the ornamental altars. Here he again stood staring, but in a moment wheeled about and returned to his former place. Just then he recognized me, and perceived, I suppose, the puzzled gaze I must have fixed on him. He saluted me frankly with his hand, and at last came toward me. I fancied that he was in a kind of nervous tremor and was trying to appear calm.

"This is the best place in Rome," he murmured. "It's worth fifty St. Peters'. But do you know I never came here till the other day? I left it to the *forestieri*. They go about with their red books, and read about this and that, and think they know it. Ah! You must *feel* it—feel the beauty and fitness of that great open skylight. Now, only the wind and the rain, the sun and the cold, come down; but of old—of old"—and he touched my arm and gave me a strange smile—"the pagan gods and goddesses used to come sailing through it and take their places at their altars. What a procession, when the eyes of faith could see it! Those are the things they have given us instead!" And he gave a pitiful shrug. "I should like to pull down their pictures, overturn their candlesticks, and poison their holy water!"

"My dear Count," I said gently, "you should tolerate people's honest beliefs. Would you renew the Inquisition, and in the interest of Jupiter and Mercury?"

"People wouldn't tolerate my belief, if they guessed it!"

he cried. "There's been a great talk about the pagan perse-
cutions; but the Christians persecuted as well, and the old
gods were worshipped in caves and woods as well as the new.
And none the worse for that! It was in caves and woods and
streams, in earth and air and water, they dwelt. And there—
and here, too, in spite of all your Christian lustrations—a
son of old Italy may find them still!"

He had said more then he meant, and his mask had fallen.
I looked at him hard, and felt a sudden outgush of the compassion we always feel for a creature irresponsibly excited. I
seemed to touch the source of his trouble, and my relief was
great, for my discovery made me feel like bursting into laughter. But I contented myself with smiling benignantly. He
looked back at me suspiciously, as if to judge how far he had
betrayed himself; and in his glance I read, somehow, that he
had a conscience we could take hold of. In my gratitude, I was
ready to thank any gods he pleased. "Take care, take care,"
I said, "you're saying things which if the sacristan there were
to hear and report—!" And I passed my hand through his
arm and led him away.

I was startled and shocked, but I was also amused and
comforted. The Count had suddenly become for me a de-
lightfully curious phenomenon, and I passed the rest of the
day in meditating on the strange ineffaceability of race char-
acteristics. A sturdy young Latin I had called Camillo; stur-
dier, indeed, than I had dreamed him! Discretion was now
misplaced, and on the morrow I spoke to my goddaughter.
She had lately been hoping, I think, that I would help her to
unburden her heart, for she immediately gave way to tears
and confess that she was miserable. "At first," she said, "I
thought it was all fancy, and not his tenderness that was
growing less, but my exactions that were growing greater.
But suddenly it settled upon me like a mortal chill—the

conviction that he had ceased to care for me, that something had come between us. And the puzzling thing has been the want of possible cause in my own conduct, or of any sign that there is another woman in the case. I have racked my brain to discover what I had said or done or thought to displease him! And yet he goes about like a man too deeply injured to complain. He has never uttered a harsh word or given me a reproachful look. He has simply renounced me. I have dropped out of his life."

She spoke with such an appealing tremor in her voice that I was on the point of telling her that I had guessed the riddle, and that this was half the battle. But I was afraid of her incredulity. My solution was so fantastic, so apparently farfetched, so absurd, that I resolved to wait for convincing evidence. To obtain it, I continued to watch the Count, covertly and cautiously, but with a vigilance which disinterested curiosity now made intensely keen. I returned to my painting, and neglected no pretext for hovering about the gardens and the neighborhood of the Casino. The Count, I think, suspected my designs, or at least my suspicions, and would have been glad to remember just what he had suffered himself to say to me in the Pantheon. But it deepened my interest in his extraordinary situation that, insofar as I could read his deeply brooding face, he seemed to have grudgingly pardoned me. He gave me a glance occasionally, as he passed me, in which a sort of dumb desire for help appeared to struggle with the instinct of mistrust. I was willing enough to help him, but the case was prodigiously delicate, and I wished to master the symptoms. Meanwhile I worked and waited and wondered. Ah! I wondered, you may be sure, with an interminable wonder; and, turn it over as I would, I couldn't get used to my idea. Sometimes it offered itself to me with a perverse fascination which deprived me of all wish to interfere. The Count took the form of a precious psychological study, and refined feeling seemed to dictate a tender respect for his delusion. I envied him the force of his imagination, and I used sometimes to close my eyes with a vague desire that when I opened them I might find Apollo under the opposite tree, lazily kissing his flute, or see Diana hurrying with long steps down the ilex walk. But for the most part my host seemed to me simply an unhappy young man, with an unwholesome mental twist which should be smoothed away as speedily as possible. If the remedy was to match the disease, however, it would have to be an ingenious compound!

One evening, having bidden my goddaughter good night, I had started on my usual walk to my lodgings in Rome. Five minutes after leaving the Villa gate I discovered that I had left my eyeglass—an object in constant use—behind me. I immediately remembered that, while painting, I had broken the string which fastened it round my neck, and had hooked it provisionally upon a twig of a flowering-almond tree within arm's reach. Shortly afterwards I had gathered up my things and retired, unmindful of the glass; and now, as I needed it to read the evening paper at the Caffè Greco, there was no alternative but to retrace my steps and detach it from its twig. I easily found it, and lingered awhile to note the curious night-aspect of the spot I had been studying by daylight. The night was magnificent, and full-charged with the breath of the early Roman spring. The moon was rising fast and flinging her silver checkers into the heavy masses of shadow. Watching her at play, I strolled farther and suddenly came in sight of the Casino.

Just then the moon, which for a moment had been concealed, touched with a white ray a small marble figure which adorned the pediment of this rather factitious little structure.

279

Its sudden illumination suggested that a rarer spectacle was at hand, and that the same influence must be vastly becoming to the imprisoned Juno. The door of the Casino was, as usual, locked, but the moonlight was flooding the high-placed windows so generously that my curiosity become obstinate—and inventive. I dragged a garden seat round from the portico, placed it on end, and succeeded in climbing to the top of it and bringing myself abreast of one of the windows. The casement yielded to my pressure, turned on its hinges, and showed for me what I had been looking for—Juno visited by Diana. The beautiful image stood bathed in the radiant flood and shining with a purity which made her most persuasively divine. If by day her mellow complexion suggested faded gold, her substance now might have passed for polished silver. The effect was almost terrible; beauty so eloquent could hardly be inanimate. This was my foremost observation. I leave you to fancy whether my next was less interesting. At some distance from the foot of the statue, just out of the light, I perceived a figure lying flat on the pavement, prostrate apparently with devotion. I can hardly tell you how it completed the impressiveness of the scene. It marked the shining image as a goddess indeed, and seemed to throw a sort of conscious pride into her stony mask. I of course immediately recognized this recumbent worshipper as the Count, and while I stood gazing, as if to help me to read the full meaning of his attitude, the moonlight travelled forward and covered his breast and face. Then I saw that his eyes were closed, and that he was either asleep or swooning. Watching him attentively, I detected his even respirations, and judged there was no reason for alarm. The moonlight blanched his face, which seemed already pale with weariness. He had come into the presence of the Juno in obedience to that fabulous passion of which the symptoms had so woefully perplexed us, and, exhausted either by compliance or resistance, he had sunk down at her feet in a stupid sleep. The bright moonshine soon aroused him, however; he muttered something and raised himself, vaguely staring. Then recognizing his situation, he rose and stood for some time gazing fixedly at the glowing image with an expression which I fancied was not that of wholly unprotesting devotion. He uttered a string of broken words of which I was unable to catch the meaning, and then, after another pause and a long, melancholy moan, he turned slowly to the door. As rapidly and noiselessly as possible I descended from my post of vigilance and passed behind the Casino, and in a moment I heard the sound of the closing lock and of his departing footsteps.

The next day, meeting the little antiquarian in the grounds, I shook my finger at him with what I meant he should consider portentous gravity. But he only grinned like the malicious earth-gnome to which I had always compared him, and twisted his mustache as if my menace was a capital joke. "If you dig any more holes here," I said, "you shall be thrust into the deepest of them, and have the earth packed down on top of you. We have made enough discoveries, and we want no more statues. Your Juno has almost ruined us."

He burst out laughing. "I expected as much," he cried; "I had my notions!"

"What did you expect?"

"That the Signor Conte would begin and say his prayers to her."

"Good heavens! Is the case so common? Why did you expect it?"

"On the contrary, the case is rare. But I've fumbled so long in the monstrous heritage of antiquity that I have learned a multitude of secrets; learned that ancient relics may work modern miracles. There's a pagan element in all of us—I don't speak for you, *illustrissimi forestieri*—and the old gods have still their worshippers. The old spirit still throbs here and there, and the Signor Conte has his share of it. He's a good fellow, but, between ourselves, he's an impossible Christian!" And this singular personage resumed his impertinent hilarity.

"If your previsions were so distinct," I said, "you ought to have given me a hint of them. I should have sent your spadesmen walking."

"Ah, but the Juno is so beautiful!"

"Her beauty be blasted! Can you tell me what has become of the Contessa's? To rival the Juno, she's turning to marble herself."

He shrugged his shoulders. "Ah, but the Juno is worth fifty thousand scudi!"

"I'd give a hundred thousand," I said, "to have her annihilated. Perhaps, after all, I shall want you to dig another hole."

"At your service!" he answered, with a flourish; and we separated.

A couple of days later I dined, as I often did, with my host and hostess, and met the Count face to face for the first time since his prostration in the Casino. He bore the traces of it, and sat plunged in sombre distraction. I fancied that the path of the antique faith was not strewn with flowers, and that the Juno was becoming daily a harder mistress to serve. Dinner was scarcely over before he rose from table and took up his hat. As he did so, passing his wife, he faltered a moment, stopped and gave her—for the first time, I imagine—that vaguely imploring look which I had often caught. She moved her lips in inarticulate sympathy and put out her hands. He drew her towards him, kissed her with a kind of angry ardor, and strode away. The occasion was propitious, and further delay unnecessary.

"What I have to tell you is very strange," I said to the Countess, "very fantastic, very incredible. But perhaps you'll not find it so bad as you feared. There *is* a woman in the case! Your enemy is the Juno. The Count—how shall I say it?—the Count takes her *au sérieux*." She was silent; but after a moment she touched my arm with her hand, and I knew she meant that I had spoken her own belief. "You admired his antique simplicity: you see how far it goes. He had reverted to the faith of his fathers. Dormant through the ages, that imperious statue has silently aroused it. He believes in the pedigrees you used to dog-ear your school mythology with trying to get by heart. In a word, dear child, Camillo is a pagan!"

"I suppose you'll be terribly shocked," she answered, "if I say that he's welcome to any faith, if he will only share it with me. I'll believe in Jupiter, if he'll bid me! My sorrow's not for that: let my husband be himself! My sorrow is for the gulf of silence and indifference that has burst open between us. His Juno's the reality; I'm the fiction!"

"I've lately become reconciled to this gulf of silence, and to your fading for a while into a fiction. After the fable, the moral! The poor fellow has but half succumbed: the other half protests. The modern man is shut out in the darkness with his imcomparable wife. How can he have failed to feel— vaguely and grossly if it must have been, but in every throb of his heart—that you are a more perfect experiment of nature, a riper fruit of time, than those primitive persons for whom Juno was a terror and Venus an example? He pays you the compliment of believing you an inconvertible modern. He has crossed the Acheron, but he has left you behind, as a pledge to the present. We'll bring him back to redeem it. The old ancestral ghosts ought to be propitiated when a pretty creature like you has sacrificed the fragrance of her life. He has proved himself one of the Valerii; we shall see to it he is the last, and yet that his decease shall leave the Conte Camillo in excellent health."

I spoke with confidence which I had partly felt, for it seemed to me that if the Count was to be touched, it must be by the sense that his strange spiritual excursion had not made his wife detest him. We talked long and to a hopeful end, for before I went away my goddaughter expressed the desire to go out and look at the Juno. "I was afraid of her almost from the first," she said, "and have hardly seen her since she was set up in the Casino. Perhaps I can learn a lesson from her—perhaps I can guess how she charms him!"

For a moment I hesitated, with the fear that we might intrude upon the Count's devotions. Then, as something in the poor girl's face suggested that she had thought of this and felt a sudden impulse to pluck victory from the heart of danger, I bravely offered her my arm. The night was cloudy, and on this occasion, apparently, the triumphant goddess was to depend upon her own lustre. But as we approached the Casino I saw that the door was ajar, and that there was lamp-light within. The lamp was suspended in front of the image, and it showed us that the place was empty. But the Count had lately been there. Before the statue stood a roughly extemporized altar, composed of a nameless fragment of antique marble, engraved with an illegible Greek inscription. We seemed really to stand in a pagan temple, and we gazed at the serene divinity with an impulse of spiritual reverence. It ought to have been deepened, I suppose, but it was rudely checked, by our observing a curious glitter on the face of the low altar. A second glance showed us it was blood!

My companion looked at me in pale horror, and turned away with a cry. A swarm of hideous conjectures pressed into my mind, and for a moment I was sickened. But at last I remembered that there is blood and blood, and the Latins were posterior to the cannibals.

"Be sure it's very innocent," I said; "a lamb, a kid, or a sucking calf!" But it was enough for her nerves and her conscience that it was a crimson trickle, and she returned to the house in sad agitation. The rest of the night was not passed in a way to restore her to calmness. The Count had not come in, and she sat up for him from hour to hour. I remained with her and smoked my cigar as composedly as I might; but internally I wondered what in horror's name had become of him. Gradually, as the hours wore away, I shaped a vague interpretation of these dusky portents—an interpretation nonetheless valid and devoutly desired for its being tolerably cheerful. The blood-drops on the altar, I mused, were the last instalment of his debt and the end of his delusion. They had been a happy necessity, for he was, after all, too gentle a creature not to hate himself for having shed them, not to abhor so cruelly insistent an idol. He had wandered away to recover himself in solitude, and he would come back to us with a repentant heart and an inquiring mind! I should certainly have believed all this more easily, however, if I could have heard his footstep in the hall. Toward dawn, scepticism threatened to creep in with the gray light, and I restlessly betook myself to the portico. Here in a few moments I saw him cross the grass, heavy-footed, splashed with mud, and evidently excessively tired. He must have been walking all night, and his face denoted that his spirit had been as restless as his body. He paused near me, and before he entered the house he stopped, looked at me a moment, and then held out his hand. I grasped it warmly, and it seemed to me to throb with all that he could not utter.

"Will you see your wife?" I asked.

He passed his hand over his eyes and shook his head. "Not now—not yet—sometime!" he answered.

I was disappointed, but I convinced her, I think, that he had cast out the devil. She felt, poor girl, a pardonable desire to celebrate the event. I returned to my lodging, spent the day in Rome, and came back to the Villa toward dusk. I was told that the Countess was in the grounds. I looked for her cautiously at first, for I thought it just possible I might interrupt the natural consequences of a reconciliation; but failing to meet her, I turned toward the Casino, and found myself face to face with the little explorer.

"Does your excellency happen to have twenty yards of stout rope about him?" he asked gravely.

"Do you want to hang yourself for the trouble you've stood sponsor to?" I answered.

"It's a hanging matter, I promise you. The Countess has given orders. You'll find her in the Casino. Sweet-voiced as she is, she knows how to make her orders understood."

At the door of the Casino stood half a dozen of the laborers on the place, looking vaguely solemn, like outstanding dependants at a superior funeral. The Countess was within, in a position which was an answer to the surveyor's riddle. She stood with her eyes fixed on the Juno, who had been removed from her pedestal and lay stretched in her magnificent length upon a rude litter.

"Do you understand?" she said. "She's beautiful, she's noble, she's precious, but she must go back!" And, with a passionate gesture, she seemed to indicate an open grave.

I was hugely delighted, but I thought it discreet to stroke my chin and look sober. "She's worth fifty thousand scudi."

She shook her head sadly. "If we were to sell her to the Pope and give the money to the poor, it wouldn't profit us. She must go back—she must go back! We must smother her beauty in the dreadful earth. It makes me feel almost as if she were alive; but it came to me last night with overwhelming force, when my husband came in and refused to see me, that he'll not be himself as long as she is above ground. To cut the knot we must bury her! If I had only thought of it before!"

"Not before!" I said, shaking my head in turn. "Heaven reward our sacrifice now!"

The little surveyor, when he reappeared, seemed hardly like an agent of the celestial influences, but he was deft and active, which was more to the point. Every now and then he uttered some half-articulate lament, by the way of protest against the Countess's cruelty; but I saw him privately scanning the recumbent image with an eye which seemed to foresee a malicious glee in standing on a certain unmarked spot on the turf and grinning till people stared. He had brought back an abundance of rope, and having summoned his assistants, who vigorously lifted the litter, he led the way to the original excavation, which had been left unclosed with the project of further researches. By the time we reached the edge of the grave the evening had fallen and the beauty of our marble victim was shrouded in a dusky veil. No one spoke—if not exactly for shame, at least for regret. Whatever our plea, our performance looked, at least, monstrously profane. The ropes were adjusted and the Juno was slowly lowered into her earthy bed. The Countess took a handful of earth and dropped it solemnly on her breast. "May it lie lightly, but forever!" she said.

"Amen!" cried the little surveyor with a strange mocking inflection; and he gave us a bow, as he departed, which betrayed an agreeable consciousness of knowing where fifty thousand scudi were buried. His underlings had another cask of wine, the result of which, for them, was a suspension of all consciousness, and a subsequent irreparable confusion of memory as to where they had plied their spades.

The Countess had not yet seen her husband, who had again apparently betaken himself to communion with the great god Pan. I was of course unwilling to leave her to encounter alone the results of her momentous deed. She wandered into the drawing room and pretended to occupy herself with a bit of embroidery, but in reality she was bravely composing herself for an "explanation." I took up a book, but it held my attention as feebly. As the evening wore away I heard a movement on the threshold and saw the Count lifting the tapestried curtain which masked the door, and looking silently at his wife. His eyes were brilliant, but not angry. He had missed the Juno—and drawn a long breath! The Countess kept her eyes fixed on her work, and drew her silken stitches like an image of wifely contentment. The image seemed to fascinate him: he came in slowly, almost on tiptoe, walked to the chimneypiece, and stood there in a sort of rapt contemplation. What had passed, what was passing, in his mind, I leave to your own apprehension. My goddaughter's hand trembled as it rose and fell, and the color came into her cheek. At last she raised her eyes and sustained the gaze in which all his returning faith seemed concentrated. He hesitated a moment, as if her very forgiveness kept the gulf open between them, and then he strode forward, fell on his two knees and buried his head in her lap. I departed as the Count had come in, on tiptoe.

He never became, if you will, a thoroughly modern man; but one day, years after, when a visitor to whom he was showing his cabinet became inquisitive as to a marble hand, suspended in one of its inner recesses, he looked grave and turned the lock on it. "It is the hand of a beautiful creature," he said, "whom I once greatly admired."

"Ah—a Roman?" said the gentleman, with a smirk.

"A Greek," said the Count, with a frown.

This Franklin Library edition of

GHOSTLY TALES

is set in Garamond No. 3,

a modern revival of the influential sixteenth-century

typeface named for its creator, Claude Garamond,

and known for its dignity and elegance.

This is complemented by the display face Benguiat Book Condensed,

selected by designer Kate Nichols.

The four part openers are the work of artist Scott Reynolds

and were specially commissioned for this edition.

The acid-free paper is 70-pound Franklin Library Vellum Cream,

made to archival standards by the P. H. Glatfelter Paper Company

of Spring Grove, Pennsylvania, for The Franklin Library.

The book was printed by R. R. Donnelley & Sons Co.,

Chicago, Illinois.